The Princess of Pride

Deborah S. Jones

PublishAmerica
Baltimore

ISBN: 1-4241-2479-4
PUBLISHED BY PUBLISHAMERICA, LLLP
www.publishamerica.com
Baltimore

Printed in the United States of America

*This book is dedicated first and foremost to my girls
who saw my potential and believed in me.
You know who you are;
I couldn't have done this without you!
And to my husband for his support.
Thank you all!*

Prologue
Who is Diamond Chantiel Skovachy?

My parents knew I was special from the moment I was born, or so they say. Much of my life seemed to come out of a fairy tale and on other days a horror movie. My mother, Nyrobi Chantiel, was the princess of the Embatu Tribe, one the largest tribes in Africa. My father, Zachary Skovachy was the only son of one of, if not, the wealthiest men in the world, Nathan Skovachy. They had met when my grandfather, was drilling for oil in the Northern part of Nigeria and his wife, Viktoria was finishing her pharmaceutical research in the Congo. Nathan had become great friends with Nyrobi's parents, Ramantu and Alee Chantiel, as he developed and dug his way through Africa. Both were men of power and persuasion. The families benefited from each other and Africa was all the better for it.

It was love at first sight for Zachary and Nyrobi. She was from a different world, but he didn't seem to care. Neither of their parents were pleased, so they tried to keep my father out of Africa and my mother inundated with school. Even though Nyrobi was unbelievably beautiful, intelligent, and educated, she was African. Zachary came from superb stock and was already the most sought after man in Europe, but he was *not* African. Zachary and Nyrobi defied their parents and against all odds eloped, threatening never to return if their parents did no accept the marriage. As much as could be said about the Skovachys and the Chantiels they loved their children and finally welcomed the marriage. Things were perfect for twelve years. The coupling of the two families was one of the best events that ever happened to Africa. I was born two years into the marriage and was the gem of both families, hence my name, royalty on one side and heiress on the other, Diamond Chantiel Skovachy.

My grandfather along with my father's help built a fortress with our name and increased the family's wealth exponentially with the development of several oil companies, real estate, and pharmaceutical companies with pivotal drugs and therapies, thanks to my grandmother, Viktoria. We had several industries locked and seemed to be taking over Africa and Europe. Our name was known everywhere. My grandfather Nathan made many enemies, as to be expected from such a powerful and influential man. Both sides of my family became, how should we say, guilty by association. He was known as a ruthless man who always got what he wanted. He took enormous risks, but they always worked out to his benefit. Investors would jump on the band wagon of any of his business ventures, but he never failed. Many had learned the hard way that passing up on an opportunity to join him early on would turn around and cripple them in the future.

Ten years later, my perfect world came crashing down. While visiting my grandparents in Africa my mother, grandparents and I were kidnapped by an uprising militia. I've pushed these things into the deep dark recesses of my mind, so even now the details elude me. The militia wanted land from King Ramantu, but it was land belonging to my grandfather Nathan. As King of the Embatus the militia thought it was his land to give and if it wasn't, he could at least persuade Nathan to give it up, since they were so close. Little did they know how wrong they were. Nathan's business, was Nathan's business alone. Word spread that all the militia wanted was the land and we would be set free.

The militia had become tired of the Europeans coming in and taking the best that Africa had to offer and leaving the natives with the scraps. It figures, the land they wanted was the most lucrative of the African oil fields and Nathan didn't take kindly their threats, vowing not to give in to greedy thieves looking to steal his hard earned money. Others had tried before to swindle him and had not succeeded. He vowed to find them before they could harm a hair on any of our heads. I was told by my father's closest friend, Armand, that my father begged for us, but he begged in vain. Within days of the kidnapping my father had transferred all his wealth under my name and as his last will and testament stated, in the care of his closest friend and confidant Armand LaVoielle, should anything happen to him. He left to find us. When it became clear that my grandfather wouldn't give in, the militia was furious. That night when the men began to attack my mother, I fought loose and wreaked havoc, resulting in one missing ear, several bruised testicles and battered shins. The leader was furious, he tackled me, throwing me so hard against a wall that I blacked out. Both my mother and grandmother were raped and tortured to death, my grandfather disarticulated, and me…well my only reasoning for why they didn't touch me was because they thought I was already dead. I managed to open my eyes long enough to take in some of the screams, the cries, the smells, and the pleas, then I would black out again. I had suffered a serious concussion when my head hit the wall and had the three inch scar to remind me, in case I ever tried to forget. I remember never shedding a single tear. It's all such a blur. I woke up to find myself in the midst of my family's mangled bodies and the stench the heat had on the blood, open wounds, urine and feces around the room was indescribable. I remembered thinking, so this is hell. At first I didn't want to leave my mother's side, but in the end thought I may be able to get help. I walked for what seemed like days and was finally picked up by a search unit. They had found the bodies and thought we were all dead. At that news, my father, without hesitation, had killed himself, a single bullet to his head. Africa was thrown into a war. Their beloved King and Queen murdered. Across the world Nathanial Skovachy was despised and looked at with disgust, for people thought his family was worth less to him than his money. I was told he was devastated. He didn't care what people thought of him, and as punishment to Africa, sold every oil field, closed every factory, and outsourced every task. Africa never saw another Skovachy cent directly and they were plunged into poverty and up to this day had not fully recovered from my grandfather's backlash.

Even at the tender age of ten my stubbornness was known. I refused to see my grandparents, allowing them only to come to Africa for the funeral, as Armand helped me plan the burial of my parents and grandparents, but refusing all contact with them. I knew my mother and father would want to be buried together. I might as well have buried Nathan and Viktoria with them because I never spoke to my grandparents again and thwarted off all their attempts to contact me. God, even then, at such a young age I was a bitch. That entire experience could have turned me into a serious whack job, and although I definitely have some idiosyncrasies, I'm certainly not crazy. Stubborn, bull-headed, vindictive, and lethal, not necessarily in that order, but certainly not crazy. My teachers and friends would say I was too proud. I never asked for help and although my independence was an admiral trait that would one day take me to the pinnacle of success, at some point I would need help and if my pride wouldn't let me ask, it could also be my doom. I've been invited into enough inner circles, political and otherwise, to know that I had grown to be a powerful woman, whose opinions and advice were well respected. I was known for being fair, ruthless, and for my somewhat superior intellect. I had a talent for finding equal ground when there seemed to be none, and presidents, royalty, and dignitaries alike had benefited from my knowledge. Revenge against the militia never once crossed my mind. Revenge against my grandfather did. I often wonder about that and whether the lack of a simple emotion like that did mean I was crazy.

To say Armand had taken care of me would be inaccurate. I've always known what I wanted and he helped me attain those things. As the years passed and I became more wealthy and powerful, it was important to both myself and Armand that I knew how to protect myself, vowing to kill anyone who tried to do me harm. I became skilled in martial arts and Armand took pride in training me himself. As I got older and entered more elite circles, those aforementioned skills became a necessity. Sometimes I felt like Armand had wasted his life on me, since he was never married and had no children of his own, but he insisted that I was his family. He lived to protect me and I kept him very comfortable so he could have women and men alike whenever he wanted. He resented the burden that marriage became after some time and was content to travel the world with me, catering to the needs of my companies and projects, and indulging in all the extravagances that brought along with it. He had lovers on every continent and reveled in his sexual freedom.

I managed by the age of twenty-eight to attain several degrees, had several publications, and had patented three inventions through my companies. In business I've never focused on one thing or one industry, except Africa. For every penny my grandfather took out I put two back in. His curse would be my cure. I had so many ideas floating around in my head that I wanted to do them all, and for the most part I always did. I named my umbrella company Genesis. The Beginning...the beginning of my new world. My products, my companies, my inventions, my investments, my drugs, mine, mine, mine. I never borrowed a penny and all ties to me were buried in endless paper trails. I hid behind my company. Things were easier that way. Armand was the face of Genesis. It was important that my grandparents couldn't find me. The things you can do when you have anonymity are endless.

I've heard myself referred to as the most beautiful woman in the world. The *Helen* of our era, but none of that interested me. There is more to me than my looks, wealth and excursions. I've never been in love, been kissed once, although my best friend Michelle is convinced Lynus McCleod's 11th birthday party doesn't count. I have to agree with her on that one. I think I want kids, but thought I should find a man first. I know what I liked and wanted in a man, but had never really found it. Not sure if I'd ever really looked. Scores of men had approached me, but there was always something that forced me to hold back and refuse their advances. I often wondered what that something was and if there was also a something that would one day make me let one of them into the confines of my heart.

Chapter 1

I awoke to the gentle pitter patter of rain against my bedroom window. Despite the overcast clouds and half-naked trees, something seemed to beckon me out from under the warmth of my down comforter. Slowly I pulled the covers back and swung my legs off the side of the bed, stepping down onto the cool hardwood floors. Living on the twenty-second floor was one of the main reasons I'd settled on this penthouse apartment after moving back to New York eight months before. Below, the streets were already busy with morning commuters off to do whatever it is they needed to do.

"Dye?" came the soft low voice of Armand standing outside my door. "Are you awake?"

"Yes, Armand. Is everything all right?" as I walked over to the bathroom and slipped on my robe.

"Everything is fine, but your mobile has been ringing quite a few times and it's in your coat pocket out here; so I wanted to make sure you knew" he said.

I opened the door and came face to chest with Armand. My face, his chest. Even as I got older and taller I thought he would diminish in size but he hadn't changed a bit. He still seemed to tower over my 5' 10" frame. Wearing what I called his uniform and he called his comfort clothes, a crisp dress shirt, usually some solid color. Today it was white, black slacks, black belt and black shoes I could see my face in them. I could count on a single hand the total number of times in all my twenty-eight years I'd seen him wear something different. My parent's funeral and all five of my graduations. He had my coat folded neatly over his arm.

"It's probably Michelle, because I know I don't have any appointments today." I reached into the pocket and grabbed my phone. "Seven missed calls? Are you kidding me? Yes, they're all from Michelle and all within the last thirty minutes. What is she thinking? It's only eight-thirty. I hope she didn't wake you," I said.

"No, not at all I've been up since five. I was just worried that you may be missing something important, but since it's just Michelle I can rest easy." He bent and gave me a kiss on my forehead as he headed back down the stairs, "By the way…good morning."

"I'm sorry. Good morning," I replied as I walked back into my bedroom. I picked up the receiver over on my end table and dialed Michelle's number as I walked to the bathroom.

"It's about friggin time!" she snapped.

"Well, good morning to you too! Did the phone even ring? What's your problem?" I asked with a little laugh.

"I talked to him! Dye, I finally talked to him!"

"I'm going to assume…"

"Yes I'm talking about Quinn. I needed to get in early to finish the prep work for the DiAngelo case opening arguments this morning and he took the elevator with me. God, he looked good. I said 'good morning' and did a great job of not staring. He held the elevator door for me and I said thank you. You wouldn't believe what he said next!"

"Did he ask your…"

"He asked my name! Said he'd seen me around the office for the past few months, but hadn't gotten a chance to introduce himself. He said he'd been following my work and my successes hadn't gone unnoticed. He walked me to my office and we proceeded to drink coffee and talk for forty-five minutes."

"That's gre…"

"I know that's great, right? Anyway, the reason for my frantic calls was that he proceeded to tell me that he's having a dinner party tonight and wondered if I could come."

"You said yes, right?"

"Actually I told him that I had already made plans to go out with my best friend."

"You what? You've been waiting to talk to him for six…"

"Months, I know. Let me finish! I told him I would be able to come if I could bring you with me! And he said sure."

"What? Tell me you aren't serious! That is so high school and I didn't even go to high school! I do not want to be the third wheel and you know I don't get along well with other people."

"You won't be a third wheel and you get along fine with people, because on top of being wealthy, absolutely stunning, and genuine, you have an IQ 200% higher than Einstein! Which means you can have a conversation with anyone about anything!"

"Meesh, that's one way of looking at it, but I look at things a little different than you do. I see a woman cursed with wealth she doesn't want, a face that leads everyone to judge her erroneously, and a knack for telling it like it is, WHICH because of her severely higher than normal IQ usually means people feel intimidated, insulted, and inadequate."

"Don't be ridiculous! You never make people feel insulted or inadequate."

"Are you saying I do make them feel intimidated?"

"No, that's not what I'm saying. What I am saying is that you're being ridiculous."

"I'm not! I'm a twenty-eight-year-old woman who has managed to get to first base once in her life and all attempts at second base were squashed when her sixty seconds ran out and they opened the closet door prematurely at Lynus' party. Don't make me do this."

"I'm not going through this with you again. I'm inviting you to a dinner party not an orgy! You are going to meet me at my house at seven on the dot! You are going to wear something incredibly sexy and we're going to have fun. Pleeeaaaase…I can't do this if you aren't there. Plus, it's Friday night and I'm tired of your sorry excuses why you can't go out. You'll never get laid at this rate and thirty is looking you square in the face. I swear there should be some type of award for the oldest virgin."

"That's not funny. Do you know what I can't understand? How it is that you can have rendezvous with perfect strangers. Sleep with half the debate team, party and behave like an animal after having only two drinks and couldn't bring yourself to introduce yourself to this man for six months and now can't go to a dinner party alone."

"It's because he's the one! That's why. I want to be perfect. I told you before I'm finished with the partying and escapades. I really want this! I want him! Diamond, please do this for me. I know if you come you'll keep me in check."

"Meesh…I…I just…"

"Please, Dye. You know I would do it for you."

"I know you would do it for me and, hopefully, sometime in this century you'll get to return the favor. I'll be at your house at seven on the dot. You owe me big time."

"Oh, thank you, sweetie. You won't regret it. You're going to have so much fun and meet all the gorgeous men in this town, and…"

"Don't push it. Let's take it one step at a time. Listen, I have to go. I just woke up and I have to get cleaned up. Since I'm up I might as well get some work done. I'll see you tonight."

"Dye, for the record, if you would just knock down that wall you've built around yourself and be a little more social you would've gotten to fourth base by now and even beyond."

"Michelle Noir, do you know what you can do? Kiss my…"
CLICK.

"Hello? Hello? No she didn't." I rolled my eyes as I placed the phone back on the receiver and instantly it rang. I grabbed it.

"Hello."

"I forgot to ask you, there was a case I reviewed when I was in law school on a state verses a school district and ummm…"

"The state of Oregon vs. Mashpee High School 1988, verdict ruled in favor of the state. You should also check out code 1375.42 on the rights of communities under the state laws."

"How did you know…"

CLICK. Umph…I hung up with a broad smile, served her right for hanging up on me. What a nerve!

Chapter 2

I was dressed and in the car within an hour. Armand insisted on driving me to the office because of the weather, plus, I think he wanted to talk to me.

"Did you hear?" he asked me after it was apparent the silence was killing him.

"Did I hear what?"

"They're in town."

He didn't have to say anything else. I knew. He learned quickly that I didn't like to hear their names.

"Yes. I did hear."

"You did? When? Why didn't you say anything to me? Were you waiting for me bump into them on…"

"I didn't say anything because you get like this when they're in town. Calm down. I only found out yesterday and I would've told you, but you were in bed when I came home last night, and cooped up in the office all morning. Plus, I knew you would get a call soon enough." It irritated him when I was so cool with him. "Why are they here? That I didn't find out."

"Neither did I, but it seems to be something more than the regular fly in and fly out, they have reserved the penthouse suite at the Fairmont, indefinitely."

"What?" I screamed causing Armand to slam on the brakes prematurely.

"Do you mind? Bloody hell, are you trying to kill us?" he snapped.

"What do you mean they're here indefinitely?" I was beside myself.

"Dye, I don't know, all I know is exactly what I told you."

"Well you've got to find out. I don't care how or when, but you have to find out. Actually, I lie, I do care when, by the end of the day I must know."

"Dye, that won't be easy. Any questions could…"

"Armand, it's never easy. Just find out." By the tone in my voice he knew to drop it. I had said all I was going to say about it.

We drove in silence until we reached my building twenty minutes later. Before I got out of the car, I placed my hand on top of his.

"I'm sorry I yelled earlier and I'm sorry I didn't tell you before. I just need you to stay on top of this. I need to know why they're here and even if there's the slightest chance that they may be staying I need to know why so I can make arrangements. You know I don't like surprises."

"Okay. I'll see what I can do," he said in a low voice, looking straight ahead. I could tell he was still upset at me.

"Armand, one more thing. I'm going out tonight with Meesh to a dinner party. Can you have Lucy get something ready from my collection and we can pick it up on my way home?"

His eyes seemed to light up almost immediately at the possibility I may attend a "non-work-related" social event.

"A dinner party? That's great. I was starting to get a little worried. You really need to get out more. You're too young to be cooped up in an office or house all day and night. You're looking thirty straight down the barrel and you aren't making any attempts to improve your situation."

"What is this? Beat up on Diamond's social life day? First Michelle and now you, what the hell? Can you contact Lucy or should I?" I snapped.

"And you tell me to calm down. Humph. I'll call Lucy. I'm just happy for you, that's all."

"Well, don't get too happy. I'm just going to a dinner party to keep her company. It's nothing special."

"If you say so. What time would you like me to pick you up?"

"Well, I told Meesh I would be at her house at seven sharp, so I guess you could pick me up here around three, that way we beat the rush and that gives me more than enough time to do some research in the office."

"That should be fine. I'll call you if anything comes up."

"Armand don't for…"

"I know, Dye. I won't forget. You'll have the information by the end of the day."

"Thank you." I gave him a tiny smile and he drove away.

It was a little before seven and I was walking into the lobby of Michelle's apartment building. She lived in one of these modern contemporary buildings with glass, steel, and marble everywhere. There was no doubt that it was a beautiful building, it just seemed so cold. As I waved to the concierge, I caught a glimpse of myself in the mirrored wall behind him, and thought, *Damn Lucy can sew.* The dress she'd sent over was absolutely stunning, she had outdone herself. Michelle would be pleased. Armand certainly would've been if he'd been home to see me. He was busy all day and got so caught up he called around twelve to tell me he was sending a driver to take me home because he had to meet someone around four. I asked him who he was meeting, but he couldn't talk. My dress was already there when I got home, but Armand wasn't. When I called his mobile he abruptly told me he couldn't talk and hung up. That alone made me want to stay home and wait for him to get in so he could fill me in on what he'd found out, but I knew Michelle wouldn't hear of it.

"Good evening, Ralph. Can you let her know I'm on my way up?"

"Good evening, Ms. Chantiel. I certainly will. Have a nice evening."

Within minutes I was knocking on her penthouse door.

"It's open!" she yelled.

I opened the door and walked in. I could hear her running around her bedroom. Her California king bed was covered with clothes. The four doors to her walk-in closets were open and shoes and more clothes were scattered on the floor. Michelle was standing in front of the one set of doors, looking like she'd stepped out of a Victoria's Secret magazine, her legs slightly spread, wearing a black lace strapless bra with matching thong and garter with black sheer stockings. Her thick blonde hair was tossed over one shoulder, and with one hand akimbo and the other hand massaging her temple she was deep in thought. She was beautiful, in a naughty teacher type of way; she just had a knack for choosing men who could never look past that. All they saw was her face and body and things usually went sour when they realized she was way more than that. Hopefully this Quinn would be different.

"Don't be mad. I'll be ready in no time. I had to change like eight times and I'm running out of options. Nothing looks right. Help!"

"I don't believe this. All the shopping you do and with all the clothes you have, you couldn't find one thing to wear?" I said with a laugh.

"I don't need your shit right now, just help me find something to wear! I don't want to be late." She turned and faced me with a complete look of desperation on her face. When she saw what I was wearing her face broke into a huge smile.

"Wow! You look amazing. Is that new? Lucy?"

"Uh huh."

"Damn she's good! You see, that's what I need, a fabulous no-name designer who dedicates her talent to creating me a couture wardrobe."

"I thought you told me you were leaving work at four."

"I did. Thanks, by the way, the opening arguments went really well."

"No problem. Well, if it's any consolation your underwear looks fabulous! You should go just like that."

"Diamond! I don't have time for jokes."

"It wasn't a joke. Look, why don't you wear the strapless raw silk dress we bought in Italy over the summer with the matching Stuart Weitzman's? That dress was made for your body. Plus, I don't think you want to show too much skin. That dress shows just enough to make Quinn want to see more."

"Ummmm, I never thought of that dress, but I broke the heel on the

Stew's, so I will have wear another pair of shoes," as she disappeared into the closet.

"You broke the heel on a pair of Stew's? I hope you said six Hail Mary's and repented, because that is surely a sin."

"I know, I was beside myself and wrote a letter to City Hall on the conditions of the sidewalks in downtown, but I got no response. Figures. Can you zip me up?"

"See how simple that was? Now hurry up. I don't do the fashionably late thing."

Chapter 3

We pulled into the gate of Quinn's estate and drove up the driveway to his 19th century mansion. There were six or eight cars ahead of us, waiting for what seemed like valets. I could feel my stomach starting to churn and my heart rate increase.

"Michelle, I thought you said this was a small dinner party! This doesn't look small. Valets? How many people are coming to this thing? The license plate in front of us says 'Consulate.' What's going on?"

"Dye, don't worry. He throws this dinner party every year for the who's who in law, business, medicine, politics, entertainment, and…well…pretty much anybody who's anybody."

"I am going to kill you! How could you do this to me? You told me this would be small! Is that why you insisted on taking your car, so I couldn't leave once I found out?"

"I don't understand why you're being like this. You need to take the stick out of your ass! You're too proud to step out on a social limb and try something new or meet someone. These are great people and this is one of the biggest parties of the year and I was invited by the man of my dreams. Why can't you just put all your issues aside for once and do this for me! Your pride is killing you! Slowly, but surely. You can't see it, but I can; you're dying inside and you're too proud to ask for help, or maybe just too stupid to know what you're doing to yourself. I don't know any more. It's not like I've brought you to some dive bar. This is the hottest ticket in town, being seen here is a big thing. A very big thing."

"You just don't get it, do you? When have I ever cared about being at the hottest ticket in town or bumping gums with the who's who! This is not pride, this is being cautious. I don't want to relive my past, Michelle. I don't want to have to answer any personal questions, or think up of appropriate answers. I don't want people staring at me and women holding on to their husbands and boyfriends tighter just because I walk by or say hello. I don't want to be surrounded by fake and wealthy debutantes. But, worst of all, I don't want to be in any place or situation where I could possibly run into my grandparents, and since they're in town it's very likely that will be here! Since we both know they are somebody."

"They're in town? Why didn't you tell me? Oh, my God! Do you think they'll be here? I'm sure they won't be here. This is a much younger crowd, but if they are we can leave. I promise." I couldn't see her eyes, but she sounded upset.

Maybe she was right and I was slowly dying inside. Michelle knows almost everything about me and felt I was living way under my potential. She thought I should be using my talents and intelligence for greater things, like helping foreign countries, building inventions that changed the world, and advising political leaders. I said she knew *almost* everything about me. She didn't know about my inner circles and private endeavors, and that was purely for her safety. She agreed that what my grandfather did was wrong, but thought I should forgive them and still try seeing them once in a while. She also thought I needed to see a therapist because I had commitment issues. Can I get a date first, and then we can talk about commitment issues? Plus, she didn't think anyone can go through what I've been through and not see a therapist.

"Diamond, say something please! I'm sorry. I knew you wouldn't have come if I told you what it was. I just didn't want to come by myself." Almost on cue a valet ran up and opened my door.

"Good evening, ladies." He reached for my hand, but I ignored it and got out of the car.

"Good Evening," I replied.

Shit! She's furious! I've known Diamond long enough to know when I'd crossed the line, and this was one of those times. The valet opened my door and helped me out of the car. We hadn't left the parking lot yet and already Dye was getting stares. People getting out of their cars, the valets, everyone was staring at her. Not that you could blame them. She didn't have to do anything, but her mere presence commanded your attention, whether you wanted to give it or not. I understood why she was so sensitive and hated things like this, but I couldn't accept it. She was such a good person and deserved happiness and she wasn't going to get it reading books and running her plethora of companies all damn day. I tried and Armand had tried, but to no avail. As she stood in the moonlight I could see the anger flickering behind her eyes, and yet she was still flawless. She turned to walk up the stairs and I stepped in front of her.

"Look at me. We've been friends for an eternity. You know that I would never intentionally hurt you, right? I just want the best for you. I'm sorry I lied, but I know you're going to enjoy yourself. Don't you trust me?" I asked.

"Yes, but sometimes I feel as though you don't really understand me, Michelle. You know what? It doesn't matter right now, let's just go in and win you this guy. I'll be fine." She was using that dismissive tone she gives people who upset her, but it wasn't the time or place to rip them a new asshole.

I could never bear it if Dye and I weren't friends or if she'd just written me off like I'd seen her do to so many people who had crossed her. She had done so much for me. She was the reason I went to law school and the reason I passed the bar. Her perspective on things always blew my mind. She had never judged me and was always there when I needed her. My family loved her and the hard part is I knew that deep down she was sad and there was nothing I could do about it. As she gave me a small smile and headed up the stairs, I promised myself I would stop pushing her. Losing my best friend wasn't worth it, but then you had to think if I did nothing would I slowly lose her anyway.

There was a huge man at the door with some type of book checking off names. Michelle walked up and gave her name then made a funny comment about probably being at the end of the list since she was just invited today. He found her name quickly and it did indicate she was bringing a guest so I was all set. We stepped through the mahogany doors into an exquisite limestone foyer; there were two large winding stairways to your left and right that took you upstairs. As your eyes traveled upward, they were met by indescribable murals on the ceiling and the magnificent crystal chandelier hanging in the center. The entrance to the great room was off to the left of the foyer. Michelle and I walked in. I could feel eyes all over me. Michelle was saying something, but I was off in my own little world so I only caught the ending.

"I'm sorry. What did you just say?"

"I said this house is beautiful and that I can't believe we're here. I'm freaking out Dye. What if he doesn't like me?"

"It's obvious he has great taste and must know a good thing when he sees it. You'll be fine," I said, squeezing her hand. We had only been there a couple minutes, but I had already surveyed the crowd. There were several familiar faces from television and a couple from my inner circles, but I didn't see my grandparents.

"Do you want to get something to drink?" I asked, motioning towards the bar.

"Sure." We turned to head to the bar and heard someone call Michelle's name.

"OmiGod! It's Quinn. How do I look?" she asked through a clenched smile, smoothing the front of her dress.

"You look gorgeous. Now stop fidgeting."

He walked up, gave her a nice hug and a kiss on the cheek, taking a step back he held her at arms length with his hands on both her shoulders.

"Wow, you look great! I was hoping you would come." His eyes were gleaming as he looked down at her. "Did you have any problems getting here?"

"None. You gave great directions. You look great as well. This is quite the party and a lovely house."

"Thanks. Now that you're here, the party should be even better. Thanks for coming. Let me get you a drink and then I want to introduce you to a few people, some of whom you may or may not already know," and moving his hand to the small of her back they turned to walk away.

"Um Um," I said, clearing my throat as loudly as I could.

"Jesus, I'm sorry. Quinn this is my best friend Diamond." I could tell Michelle was mortified that she had forgotten me, but I didn't mind.

Quinn looked a little embarrassed, "I'm sorry that was rude of me. I didn't notice you standing there. It's very nice to meet you. I guess you're the one I should be thanking, since Michelle wouldn't have come without you." Ummm, that was a first. He hadn't noticed me. I like this guy already. He was definitely cute. Quinn was about six-feet two-inches, with a slender build, wavy blonde hair, freckles scattered across his nose and cheeks, and beautiful blue eyes. He was built like a swimmer with broad muscular shoulders. He was wearing a tailored tux and looked very handsome. Since I didn't know what to expect, I was pleasantly surprised.

"It's nice to meet you as well. I've heard lots of nice things about you," I said as we shook hands. *For such a strong looking man he was a little light on the grip, but that didn't mean anything* I thought with a smile.

"Please join us. Let me get you both a drink and then we can start to make rounds," he said stepping aside to have us walk ahead of him.

"No that's fine. You two go ahead and we'll catch up later." I had no intentions of "making rounds." If anything I wanted to find a corner so I could do one of my favorite things, people watch.

"Dye, are you sure? At least let me introduce you to some of my colleagues," her eyes were pleading with me.

"No really, I'll be fine. We'll sit together at dinner. I see a few people I know so I'll entertain myself. Quinn it was nice to finally meet you

25

and I'm sure I'll be seeing you around." I ignored Michelle's protests and made my way through the crowd towards the bar. I got the bartender's attention almost immediately and requested a Bailey's Irish Cream on the rocks. He just stood there looking at me with his mouth open. After an uncomfortable amount of time had passed, I raised my voice slightly and said, "I'm sorry. Can I have a Bailey's on the rocks?" He seemed to snap out of whatever trance he was in and gave me a nice smile.

"Your wish is my command," he said with a wink. *Oh God, here we go, just give me my drink buddy,* I thought. He placed my drink on the counter and was about to start up some mindless conversation, but I said thank you, quickly grabbed the glass and scurried off to the corner.

Michelle wasn't lying. Everyone was here. So far I'd seen a couple senators, politicians, football and basketball jocks, actors, models, and more fake breasts than I care to recall. I had a couple brief conversations with a few people from my inner circles, but tried to move on quickly since I was out of my element. I made my way over to the open French doors that led out to the courtyard, where there were people mingling and two Asian women playing the harp at the bottom of the steps. The weather had cleared up nicely from the showers that had persisted until early afternoon, so the air was cool and slightly damp. There was a young man standing in front of me surrounded by a school of women all doting on him and laughing at his jokes. I found their conversation and women's behavior rather amusing. He had a thick Spanish accent and I thought I recognized his voice, but I couldn't see his face. He was asking something about a dish he tried at a French restaurant he had recently been to. He couldn't pronounce it but thought this ingredient began with an "F." He was going on and on about how much he paid and it was a delicacy he wanted to try it again but wasn't sure what to ask for. He asked the women if they knew what he was talking about and a busty blonde chimed, "Was it fish?" I almost died trying to keep from bursting out with laughter. Fish? I felt bad for the poor thing. He rolled his eyes and impatiently replied, "I said it was a delicacy, fish isn't a delicacy." Eager to stay in his favor the other girls started yelling out their suggestions: Caviar? French something? Filet mignon? Finally he got frustrated and said never mind he'd just have to call the restaurant and find out.

I don't know what got into me, but I said, "Was it Foie Gras?" Everyone in the group turned to see who had said it. They were all pretty shocked when they saw me standing off to the side.

"That's it! How do you pronounce it? Flug Grass?"

He stepped out of the crowd and stood in front of me. His eyes seemed to be drinking in the sight of me. His entourage didn't appear too happy as I saw lips start to pout, arms fold, and eyes begin to roll. Now I knew who he was, Juan Estapa, the young Spaniard that had taken the soccer world by storm, leading the US team to victory in the recent World Cup Finals.

"It's actually pronounced, f-wah gra," I replied.

"And what is it? No one with me at the restaurant seemed to know."

"I'm not sure you want to know."

"Yes, I do."

"Well it refers to the methods farmers use to turn duck and goose livers into the "delicacy" known as pâté de foie gras," everyone seemed interested so I continued. "Umm…the term delicacy is really a contradiction, since there isn't anything remotely delicate about the process. Foie gras is a French term meaning "fatty liver" and it's produced by force-feeding ducks and geese. These birds are compelled to consume much more high-energy food, mostly corn, than they would eat voluntarily. They are force-fed tremendous amounts of feed via a 12- to 16-inch plastic or metal tube, which is shoved down their throats and attached to a pressurized pump. The force-feeding may be performed twice daily for up to two weeks for ducks and three to four times daily, for up to twenty-eight days for geese. The force-feeding causes the liver to increase in size about 6-10 times compared to the normal size for a bird. This damages their liver and often kills them. Then tah dah, you've got your delicious foie gras." I was slightly out of breath and everyone looked completely shocked.

"That is absolutely fascinating. *You're* absolutely fascinating. How do you know all that?" Juan replied stepping into me with an out stretched hand.

"I'm sorry, I get a little carried away sometimes. I like holding on to useless pieces of information. If you'll excuse me," I said as I turned to leave, and he took my elbow.

"Please don't go, join my private party. My name is Juan Estapa and you are?"

"I know who you are and I'm *not* a fan of pâté de foie gras. Have a nice evening," I replied over my shoulder, and without stopping, I slipped my hand free and walked through the crowd out onto the patio. I spent the next hour avoiding Mr. Estapa and chit chatting with a couple senators and their wives. I was deep in a conversation about the recent controversy over the cost of NASA experiments when someone tapped me on my shoulder.

"There you are I've been looking all over for you." It was Michelle, looking relieved. "Can I steal you for a moment?" There were a few protests and comments about finally talking to someone with such an interesting perspective on things. I promised to return and Michelle and I walked inside.

"You seem to be having fun," she said.

"So far so good, that group was pretty nice. How about you? How are things going with Quinn?"

"Great. He's hoping you weren't offended by him not seeing you. I'm sorry about that. I just got so caught up in his voice I…"

"Offended? Please, I was actually flattered. That was a first for me. He seems really nice. You two look good together."

"You really think so? Dye, he wouldn't let me leave his side. He's introducing me as his friend and colleague, but he's held my hand a couple times. Anyway, I was worried about you. Dinner is going to be served soon so I wanted to grab you so you could sit with us." She was leading me into the main dining room where the guests had already started to be seated.

"Where are you sitting?" I asked.

"Somewhere up front."

"Figures," I said, a little annoyed.

She lowered her voice, "There's someone I want you to meet. He's Quinn's best friend and one of the top lawyers in the country. You'll like him, but watch out for Lola, she's his ex and a complete bitch. No one in the firm likes her, but I'll fill you in on her later."

"Michelle, no matchmaking please! I've been enjoying myself, don't spoil it." I could see Quinn just ahead of us in a group of five or six people.

"Found her! Everyone, this is my best friend Diamond Chantiel. Dye, this is Quinn's sister Erin and her boyfriend Richard, Todd, Lola, and Quinn's best friend Jonathan, all of whom work at the firm. Actually, Jonathan is the head partner, so technically my boss," Michelle announced with a smile. I was trying not to stare, but Jonathan Hamilton could very well be the most beautiful man I'd ever seen.

"It's nice to meet all of you," I said as I did a general wave and smiled. They all responded with smiles, the only one I didn't seem to get a favorable welcome from was Lola.

"Oh, my God, that dress is absolutely stunning! Who's it by?" Erin asked, all but drooling on me.

"Umm, a friend of mine made it for me."

"Made? Well, it's beautiful, it fits you perfectly. Mine is a Vera Wang original."

"It's lovely. Quinn, this is a very nice party." I hoped it wasn't too obvious I wanted to change the subject.

"Nice? Do you get out much? A 4th of July cookout is nice. Your mom's birthday party is nice, but this is the party of the year. Only the crème de la crème are here!" Lola said, obviously annoyed by my unintentional downplay of the "party of the year." The others seemed a little taken back by her tone.

"I guess I should be thankful I got in on the hem of Meesh's skirt since it was intended just for the crème de la crème," I said in an almost grossly sweet tone. Her name had now been placed in my mental black book. Rarely did anyone ever get out of that book and back on my good side.

"Lola, give me a break," Jonathan said. "This whole thing started out pretty benign and over the past three years you've managed to turn it into a celebrity circus. Diamond, I agree that it's nice, but it used to be even nicer, and fifty percent smaller," he said, smiling at me. We all laughed, except Lola. God, he had a beautiful smile, and that voice. Was I just holding my breath while he was talking? What the hell was wrong with me? I couldn't stop looking at him, and I must've been imagining things because I could swear he was looking at me as well. Lola practically did a somersault to get beside Jonathan as we made our way to the dinner table, so I ended up sitting between Michelle and Erin, directly facing Jonathan who was between Quinn and Lola. They talked shop for a little bit and then Quinn switched the subject asking me what I did for a living.

"That's hard question," I said with a laugh, "I do a little of everything."

"Are you a lawyer?" Lola asked.

"Yes and no," I replied.

"What does yes and no mean? Either you are or you aren't, it's really not that difficult," Lola responded with total disdain. This bitch must be out of her mind! She obviously didn't know who she was dealing with. Michelle was squeezing my leg under the table, because she knew I was two seconds away from telling this heifer where to go and how to get there. It was moments like these where I could feel my mother's side of the family coming out in me.

"Well, I *did* go to law school, and I *did* pass my bar, so technically I *am* a lawyer, but I don't practice law on a daily basis. I really only studied it for the knowledge. I have my own company, hence my yes and no answer." *That should shut her up,* I thought.

"What type of company?" asked Richard.

Here we go? It's time for the pry into Diamond's life section of the evening. I briefly explained my company and the various industries from oil to biotech and left everyone for the most part dumbfounded. I fueled a few more questions before Jonathan jumped in and suggested that if they didn't want to scare me off, they should stop with all the questions. They all started laughing.

I had to admit they were pretty nice. When everyone was seated in the ballroom, Quinn said a brief welcome and the feast began. The food just kept coming. The conversation was great and I was honestly enjoying myself. Quinn couldn't keep his eyes off Michelle and they

30

seemed very *into* each other. Much to my dismay, Señor Estapa stopped by and all but forced himself between Michelle and me, asking if anyone at the table would care to give him my name. He went on to say how Cupid had shot him tonight with my arrow and I was refusing his advances. There were a couple dramatic "awww's" from Michelle and Erin. I wondered if there was a way to nip this in the bud without completely humiliating him. Everyone seemed to be enjoying his broken hearted performance, except me.

"If I give you her name will you leave her alone?" Michelle asked, obviously sensing my increasing frustration.

"Don't you dare," I whispered through a clenched smile. "I'll take care of this myself." Turning my attention to Juan, I gave him my sweetest smile, "El señor. Perdón, pero el corazón es prometido a otro, y él no toma amablemente a insinuaciones indebidas. Aprecio el cumplido, pero si usted abriga su vida y la pierna que patean, entonces sugiero que usted sale y desiste de molestarme. Y significo esto en la manera más agradable posible."

"My apologies," he replied, taking my hand and holding it to his lips, "El es sinceramente el hombre más afortunado en el mundo." And with that he turned and walked away. My table was in complete silence as I could tell people were trying to do a mental translation.

Todd finally asked, "What did you just say to him?"

Quinn replied, "I understood 'my heart and compliment' and then he said something about the most fortunate man in the world." Soon everyone was piping in with their answers.

"Well, what did you say?" probed Michelle.

"Nothing. I told him my heart was promised to someone else and that I appreciated the compliment. It doesn't matter what else I said. What does matter is that he's gone," I said with a smile. There was an eruption of laughter and I couldn't help but join in, especially since I'd left off the part of the translation where I threatened to break his kicking leg. As the evening progressed, I had to force myself to stare at my plate so that I wouldn't keep looking at Jonathan. I was becoming a little embarrassed by the thoughts that were going through my mind. Then it happened.

I could feel someone come and stand behind me and from looking across the table at the others I knew the person was someone Jonathan and Quinn seemed to know.

"Gentlemen, you have outdone yourself this time around. I apologize for being late, but my wife and I had a few appointments," the German accent was subtle but definitely there.

"Nathan, it's wonderful to see you again." Jonathan said as he got up and the man walked around the table to shake is hand. "When did you get in?"

"Viktoria and I came in yesterday…" he said as he slowly surveyed the table. No running, now he'd seen me. The shock on his face was clear and everyone turned their attention to me.

Chapter 4

"It can't be," my grandfather said, his voice barely audible and coarse with emotion. I wiped the corners of my mouth and stood up. "Diamond, is that you?"

"Dye," Michelle said in a low voice, she was squeezing my arm, "Let's go."

"Diamond, please don't leave." Everyone was clueless as to what was happening, but no one took their eyes off of us. He stepped forward and reached out his hand to take my arm and I jumped back so suddenly I bumped into the waiter clearing plates from the table behind me and both him and his wares when flying. There were gasps all over the room. Anyone not paying attention to what was happening was now completely focused on us. I was completely mortified.

"It was very nice to meet all of you. I apologize for the mess. Please let Michelle know what the damage is and I will surely take care of it." I took my purse up and with my head held high and my mind spinning, I started to make my way through the tables, focused only on the exit. Michelle was scrambling at my side trying to keep up. I could hear Quinn's voice calling after her and my grandfather's voice high above his.

"Diamond. Diamond, please." I could hear him calling me. "Diamond Skovachy, enough!" Nathan finally yelled. I stopped dead in my tracks and turned to face his direction. Skovachy. The pain and anguish seemed to come back immediately. It had been so long since I'd been called by that name. My eyes told the story as I made my way back to the table. My lungs hurt. It hurt to breathe. Were the walls spinning? *Shit, Diamond pull yourself together. You will not rip his heart out. You will not make a scene. And you will not pass out.*

"My name is Diamond Chantiel," I heard myself saying. Michelle was pulling me towards the door and I kept pulling free. I stopped when I was a few feet in front of him. "My name is Diamond Chantiel, and don't you ever forget it, you son of a bitch. The name Skovachy was buried eighteen years ago with my parents and my grandparents." My voice didn't seem to be my own. It was laced with something. I could hear the whispering around the room start.

"Please, I just want to talk to you. We just want to talk to you. You owe your grandmother that much. We love you. We've been searching for you for so long. I need you to forgive me." His tears were falling now.

"Owe? I don't owe *you* anything! *You* owe me my family," I snapped. He had opened the flood gates, so I hope he'd brought his boat. "It was *you* that allowed them be raped, tortured and slaughtered, over a fucking oil field. *You* thought too much of yourself to save your son's wife and his daughter. Or should I say you thought too little of us. It's because of *you* my father killed himself. I owe *you* nothing! *You* owe me everything!" Now I knew what my voice was laced with. Hate. "How dare you say that to me? Owe? It's been eighteen years, do you really want to bring up who owes who? You selfish, thoughtless bastard!"

No one around us said anything, they were all just quietly putting the pieces together.

"There isn't anything I wouldn't give to take back everything that happened and for you to forgive me."

"It's a little too late for you to start giving things up now, Nathan. Eighteen years to be exact! The one time when it mattered most your greed wouldn't let you."

"I made a terrible mistake that I live with every day. I broke my wife's heart and I lost you. Don't you understand? We came here for you. We never stopped looking for you."

"For me?" I looked incredulous.

His eyes were darting back and forth as he realized we were the center of attention. "Diamond, this isn't the place. Let's go some place private and talk." The function's hired photographer was taking pictures. Even then my grandfather was still thinking about his image.

"This is as good a place as any. Why would you come here for me?" I didn't care who heard us or who recognized me.

"For your grandmother," his voice was heavy with emotion and his tears continued to fall.

"Why? My grandmother what?" I pressed.

"Your…I don't know how to say…your grandmother…Viktoria is dying." He looked like he was in such pain. "Her final wish is that she sees you again."

I felt like someone had knocked the air out me. I think I actually stumbled, Meesh caught me.

"Dying? From wh…how long does she…" I could barely hear my own voice. My mind was spinning. Why did I even care?

"Ovarian cancer. They've given her less than three months. She wanted to come here as soon as she found out, because this is the last place we heard you were."

I was silent for a long time. "I wasn't expecting this. I've played this meeting out so many times in my head and each time it ended the same way, with one of us not breathing. I need time to think. I'll call you at the Fairmont."

"How did you know we were at the Fairmont?"

"I like to know where you are, so I will know where not to be. If it weren't for Michelle, I would never have been here. You should thank her."

"I'll wait to hear from you," my grandfather responded not even glancing at anyone at the table. He turned, brushing past the photographer and left.

"Dye I'm so sorry," Michelle said in a low voice

"Don't be. It was only a matter of time." I said. As I turned to leave I heard Michelle telling Quinn good bye.

"Michelle, you don't have to leave. I'll take a cab home."

"No, you shouldn't be alone right now. I don't mind."

"No, I would actually prefer to be alone. You stay and we'll talk tomorrow." Turning to Quinn, I apologized for the scene I'd caused and left, never looking back in their direction.

I rushed out into the night, gasping for air as the intense pressure between the walls of my head grew and my chest tightened. I stood there with my eyes tightly closed and let the cool night air sweep across my face and instantly had the urge to cry. My grandmother was dying. They still loved me. They'd been looking for me. I wanted someone to hold me and kiss me and tell me that everything would be all right, but there was no one. A wave of nausea came over me and I felt myself swaying. Just when I thought my knees would give, a strong arm slipped around my waist and steadied me.

"You're not all right. Let me have my driver take you home." Jonathan was standing beside me and looking at me intently. I started to feel warm, almost feverish, as I pulled away.

"That's not necessary. I'll be fine, I just got a little light-headed," I said, as I fished for my mobile in my purse.

"Diamond, you are not all right. I want to take you home." There was a kind firmness in his tone that I recognized. That was the way Armand spoke to me when the subject really wasn't debatable. "I won't take no for an answer. I don't have to tell you that from a legal perspective if anything were to happen to you I would be liable," he said with a smile.

"You shouldn't leave your guests."

"These are really Quinn's guests, and with Michelle here, I don't think he will notice I'm gone."

"I'm sure Lola will notice though." Why did I say that? What was I thinking? That didn't even sound like me.

"I couldn't care less what Lola noticed," he responded in a nonchalant way. He motioned to one of the valets that he was ready and in no time they brought his car around.

"Where is your driver?" I asked.

"Well, if you had said yes to the driver, I would've borrowed a valet's hat," he said with a smile as he opened the door for me and helped me in. He got in, reached over and fastened my seatbelt, started the car and we were off. God, it was hot in here, I was burning up. What was I doing?

"How do you open your windows?" I was almost frantic looking for buttons on his door but there were none.

"They're right here. Let me," as he reached the center console and lowered my window. The cool air felt soothing against my hot flesh. After we drove for a few minutes, he asked "Are you feeling any better? You certainly have more color now than when I saw you outside the house. Let me know if you need me to pull over."

Damn right I have more color, you make me hot. "Thank you. I really appreciate this. You didn't have to come outside to check on me."

Not taking his eyes off the road, he responded, "Don't thank me, I needed to know you were okay. It was ninety percent concern and ten percent selfish reasons."

"Needed is a strong word, don't you think? What are the selfish reasons?"

"I feel a little stupid even…even…never mind. Listen, this would be a good time to get your address or directions so I know where I'm supposed to go." He seemed uncomfortable, he started fidgeting and then he rolled his window down as well. I think I made him uncomfortable.

"Jonathan, are you married?" That question was too personal. What the hell was I doing? Who is this woman?

He chuckled trying to hide his discomfort, "Umm, no. Why?"

"Do you have a girlfriend?" That's it, I had completely lost my mind and there was no turning back now.

"No. I broke up with Lola a little over a year ago and I've been on a couple dates, but nothing serious. I just haven't had the time. Again, I ask why? Are you married or seeing anyone? I wouldn't want anyone to break my kicking leg," he said with a smile. The confusion had left his eyes and intrigue remained.

"You're funny. Why didn't you tell me you could speak Spanish? I hope you know he had it coming."

"Believe me, if you hadn't said something I would have." We both started to laugh then. "You never answered me," he pressed.

"No to both your questions. And I was asking because I lied earlier. I really don't want to be alone tonight and if you had a spare room at your house and I wasn't stepping on anyone's toes, I would ask to spend the night."

There was a slight pause as he tried to read my eyes. He was hesitant, "Sure you can spend the night. I have a couple spare rooms so you can take your pick and if you need to talk I'll be there as well." He didn't seem as uncomfortable as before.

We drove a little while longer. "Jonathan?"

"Umm"

"Just so you know I've never done anything like this before. I mean sleeping over at a stranger's house."

"I didn't think you had and I would hope that I was a little more to you than a complete stranger seeing that our best friends are head over heels for each other. I'm just glad I was here to help. It will all work out."

Chapter 5
Love At First Sight

I can't believe Diamond Skovachy was sitting in my car. I noticed her the moment she walked into the main ballroom. I didn't recognize her at first, but when I saw Nathan's face I began to put it all together. God, she was exquisite. Quinn and I were talking when they walked in. I would've gone over and introduced myself, but I assumed he would bring them back to introduce them to the group. He brought Michelle, but Diamond had gone to the bar. That was it. After that I couldn't pay attention to any conversations going on around me. I just found myself constantly surveying the crowd looking for her. I spotted her in a few deep conversations with some very important people, but by the time I finally made my way over the group she was gone. When she came over before dinner, it took every ounce of willpower I had not to stare at her. My heart was beating a million miles a minute. Then I listened to her talk and realized I never met anyone like her before in my life. I've known my share of beautiful women and none of them intimated me, but her beauty far surpassed any I'd ever known and she left me feeling weak. There was something about her that kept drawing me in. Our eyes kept meeting and it was obvious she was trying to focus on other things. After everything happened and she left, I excused myself and went after her. I couldn't let this be it. After tonight I had to see her again. I know it seems selfish, but I needed to make sure it wasn't just the alcohol, or that dress, or the atmosphere and mostly that I wasn't crazy. It's funny, but I saw myself taking care of her and then I found her standing outside. I didn't know what was wrong with me but I wanted to see her again. I wanted to learn all the secrets I saw hidden behind those eyes. I wanted to make all her pain go away.

The mere thought of her made me hot, I was thankful when she opened her window, I thought that would help but it didn't. The scary part was that it wasn't only physical, everything about her I found attractive and unbearably sexy. How she handled Lola and the Spaniard, the way she laughed, how her skin felt when I touched her. She made each of my senses burn. Her eyes told a story that I wanted to read in its entirety.

Nathan Skovachy was a close family friend and I had known him most of my life. He was my late grandfather's dearest friend up until they had a falling out and had been a mentor to my father and uncle. He was one my father's first clients and had singlehandedly shown my uncle the tricks of the oiling trade. There wasn't a corner of the world where the story of his family's murder didn't reach. My parents were deeply upset and left with my grandmother as soon as the news broke to console the Skovachy's. My grandfather was already there. It was during my first year of college and I remembered watching the funeral on television. Seeing Diamond walking alone behind the four caskets broke everyone's heart. I felt sorry for her that she had to walk alone. I had never met her before tonight but had never forgotten her face. As I looked over at her with her eyes closed and arms folded across her chest, I vowed she would never have to walk alone if I had anything to say about it. I wanted to be her friend.

Chapter 6

I woke up to Jonathan tapping me on my shoulder. "Diamond, we're home," he said.

We're home I thought. *We are home.* God that sounded so good to me. I smiled and opened my eyes.

"What time is it?" I couldn't believe I'd fallen asleep under the circumstances.

"It's a little before one. The drive only took forty-five minutes or so."

We got out of the car. His house wasn't what I expected after seeing Quinn's. It was big, but seemed more quaint with the ivy growing up the side. I could tell he had a garden, because I could smell the jasmine and the lady-of-the-night plants. It was dark, but the moonlight put a warm glow on everything.

"Come on in. Let me give you a quick tour, show you your room and if you want to take a shower or anything, let me know. I've got some pjs I got for my birthday from a great aunt that are way too small. She obviously thinks I'm still sixteen," he said jokingly.

He showed me around downstairs, and then we went upstairs. I couldn't stop staring at his butt as he walked up the stairs. What was wrong with me? I couldn't think straight and what I was thinking was a little embarrassing. I felt like a completely different person with him, almost like caution was thrown to the wind.

His room was very masculine, but beautifully decorated. The dark wood added to the cozy feeling you got throughout the house. We ended in my room which was down the hall from his. There was a nice balcony with a lovely view of the city. He opened the doors and we stepped into the cool night air.

"That's it. Abode de Jonathan," he said with a smile and his arms outstretched.

"You have a beautiful home."

"Thanks. So would you like to take a shower or I could make you some tea or hot chocolate. You let me know, I just want you to be comfortable. I'll bring those pajamas so you can get some sleep." He turned to leave.

"All they wanted was an oil field," I whispered. He stopped when I started talking and sat on the chaise in the corner of the room reaching out his hand for me to sit beside him. I took it and sat close to him. "We were more worthless to him than his oil field. Countless times I wished my grandparents had died instead of my parents. I wanted them to feel the pain I felt. All the visions and smells came back tonight. The minute I saw his face everything that I'd tried to forget or bury deep in the reservoirs of my mind came flooding back. And yet, after seeing him tonight, I know now I still love them. I'm so confused. I just want the pain to go away. *I* just want to go away." Jonathan just listened. "I've tried to forget, but I can't. I pride myself on being so strong, on never shedding a tear over this tragedy, on no one ever knowing how much this had all hurt me, on never needing anyone. I needed to be strong, or should I say, I needed to appear strong. I didn't want pity, 'poor Diamond, poor little girl.' I wanted to be strong for my parents. They would've wanted me to be, and that's been my life's motto whenever I felt the dull pain of sorrow trying to creep into my heart or my mind. Michelle hates that about me. Up to this evening, she was telling me how my pride was going to kill me. She calls me the princess of pride.

Maybe I do need to see a shrink. I don't know anymore." I stood up and started walking back and forth. "I don't want to need or love them, and right now I hate my traitorous heart for turning on me so quickly after all these years. I want to hate them. It's all I know." I sat down, leaned back on his shoulder and closed my eyes and saw a vision my mother naked displayed for the entire world to see, lying in a pool of blood and excrement, her legs spread and body maimed, where chunks of her flesh had been removed down to the bone. Her eyes were open, looking at me. I could feel the nausea rising. I tried to get up, but my legs wouldn't obey. My throat was burning and my mouth was full. I stumbled on the patio trying to reach the decorative urn in the corner, but the vomit kept coming. I couldn't stop it. Every time I thought it was over another wave would wash over me. My stomach muscles hurt, but I couldn't stop. Jonathan had gotten towels and was on his knees beside me, rubbing my back and holding me as the waves caused my body to convulse. Then the tears came. They just poured out of me. My voice wasn't my own. I didn't recognize the guttural sounds I was making. Jonathan just held me and told me it would be okay. He told me he was there for me and to let it all out. I beat his chest and wailed. I tried to turn away, but he wouldn't let me go.

"No," he said, "Let it all out. Leave it all here. This was long overdue and you can't fight it anymore." He held me tight and I beat his chest and wailed even more. My body shook as I finally let my pain out. I could taste the saltiness of my own snot and tears running into my mouth, mixing with the fowl taste of my vomit, and I couldn't stop. I tried to pull myself together, gain my composure, but my mind and body wouldn't let me. I sobbed until my eyes were painfully swollen and my throat was raw from my wails. I was weak from exhaustion. My chest and shoulders hurt. When my cries turned to moans, Jonathan picked me up and carried me to the bed. He took my shoes off, walked into bathroom and came back with more towels and a glass of water. I tried to drink it, but started to gag again. He ran downstairs and this time he came back with a bowl of water and started to wipe my face with a cool damp cloth. That felt good. He felt good. For eighteen years I'd held myself together, and the first night I meet a man that makes my skin tingle and tummy flutter, I had to have a major meltdown. I was so embarrassed I didn't want him to look at me anymore. I couldn't even begin to imagine what I looked like at that moment. I felt disgusting. I held his hand from wiping my face and told him 'thank you' and drew my legs up to my chest and turned on my side toward door.

"Please don't turn away from me. I know what you're thinking. Let me help you through this." He placed his hand on my hip and gently pulled me toward him until I was flat on my back.

"I'm so sorry and embarrassed. I don't know…" My voice croaked. It was unrecognizable.

"You have nothing to be sorry or embarrassed about," he said, rubbing the back of my hands. "Absolutely nothing. Now try to get some sleep. I'm here. I'm not going to leave you."

I gave him a crooked smile, pulled his hand to my lips and placed a slow deliberate kiss on his knuckles.

"Thank you." I closed my eyes and the last thing I remembered was Jonathan's smell.

When I awoke and peeped through my swollen eyes at the clock, it said 7:45. Jonathan had pulled the chaise beside the bed and was holding my hand as he slept. He looked uncomfortable. I slipped my hand out of his and turned onto my side so I could get a better look at him. He'd changed into a white t-shirt and flannel pajama pants. He was a gorgeous specimen. I smiled as I thought, *Now that's a face I wouldn't mind waking up to every day for the rest of my life.* I could see the definition of his muscles rippling under the shirt and got a peek at his flat stomach where his t-shirt had raised up, from his awkward sleeping position, to reveal the hint of a tan line above his pajama pants. My God, what a bulge. I forced myself to look away. Ummm he had nice feet, his thighs were muscular, and…shit! The bulge again. I hit my forehead with the palm of my hand and I swung away. I looked down at myself still wearing my dress and then glanced out on the balcony and the reality hit me of what I had done and how I'd behaved last night. I could see where I'd missed the urn. I was mortified. I slipped out of bed, ran down stairs to the kitchen. After a few minutes of rummaging around I found all the cleaning supplies I needed. I ran back upstairs, closed the balcony doors so I wouldn't wake Jonathan and scrubbed the floor clean and put the dirty towels in the wash. When I was finished, I found my pajamas just where he'd left them at the bottom of the bed and went into the bathroom and had a shower. When I emerged I felt so much better. Using a wash cloth and toothpaste I scrubbed my teeth and my tongue. Jonathan was still sleeping when I came back into the bedroom. Even though I could tell he'd never worn the new pajamas they still smelled like him and I found myself bringing the shirt up to my nose to take in the scent of him.

I went back down to the kitchen and while a pot of coffee was brewing I made a few calls. When I was finished I called Armand through our service so that Jonathan's number wouldn't come up. I wasn't ready for the questions. He picked up on the first ring.

"Diamond?"

"Yes. It's me."

"Jesus Christ! Are you okay? Where are you? Do you know how frantic I've been? Michelle is beside herself. I had to give her two Ativan just so she would go to sleep. Where are you?"

"I'm at a friend's house."

"What friend?"

"No one you know. Listen…"

"Are you okay? Meesh told me what happened."

"Yes. I'm better now. What did you find out?"

"Viktoria has been diagnosed with late stage ovarian cancer and they had apparently hired a slew of private investigators to find you. I have their room number at the Fairmont and a complete copy of her chart. Are you sure you're okay?"

"Yes, Armand, I'm fine. Can you do a couple things for me? Fax the entire chart to the attention of Dr. Kimora at Genesis Cancer Research Institute, but use his home fax number. I've already spoken to him and he's expecting it. Contact my grandparents and ask them if they're available tomorrow night for dinner at the Peabody just a couple blocks away from the Fairmont. If they're unavailable then maybe we can schedule something for later in the week. If they are available, make a seven o'clock reservation for four and leave the details on my mobile. Who is our contact at the Fairmont? I need to know every move they make."

"Raquel Welch."

"Well, I need you to contact her immediately and let her know that I should be informed of my grandparent's activity immediately, who comes and who goes. Everything. Is there anything else you think I should know about? "

"Ummm, who else will be joining you for dinner at the Peabody, you said the reservations should be for four?"

"I'm not sure if anyone will be joining me, let's just reserve four seats for now. Anything else?"

"I don't think your grandfather is well either. I was told he's been seeing a cardiac specialist at Lancaster Hospital, but I don't think Viktoria knows. My source also told me that they've made no changes to their will and as it stands, you are still their sole heir."

"I'm not interested in their will and you should know that. I want to see…"

"I've already requested it."

"Requested what? You didn't let me finish."

"I've already requested a copy of your grandfather's chart. Isn't that what you were going to ask me for?"

"Yes. Listen, I have to go. If you need me, call my mobile."

"Diamond, be careful. I don't know where you're staying and I figure if you wanted me to know you would've told me by now. Do you want to talk to Michelle?"

"Is she sleeping?" I asked, completely ignoring the first part of his comment.

"Yes, those Ativan knocked her off her feet. She's curled up in your bed like a baby."

"Then, no, don't wake her. Tell her I'm fine and that I'll talk to her later. I have to go. Thanks for everything."

"All right."

"Oh, oh, oh, Armand?"

"Yes?"

"I need you to send something nice, very nice, to Quinn Holt at his home address, for delivery today. The note should read: *I apologize for the scene I made last night. Accept this as a token of my appreciation for your hospitality. Diamond Chantiel .*"

"Right away."

"Thanks."

"You're welcome."

I hung up and set up a bed tray with a pot of coffee, toast and sliced fruit and went back upstairs. I place the tray on the bureau, poured myself a cup of coffee, grabbed some toast, and went out onto the balcony. The strong scent of PineSol hit me and I realized that I may have gone a little overboard with the cleaning solutions. What a view. It was so beautiful and quiet here, the whole atmosphere was conducive to productive thinking. Quiet and serene. I turned as I heard Jonathan start to stir. No wonder he was stirring, the morning sun was shining through the French doors and directly in his face. I quickly stepped back inside, closed the doors and pulled the shades.

He opened his eyes and squinted at me, a smile playing across his lips. Ummm those lips.

"Well, good morning."

"Good morning to you too. What time is it? How long have you been up?"

"It's almost ten and I got up a little before eight."

He made a low moan and he sat up and rubbed his neck. "Sleeping on this thing was a bad idea."

"I'm sorry. I should've made you go to bed."

"Don't apologize. I wouldn't have had it any other way. What's that smell?" he asked crinkling his nose.

"Umm, I cleaned the balcony and got a little carried away with the PineSol and bleach." I said with a little laugh.

"You didn't have to do that. I would've taken care of it."

"No. I wouldn't want you to clean up my mess."

"I wouldn't have minded. The pajamas look good on you," he said playfully pulling at the bottom of the oversized top.

"Thanks. They're pretty comfortable," as I stood in front of him twirling.

"How are you feeling?" he asked as he reached out and took my hand.

"A lot better than I look. I've had a shower and some caffeine, so I'm good to go," I replied with a smile. "Jonathan?"

"Umm."

"I can't begin to tell you how much I appreciate you letting me stay here last night and being with me during my…"

"It wasn't a problem, and as I said before, I wouldn't have had it any other way." He was looking up at me and smiling. He was easily the most glorious thing I'd ever laid eyes on. I felt stupid for thinking the same thoughts over and over again, but it was the truth. In a tuxedo or pajamas it looked like God had personally chiseled each part of him.

"Would you like some coffee?" I asked as he stood up and towered over me. Everything about him made me nervous. No one ever made me nervous. I needed to get out of his personal space before I did something I regretted.

"Yes," he said, gently squeezing my hands. "Coffee sounds nice. How about I wash up and we can enjoy it out on my balcony. There are lounge chairs out there that I never get to enjoy. Plus, it would be minus the PineSol."

"Sure."

"Why don't you bring the coffee over and I'll join you in a couple minutes." He released my hands and turned to walk away.

I placed my hand over my mouth as I gazed at his tight round rear end as he left the room. I didn't trust myself not to make the "umm umm" sound.

Chapter 7

I walked into his bedroom and placed the tray on the table out on the balcony. I could hear the water running in his master bathroom and I found myself getting hot again. My heart was beating out of the stadium. Jesus, Diamond, it's only coffee on a balcony, not strip poker. I found myself thinking back to the novels I'd read growing up and visualizing myself with Jonathan. I wanted to kiss him so badly. I had been dwelling on it since last night when he was holding me, but there was a part of me that was afraid to disappoint him. I had heard of Jonathan Hamilton and he was the most sought after bachelor in town. I'm sure he'd been with many women. What was I thinking? I shouldn't be here. I should quit while I am ahead. Society would probably look at me and think I too had been with many men, but little did they know how wrong they were. I looked out onto the balcony and then my eyes trailed back into the bedroom and focused on the bed. The water in the bathroom had stopped running. I can't do this. I don't know who I thought I was fooling with this spending the night thing, being Ms. Adventurous, but in a minute it won't be him and he will see how truly inexperienced I am. I turned and headed for the bedroom door, but stopped in my tracks as he came out of the bathroom. I swung around looking like a deer caught in the headlights. Shit!

"Did you forget something?"

"Umm, no," I said looking down.

"Then where are you going?"

"Nowhere." I was still looking any and every where except at him.

"Are you okay?" he asked, walking toward me. With every step he took toward me, I took a step back. "What's wrong?" I was burning up again.

"Nothing. I just...I just can't do this."

"Do what?"

"This!" I said pointing toward the balcony. "You!" Now I was looking at him intently. "I've always been an honest woman and was never very good at hiding my feelings. You make me feel things and think things that I can't control and I honestly don't like it. I look at you and find myself envisioning these thoughts and imagining. I..."

"Diamond."

"No, let me finish. I've already embarrassed myself and now I feel like I can only make it worse. I've known you less than twenty-four hours and already you have seen a part of me that no one else has ever seen." I could feel the tears burning my eyes, but I wouldn't let them fall. He walked towards me, and with my back against the door I had nowhere to run. I realized I'd still not gotten last night out of my system. I turned my face to the door and then the tears fell. He was right behind me and I felt his large hands on my shoulders.

"Please don't," my voice pleaded.

"You're right, we haven't known each other very long, but there is one thing I'm certain of, and that is I'll never hurt you." He turned me to face him and looked at me. "I've been feeling things and having thoughts about us since the moment I laid eyes on you last night and I promise you that I won't let anything happen that you don't want to happen. I didn't mean anything by this," he said looking around the room. "I just thought it would be nice to have breakfast on the balcony. I have no problem going down to the kitchen; we could eat in the garage or on the roof for all I care. Since we're being honest with each other,

I really just want to be close to you."

All I could do was stare at his lips. His breath was minty from the toothpaste and his face smelled like soap. What did he just say? Something about having thoughts as well? Damn, I couldn't focus on what he was saying when I was so close to him. My body seemed to have a mind of its own, shit; my mind seemed to have a mind of its own.

"Please don't go. You stay here and I'll bring everything down to the kitchen." He turned to walk away but I held his arm.

"Jonathan?" He turned back to answer me.

"Umm…" but my lips were already on his. At first it was just my lips on his, warm and sweet with a hint of saltiness from my tears, then after a few moments I pulled away and looked at him. He was staring at me and looking confused. He licked his lips, as if trying to taste every bit of the sweet moisture I'd left on his mouth, then he turned away.

"I'll grab the coffee…" he started, but I didn't let him finish, my lips were on his again. This time I opened my mouth and took his bottom lip into mine, running my tongue across it. Back and forth. I was hesitant at first, conscious of where my teeth were and making sure I didn't bite him, then I became more confident. I closed my eyes and his arms were still at his side, so I slipped mine through his and up his back, pulling him closer to me. That seemed to be the invitation he was waiting for. He opened his mouth and slipped his tongue deep into my mouth. He wrapped his arms around my waist and brought me even closer. His tongue darted in and out of my mouth and he made tiny circles around my tongue with his own. Damn he was good! I moved my mouth away from his and down to his chin, sucking on it slowly. His stubble felt prickly against my tongue and lips, but I didn't care. I had never tasted anything like him before in my life, so sweet. My face was now buried deep in his neck as I kissed and suckled below his jaw, running my tongue in large deliberate circles across his neck.

"Mmmm…" He let out a soft moan and brought my face back to his, kissing me all over with quick little kisses. I smiled and took his mouth again. I had never felt like this before. It was a while before I noticed how my nipples ached. They were straining upward and outward, trying to break free from the confines of my brassiere. There was a similar pain low in my abdomen trailing to my womanhood. I didn't know how long we were standing there, but it seemed like forever. Neither of us wanted to stop, but he was the one that finally broke free.

"Dye...I...I umm...need to sit down," he said with a smile, pulling me over to the beautifully upholstered bench at the base of his enormous bed. "Come sit." His voice was deep. I was thankful to sit down because I could squeeze my legs together tightly to dull whatever sensations was going on between them. I felt light-headed. I was drunk off of Jonathan's wine and hadn't even finished the glass.

God, this woman didn't know what she was doing to me right now. It was taking every ounce of my strength not to rip her clothes from her body. I wanted to be buried deep inside her so badly, but I was afraid of scaring her away. We would move on her time. It was interesting to me how she could seem so fierce and innocent all in the same breath. I could feel her nipples growing hard when we were against the door and she was pressed to my chest. I had to sit down, since all the blood was rushing from my brain and legs and heading elsewhere. I don't remember ever wanting any woman as badly as I wanted her right at this minute. She was perfect; the way she smelled, the way she laughed, the way she kissed me, but most of all the way I could feel her body responding to mine. Her already full lips had become a little swollen from playing in our rhythmic lip symphony. As we sat she crossed her legs and looked at me. God she was beautiful, she left me breathless. I took her face between my hands and kissed her deeply. I thrust my tongue as deep into her mouth as it would comfortably go and she opened her mouth to receive it willingly. As our lips twirled in their own private salsa she raised onto her knees, resting her buttocks on her heels, she started to make low moans. My member was growing to huge proportions and I was hoping she couldn't see or feel it stretched against my, now too tight, pajama pants.

"I've...never...felt...like...this," she said softly between kisses.

"Neither have I," I replied slightly breathless. She stopped kissing me and pulled away.

"You don't have to do that," she whispered.

"Do what?"

"Lie about how I make you feel, or feel the need to exaggerate your feelings to make me comfortable. I know you've been with plenty of women and many I'm sure, who don't fumble and bumble their way through their first kiss." I placed my finger on her lips.

"First of all, I would never lie to you! And secondly, if you call that fumbling and bumbling, then I don't know if I could handle your experienced kissing. Everything you do and how you do it is perfect to me." I reached for both her hands. "Believe me."

"I'm sorry. I shouldn't have said that. I was worried I would disappoint you in some way. I'm glad I didn't." She seemed almost proud of herself.

"Don't worry about it; I don't think your disappointing me is even possible. What are you doing today?"

"Honestly?"

"Always."

"Well, I was hoping I could spend the day with you, and if my grandparents agreed to meet me at the Peabody for dinner tomorrow night, that you would join me." I was hoping she would say something like that. Dinner with Nathan might be a little awkward, but I wanted every opportunity I could get to spend some time with her.

"If you really want me to, I have no problem joining you for dinner, a day with you sounds like a plan. I'm supposed to be going to an anniversary party tonight for my parents. It's their 40th wedding anniversary. Would you like to join me as my date?"

"Really? Are you sure? I don't want things moving too fast. Doesn't the meet the parents' part come later down the road?"

"Down the road where?"

"After a few dates or something like that. Listen," she said with a smile, "I may be a little inexperienced and even naïve when it comes to this type of thing, but since you aren't married and aren't seeing anyone, and we've just spent the last hour making out, I was wondering if you would like to be my boyfriend." I couldn't help it. I had to burst out laughing. She looked so innocent.

"Now all we need are the two boxes that say, check here for yes and here for no," and we both started laughing. "You're a living contradiction. You don't want things moving too fast in one breath and in the other you're asking me to be your boyfriend."

"I don't know what's gotten into me. I've become so corny, this isn't like me at all. I guess I've never really believed in the casual dating thing. Neither of us is seeing anyone so it just makes sense that we should become a couple. Don't you agree? Maybe I'm wrong and this isn't how this works. Contradiction or not, you didn't answer the question." she said between smiles.

"Yes and yes. Yes, I agree and yes, I would love to be your boyfriend. I've always been a big fan of corn." She made me happy.

"This is wonderful! I can't believe any of this is really happening. I know these things usually don't happen this fast, but it feels right. You feel so right." With that she gave me a huge hug. "Where do we go from here? What are we supposed to do?" She seemed almost like a kid in a candy store.

"I guess we should start by exchanging telephone numbers, spending lots of time together and kiss incessantly. Not necessarily in that order." I added with a smile.

"Sounds good to me. Let's start with the later," and with that she kissed me again. Her tongue curled around mine and danced across the roof of my mouth, sending shivers down my spine. Damn she was good. Could I be in love?

Chapter 8

Once we managed to pull our lips apart, our breakfast on the balcony was wonderful; we talked about anything and everything. I learned how he'd grown up and met Quinn and how he had a vision of building his own corporate and civil law firms. I told him about growing up with Armand and traipsing around the world with my ideas and how I'd met Meesh. Talking to him came so easily. I checked my messages during breakfast and there was one from Armand saying that my grandparents could do dinner tomorrow and asking me to give him a call. I was about to call him back when the buzzer for Jonathan's front gate went off. He looked almost as surprised as I did.

"I wonder who that is?" he asked to no one in particular.

"If you need to run downstairs, it's okay, I'll stay here." I actually didn't want anyone to see me there in pajamas having a late breakfast. The rumor mill would start turning.

"No, I can check from here. Whoever it is will have to come back." He turned on the flat screen television against the wall, entered a channel and his front gate came up on the screen. It was Lola, looking like a younger Jackie O with large sunglasses and a beige trench coat, sitting in her red convertible. "Humph, what does she want?" again to no one in particular. I was already making my way into the bathroom to wash my hands. I didn't want to seem nosey. He pressed the intercom close to the bed. I was very interested in how he handled this, but didn't want him to see just how interested I was.

"Hello?"

"Jonathan, it's me. Lola."

"I know. What is it?"

"Can I come in?"

"No. This really isn't a good time."

"Let me in."

"For what?"

"What do you mean for what? It won't take very long. We need to talk. You left last night without saying goodbye and no one knew where you went. I was worried."

"Listen, something unexpected came up and I had to leave. Lola, we really don't have anything to talk about. I've said all that I'm going to say to you. I have to go."

"Jonathan, please. It will only take a minute."

"Fine, Lola. Only one minute."

"Okay."

He pressed a button and his front gate opened up.

"Diamond, it's Lola, I have to run downstairs. I won't be long," he said as he grabbed the coffee tray and went down the stairs. It was reassuring that he had no problem telling me who it was. Once I heard the front door open, I tip-toed out of the bedroom to the top of the stairs and stood where they couldn't see me. I didn't want to eavesdrop, but had every intention on doing so. I saw Jonathan walk over and lean on the bookshelf, his arms folded across his chest.

"Well?" she asked.

"Well, what?"

"I don't even get a hug?"

"Lola, I don't have the time or patience for this. What do you want?"

"You, I want you!" she practically yelled. "This past year has been miserable for me and seeing you date these worthless bottom-dwellers

56

infuriates me," and with that she opened her trench coat letting it fall to the floor. She was completely naked. *Holy shit*, I thought, *this woman is crazy!*

"What that hell are you doing? Put your clothes on. Now!"

"Why? I know you miss me. I saw how you were looking at me last night. Smiling and laughing with me like it was old times. We were the best lovers. No one has ever satisfied me the way you do."

"What a contradiction! Do you hear yourself? *You're* the one who cheated on me! *You're* the one with the sexual appetite that couldn't be sated!"

"I made a mistake! Please forgive me! You've cheated on me as well, so don't play high and mighty with me. Plus, what was I supposed to do? You would be gone for days at a time on business and you never had time for me. Even when you were around it was like I didn't exist."

"Yes, I did cheat on you, in college over ten years ago! It wasn't after we were engaged! You're right, I was completely devoted to my firm and that hasn't changed, so I'm afraid I would still be away for days at a time."

"I don't care anymore. I understand how much it means to you and I won't have any problems with your work schedule. I know you love me. We've been together too long for you to just throw everything away like this!"

"*Me* throw this away! Let's get this shit straight okay. You didn't make *a* mistake, you made several, eleven to be exact that I've been told and with many of my colleagues. News flash, Lola, I don't love you anymore! I actually fell out of love with you soon after I thought I fell in love with you. Maybe, when my feelings changed years ago, instead of going along for the ride and being too comfortable to start over with someone else, I should have told you instead of letting you and your family pressure me into giving you a ring and for that I'm sorry."

"Stop this! I know you want me. Just touch me and it will all come back. Please." She seemed desperate. I could see her stepping forward trying to touch him and he would brush her off.

"Leave, Lola."

"Jonathan…"

"Get out!"

"Jonathan, please just one more time. I need to feel you inside me one more time!" She was rubbing her nipples and biting on her bottom lip.

"You're sick, and I'm going to count to three before I throw you out on your ass! ONE!"

"What is it? You've never treated me like this and now is seems you can't even bear the sight of me. What has gotten into you?"

"You! You've gotten into me. Your lies and deception. You are so shallow and conniving, that I wonder why I ever stayed with you this long. I thought I couldn't keep my eyes off of you last night and now I can't bear the sight of you?" He walked over and picked up her coat and held it out to her. "Even now you can't get your lies straight. Now leave, and if you ever pull anything like this again, I'll fire you. Now get out!"

She snatched the trench coat and slipped it on, walking towards the door. With one hand she held the door and with the other squeezed the opening of the trench coat. She seemed embarrassed and totally defeated, as though no man had ever refused her.

"Fine! For the record, I'm keeping the engagement ring. You're going to regret this! You will never find anyone that will treat you the way I did."

"For the record, I hope not!" and with that Jonathan slammed the door in her face. Ouch! Jonathan sat on the back of the sofa and leaned forward putting his head in the palms of his hands. He was upset. Outside I could hear the car door slam and Lola speed away.

I could see Jonathan's back rise and fall as he took deep breaths. He stood up, walked over to the door and locked it. I quickly moved from the top of the stairs to the guest bedroom to call Armand.

Chapter 9

It was bothering me that Diamond hadn't told me where she was. She had never kept secrets from me until now and she was definitely hiding something. Friend? What friend? Michelle was her closest friend and anyone else that she would remotely call a friend was thousands of miles away and the fact that Michelle didn't know where she was last night wasn't helping either.

I could hear Meesh upstairs walking around, "Armand?" she yelled.

"I'm in my office."

She ran down the stairs and walked into the office. "Is she here yet?"

"Uh, no, but she called?"

"She did? When? Where is she? Why didn't you wake me?"

"I don't know where she is. She called shortly after you fell asleep and called through our operator so I couldn't identify the call. She said she was fine and that she was staying with a friend?"

"What friend?"

"Thought I might ask you the same question because I have no idea who it could be." Saying it out loud made me even more upset at the thought there could be a facet of her life I wasn't aware of.

"Who could it be? Damn it! I shouldn't have let her leave alone last night."

"Don't upset yourself; she sounded fine, almost happy when she called. I just don't like not knowing who she's with; I'm not worried about her. She said she would talk to you later."

"Do you think she's mad at me?"

"If she was, I couldn't tell. We both know how good she is at hiding her feelings."

The phone rang and almost immediately both Michelle and I jumped for the receiver, but she got a better grip.

"Chantiel residence," she said, playfully sticking her tongue out at me.

"Michelle?"

"Dye? Where are you? Are you okay?"

"Yeah, I'm fine. Let me talk to Armand quickly and then I'll talk back to you."

Michelle handed me the phone and impatiently folded her arms mouthing, "Hurry up."

"Diamond, where are you? Who is this friend? Did you get my message?"

"You know what, this isn't going to work. Put me on speaker-phone." She sounded annoyed. I held down the intercom button and hung up the phone.

"Hello?"

"Go ahead, Dye, you're on speaker-phone," replied Michelle.

"Good. Now I can kill two birds with one stone, since you'll both be asking me the same questions. Armand, I got your message, so if you haven't already, then I guess you can go ahead and hold the Peabody around seven."

"Should the reservation still be for four?"

"Ummm, yes, let's leave it for now. I'll be home later tonight so we can firm it up then."

"Later tonight?" Michelle chimed in. "That's it, Dye, enough with the secrets and the suspense we can't take it anymore. Where are you, and who is this friend that you're with? Should I be jealous?"

"You both have to let me finish without interruption and I will not be bombarded with questions. Agreed?"

"Agreed," said Michelle without hesitation.

"I don't like this one bit," I whined.

"Armand, do you agree or not?" asked Diamond.

"Well, I don't have much of a choice do I? I agree."

"All right then, last night after I left the party, Jonathan Hamilton offered me a ride home…"

"What! You left with Jonathan!" Michelle grabbed my arm and screamed into the speaker phone. "I knew it was strange when he didn't come back. Did anything happen?"

"Didn't I say no bloody interruptions? Which part of that didn't…"

"I'm sorry, I'm sorry, go on." Michelle said, she was wearing the biggest smile and silently jumping up and down with her mouth open.

"As I was saying before I was so rudely interrupted," Diamond said with a little laugh, "Jonathan offered me a ride because I honestly didn't feel like being alone, so I asked him if he wouldn't mind terribly if I spent the night at his house."

"You did what?" Now it was my turn to do the yelling.

"You little tart!" Michelle exclaimed with a smile. "Who said you never learned anything from me, was wrong."

"This is not funny! Diamond, are we talking about Jonathan Hamilton of Hamilton & Holt law firm, the fastest growing firm in the country? The same Jonathan that is most wanted on the worldwide bachelors list and went through a very public break up with a long time girlfriend?"

"I don't know all the details, Armand, but yes. I was a different woman last night after I saw Nathan. I don't know what came over me."

"I do. You've gone completely mad! What possessed you to go home with a complete stranger?"

"Armand, let her finish." Michelle was turning red from obvious excitement.

"I am very much aware of who he is Armand, and I am certainly not a tart, Michelle." She let out a long sigh. "Listen, he has been a complete gentleman and has in no way tried to take advantage of the situation. Armand, you have nothing to be worried about, I didn't learn that much from Michelle or else I wouldn't have slept in the guest room in the same dress I wore to dinner. I actually like him. He does something to me that I really can't explain."

Michelle was twisting my arm before she said, "Dye, I…we trust you completely. You should stay as long as you want. We were just worried, right, Armand?" nudging me with her shoulder, still twisting my arm.

"Yes, we were just worried. I know you have impeccable judgment."

"Thanks. Listen, I have to go, I'll talk to both of you later."

"Dye, call me!" Michelle was yelling as though she didn't understand the concept of speaker phone.

"Don't worry, I will. Bye."

"Bye." I pressed off the phone and walked over to the window. Jonathan Hamilton, umm, she had aimed a little high her first time around, but I was impressed. Should I be worried? I didn't think so. I knew Dye had never *been* with anyone, and as a parent I was proud of that. As her friend, that was another story. I knew she was missing something in her life that she could only get from a companion or lover in a social relationship. Before the day was over I would know everything and more on Mr. Hamilton. My little Diamand had spent the night at a man's house. I smiled inwardly. I'd been waiting for this a long time. Michelle was still screaming and jumping around my office, throwing herself on my leather sofa and burying her face in my pillows, kicking her feet like a teenager.

"Michelle Noir! For the love of God and all that's holy, shut up! I can't even finish my thoughts with you behaving like a madwoman."

"I can't believe this, Armand. This will be so perfect if it works out! I know you're hesitant, but he really is a fascinating guy. The woman he was with before was a complete slut. He and Diamond will be perfect together. You don't have to worry."

I walked over and placed my hand firmly on her shoulder, looking directly into her eyes. "I may seem worried, but I'm really not. I promise you, if he hurts her in anyway, I'll kill him myself. Do you understand me? *I will kill him myself,*" and with a cold smile I left the office. Michelle was completely shocked. If anything ever happened to Diamond, she would learn very quickly that I wasn't exactly who I appeared to me. I could slit his throat during communion and not give it a second thought. As with Diamond, Michelle knew *almost* everything about me.

Zachary and I had been friends since primary school and for the most part had been inseparable up until I joined the army out of prep school. The next eight years I spent working my way up the ranks and leading one of the best Special Forces outfits Her Majesty's Territorial Army had ever seen. My talent for being stealth and deadly came in handy when I returned and joined in Zachary's quest to build up the Skovachy Empire. Believe it or not, services like mine were in high demand. It all depends on how powerful you wanted to be. And the Skovachys wanted to be powerful. Some people thought it was convenient that Nathan's son happened to fall in love with the daughter of the man that could grant him unlimited access to Africa's resources, but I knew for a fact, Zach truly loved Nyrobi. He was hooked the minute he laid eyes on her, and who could blame him? She was a rare beauty, just like Diamond, and she instantly became my family the moment they said "I do." Then once Diamond was born, I was of no use to anyone, falling completely in love with her and watching her grow up. Zach traveled so much that I saw Dye more often than he did, but that didn't matter because when he was home, they were his all. Those bastards caused my best friend to take his life and if it weren't for him entrusting Diamond in my care I would've killed every and anyone I thought had information on their kidnapping. I went through phases where I hated him for not sending me to Africa instead and for killing himself, but someone with a higher power knew why things turned out the way they did. Becoming a father changed my entire perspective on things. Diamond became my priority. She became my all. And as she grew into a beautiful and powerful woman, my *talents* were needed yet again to deter all who thought because she was female she was weak and could easily be taken advantage of. In the beginning I took care of the "problems," but after she hit twenty, she took care of them on her own, insisting that her wrath was better felt when it came directly from her and not through her "muscle." People would fear me and not truly have respect for her and that's not what she wanted. She was vicious when she needed to be. I pitied the people dumb enough to cross her. She carried a hate and rage buried so deep in her that even if they witnessed a spark, it was enough to obliterate them. That's why I wasn't worried about her relationship with Jonathan Hamilton, because in many ways Diamond was far more dangerous than I.

Chapter 10

I hung up with a smile. Sometimes I couldn't believe those two. Well, Michelle, I could, but Armand was a different story. He's always behind me about getting out more and now that I was, I wondered how he would handle it. For a long time he's been the only man in my life. I called Lucy and had her send over some clothes for the remainder of the day and my dinner with Jonathan's parents tonight. She was thrilled the dress was such a hit and was pleased I needed more so soon. I finished up the call and went back downstairs. Jonathan was standing at the sink washing up our breakfast wares. I walked up behind him and slipped my arms around his waist and rested my face on his back. I had always wanted to do that. I felt so close to him, almost like I'd known him all my life.

"Are you okay?" I asked. He seemed tense even though I could feel he'd relaxed a little when I squeezed him.

"I'm fine, just a little upset. How much did you hear?" He turned off the water and leaned back into me, still looking out the window.

"Most of it, I'm sorry." A wave of guilt came over me for eavesdropping.

He turned and put his arms around me. "Don't be sorry. I should apologize. I got so caught up in the moment that I started yelling. I shouldn't have let her in. I'm sorry I put you in that position."

"Don't be. It sounded as though you got things off your chest that needed to be dealt with a long time ago." I hugged him and said, "If you want to be alone this afternoon, I have no problem seeing you tomorrow or during the week." Actually I didn't want to leave, but if he needed space I wouldn't mind.

He stepped back and turned to look at me. "Do you want to go?"

I think in the movies and the books, this is where the girl says "only if you want me too," should I say that or tell him exactly what I was thinking?

"Dye, to do you want to go?" he repeated.

"No, I don't want to go. I don't want to leave your side. I want to stay and make you feel better. Forget the movies and the books!"

"What movies and books?"

Shit! I wasn't supposed to say that part. "Umm, never mind. I want to stay, as long as it's fine with you?"

"Of course I want you to stay," he said with a smile. He picked me up with ease and kissed me. My stomach muscles started to tighten and I instinctively squeezed my legs together. Immediately there was a warmth deep inside me as though in the instant our lips met someone blew on the ambers of my desire and flames flickered to life again. I couldn't get enough of him. Twirling my arms around his neck, I returned his kiss. He felt so good. Finally I slipped back to the ground and opened my eyes and looked at him. His eyes were still closed as though he was still lost in the moment.

"Jonathan," I whispered.

"Umm?" he moaned opening his eyes.

"Is this normal?"

"Is what normal?"

"This…what's happening between you and me? It can't be. This type of thing only happens in fairytales. We haven't even known each other a full day, and…"

"And?"

"And yet..." I closed my eyes and rested my head against his chest.

He ran one hand through my thick curls and gently pulled my face away from his chest so he could look at me. "And yet we seem to share something that can't be described. And yet there's an invisible comfort level between us that causes us to want to share our deepest thoughts and dreams. And yet the physical attraction is so strong, but the emotional attraction is even stronger." He kissed me tenderly. "I can see in your eyes that this scares you and it makes you nervous when you don't know what's going to happen next, but I need you to trust me. Trust that I will never hurt you. Trust that my number one goal is to please you completely. Trust that even though I've been in several relationships, I can tell you right now that this one will be drastically different, that I am sure of, with every fiber of my being. Trust me when I say that after last night I feel as though I've lived my life and been through everything I've been through for this moment right here. This moment when I prove to you that I can make you happy. Don't be afraid because I've learned from my mistakes and will treat you right, the way you deserve to be treated, so that you never have an excuse to leave me. Dye, I can't tell you that you're supposed to be in a relationship for six months or a year or six years before you start saying these types of things to the person in the relationship with you. I can't tell you that, because everyone and every relationship is different. I'm standing here wishing I could tell you that. This moment is going against every rule I've tried to live my life by." He paused and smoothed his hand over my hair. "What I can tell you is that I have never felt this way before. It's in my nature to hold out from sharing my feelings as long as possible when I'm in a relationship. I've been in love once, and in lust several times, and now that I've spent these past few hours with you I'm questioning whether I was ever in love at all, because no one has made me feel the way you have." I closed my eyes and the tears rolled down my cheeks. What the hell was wrong with me? He bent his head and gently kissed my tears away. "Dye...please...don't...cry."

"I don't know why I'm crying. These are tears of joy not sadness. I need to know this isn't just physical. I'm going to hold you to everything you just said. I don't know what's gotten into me! I've gone from never crying at all to crying every minute I'm in your arms."

"You? I don't know what's gotten into me. I never had the urge to tell a woman how I really felt and I've managed to do it twice already today."

"You can tell me anything."

"I know," he said as he planted a kiss on my forehead. "Listen, it's about one and my family's dinner is at six. What do you want to do with the next five hours? We could just lie around and talk?"

"It doesn't matter to me. Talking sounds good, plus I'm actually expecting a delivery in a little while, so we probably shouldn't go anywhere."

"A delivery?"

"Yes, I'm sorry. I forgot to mention it, but I'm having some clothes dropped off so that I don't have to wear your great-aunt's pjs to dinner," I said with a smile.

"Oh, okay. Did I ever tell you how beautiful you looked last night? Erin beat me to drooling all over you and that dress," he said with a little laugh.

"Thanks. Lucy outdid herself on that one."

"Who's Lucy? The friend you mentioned that made it?"

"Yes. Her mother designed for my grandmother and when Lucy and I met at her design school's fashion fair, we hit it off right away. Armand hired her and she's been my seamstress ever since." He took my hand and led me out to the sunroom off of the kitchen. It was a beautiful room, windows everywhere that filled the room with natural light. He plopped down onto the oversized sofa and dragged me with him.

"Tell me more. I want to know everything about you."

"Fashion has never been my forte and she makes it easy for me."

"Wow, you must make lots of women jealous."

"I doubt it. I try to keep things like that private. Showing off was never in my nature."

"That must be hard."

"What?"

"Trying to go through life unnoticed, while wearing clothes that make heads turn."

"I don't try to go through life unnoticed."

"You could've fooled me. I know how hard it was for Michelle to get you to come out last night and how annoyed you were that we were sitting up front."

"You don't understand. People never do. It's different for me. I try not to be the center of attention, not necessarily go unnoticed. Do you know what's hard? Going through life and not knowing who to trust, because of your face or your wealth, you never know what people really want from you. They always have ulterior motives. They befriend you so that they could find ways to hurt you or steal from you or quite simply put, to screw you. People see me, but they don't really *see* me. They think they know me but they really don't."

"We aren't all like that, Dye. I'm not like that. Look at Michelle, you let her in."

"I know, not everyone is like that and Michelle is different. Don't get me wrong, it's not like I don't have any friends, because I do. They aren't abundant, but they're great friends. People I can count on for anything. There's just something that causes me to let people into my life or not. For me there's no in between. In between could get me killed."

"Killed?"

"Yes, Jonathan killed." Why did I just say that? The last thing I want to do is get to the point where I forget who I am around him. I still need to protect myself and be wary. "Have you really thought about who I am?"

"I know who you are. I guess up until just now I hadn't really put it all into perspective how that could affect our relationship." He propped himself up on one arm so he could lie on his side and look at me.

"Does it make you feel any differently about me or should I say us? Do you still want to go through with it?" I asked, searching his eyes for some hint of uncertainty.

"No, I don't feel any differently about you. Your wealth, private endeavors and secret societies aren't important to me, unless there's some tall dark and handsome suitor trying to sweep you off your feet." He raised an eyebrow and looked at me. "Well, is there?" he asked jokingly.

"Is there what? Wealth, private endeavors and secret societies? Yes."

"No, silly. You know what I mean. Is there any man other than Señor Estapa that I should be worried about?" he said with a laugh, trying to tickle me. I tried to squirm away.

"There's no one," I said between chuckles. "I was serious when I said you are the first man I've really kissed."

He stopped tickling me. "No you weren't." He looked completely dumbfounded. "I thought you were pulling my leg."

Ouch, that hurt. "Well, I wasn't. I don't joke about things like that." A wave of embarrassment came over me and I tried to sit up.

"I'm sorry. I didn't mean anything by it," he said, reaching for me. "You have to admit that it's unheard of for someone like you not to have *been* with a man before." He didn't say it in a mocking tone, just matter-of-factly.

"I know it's rare, but it's not unhealthy or anything like that. Michelle thinks I need to see a therapist. What do you think?"

"I think the right person just hasn't come along and it's impressive that you've waited."

"Exactly! I always viewed my heart as a lock and no one ever found the key." Until now. His eyes were dancing. I could only guess what he might have been thinking. "I may have kissed you, mister, but I have no intention of sleeping with you." Lie. I had every intention, if he'd have me.

"Well, whatever you want is fine by me," he said. Another lie. He had become quiet, simply rubbing my arm as he looked up at the ceiling.

"I know what *I* want, but what do *you* want?" I asked, determined to have him tell me the truth.

"I told you, I want what you want," he replied.

"No, I don't believe you," I said firmly. "What are you thinking?"

"I'm thinking that I really don't deserve you. You're too good to be true and I'm afraid that I'm going to mess this up. I don't know," he said as he closed his eyes and ran his hands through his hair.

I turned his face to mine and said, "That's bullshit. Because I'm a virgin doesn't mean I'm pure. We all have skeletons. I am no better than you, so please don't start to treat me differently. I want you to treat me like any other woman."

"That's the thing—you aren't like any other woman."

"Tell me what you want, Jonathan. I want the truth, not the sugar coated stuff." I wanted him to say he wanted me.

"I am telling you the truth…just not all of it," he said with a small smile. "I really do want what you want, but I also have every intention of further down the road, when the time is right for you, making sweet passionate love to you in ways you could only imagine. Now that I've tasted your lips there's no way in hell I'll ever let you kiss another man, but I don't want to scare you away either, so we'll move at your pace. What I want is you, the whole you." There he'd said it.

I breathed a mental sigh before I said, "Then you shall have me. I just need a little time."

"Take all the time you need. I'm not going anywhere."

We laid in each others arms and talked the day away until the buzzer for the front gate went off a little after four and we realized how late it was. Jonathan ran into the kitchen to check the monitor and yelled that he thought it was for me. Sure enough, it was Lucy sitting in her little Volkswagen. That's why I loved her. I paid her close to seven figures a year and she still drove her beat up VW bug.

Jonathan pressed the button and said, "Hello."

" I'm looking for Diamond Chantiel. Is this the correct address?"

"Yes, you must be Lucy. Come on in."

Jonathan went to open the front door and I ran upstairs to get the dress and shoes. By the time I got back downstairs Lucy was coming through the door with her bags and boxes.

"Hi. Let me help you with all this," Jonathan said as he took some of her bags. "My name is Jonathan."

With an outstretched hand Lucy introduced herself. "Lucy. Nice to meet you. Where's Dye?"

"Here I am," I announced as I came down the stairs. "I had to get the dress."

"Hey, beautiful," Lucy said giving me a big hug. "Sorry I didn't get here sooner, I wanted to put a couple finishing touches on the dress for tonight."

"I know I told you this morning, but you really outdid yourself with that one last night."

"Diamond's right. You are very talented. She was by far the most beautiful woman there," Jonathan added.

"I should really be thanking Diamond. I could put her in a trash bag and she would still look fabulous. She's a designer's dream, effortlessly stunning."

"All right, all right, enough of that," I said, nudging her with my shoulder.

"Not to mention way too humble," Lucy said with a smile.

"Thanks for bringing everything over. Are you all set otherwise? Anything going on?"

"I'm actually a little shocked that you're in such high spirits. I thought for sure you would be livid and having people fired left and right."

"If you're talking about last night, I was pretty upset, but I'm much better now."

"You haven't seen it, have you?" Lucy's facial expression changed completely and she started taking tiny steps backwards towards the door as if she expected me to explode any minute.

"Seen what?"

"Dye, you should call Armand."

"I'm not calling Armand. I'm asking you. Now tell me."

"Trust me to be the one to open my big mouth," she said with a loud sigh. "A story broke a couple hours ago on all the major networks about last night, and it's not painting a very pretty picture of you or your family."

"What?" My blood was starting to boil.

"If you turn the telly on, you should see it." Jonathan was looking for the remote and I sat on the sofa. "Try channel seven," said Lucy.

"What picture could they possibly be painting? I had an argument with my grandfather." We all got quiet at the news anchor was talking.

"…sources at last night's gala had some unexpected entertainment

72

when billionaire Nathan Skovachy ran into his estranged granddaughter Diamond Skovachy at the who's who affair. You may all remember the vicious murder of Nathan's daughter-in-law Nyrobi Chantiel and her parents, the King and Queen of the Embatu tribe, which resulted in the suicide of his only son, Zachary Skovachy, almost twenty years ago. Sources at the party state that Diamond verbally attacked her grandfather, blaming him for the murder of her parents. Mr. Skovachy was said to be in an emotional apologetic state, repeatedly asking Diamond's forgiveness and revealed to her that his wife was dying and her last wish was to fly to America and find their granddaughter. Diamond is said to have shown little to no emotion after learning this. The Skovachys have done a tremendous amount for Europe, and the world for that matter, through their major industries bringing economic stability and jobs to many of the world's impoverished regions. Sources close to them state that they never recovered from the tragedy, still making a point to search for their long lost granddaughter even though it was members of the Embatu tribe leading the militia that killed her mother and ultimately led to the death of her father. Diamond Skovachy, on the other hand, has managed to stay out of the public eye ever since her parents' untimely deaths. Many state that she has turned her back on her country and grandparents since then as well…"

I wasn't quite sure who turned off the television, since I had lowered my head into my hands, but I was furious. Jonathan was the first to speak.

"Dye," he walked over and held my shoulders, but I refused to look up. "Anyone that was there knows it wasn't like that. The media tries to put a different spin on things so that they can increase their ratings."

"Diamond, you've never cared what people thought before, especially the media, don't start now," Lucy chimed in. "They're scum!"

"Please say something," Jonathan pleaded.

"*I'm* the bad guy? They've made *me* out to be the bad guy. How could they be so wrong? Every penny I've ever made I've poured into Africa. Just because I don't broadcast every contribution, invention, or treaty I've done, I've turned my back on my mother's country?"

"Diamond, no one knows all the things you have done because that's the way you wanted it. Armand is the face of Genesis. Now, you could change all of that, but I don't think you should. Who cares what they say, anyone who knows you, knows the truth and how much you've done."

"Dye, she's right," Jonathan added.

"Fine. For now I will let this slide and won't destroy all of their careers," I said, walking over to the window. "But with you both as my witnesses, if they continue to slander my name, I will crush them!"

There was a fire ablaze in my eyes that Jonathan was now seeing for the first time. Right now I will contain it, but God help the person who crossed me next.

Chapter 11

I admired myself in the bathroom mirror. Once again Lucy had certainly outdone herself. I was trying to smile, but I was still extremely upset. Jonathan hadn't said much after Lucy left. He was trying to give me some space. My mind was racing. Armand and I hadn't talked about the kidnapping since I was younger. It was an unspoken rule that we didn't bring it up. I never asked any questions and now my mind was reeling. Was the news right? Were the Embatus leading the militia? Or were they wrong like they were about so many other things. I needed to stop dwelling on it. I would have all the answers I wanted soon enough. I touched up my lip gloss, grabbed my clutch purse and headed for the bathroom door. As I came down the stairs, Jonathan was fixing his tie in the hallway mirror. I looked at him and immediately felt better. He was the most handsome man I had ever seen in his tailored navy blue suit.

"Ready?" I asked.

"Yes. Let me just…" he paused as he turned and looked at me standing on the stairs. I smiled, what I hoped was my best smile. In a low voice he said, "You take my breath away," and reached for my hand. I stepped down onto the landing and took his hand.

"You don't look too bad yourself," I replied, leaning into him and straightening his tie. He didn't move or say anything; he just kept looking at me. "At this rate we're going to be la..." I didn't get to finish because his mouth was on mine. He slipped the tip of his tongue between my lips, searching until he found mine and then our mouths performed an encore of our own private salsa. I didn't want to leave his arms.

"I'm sorry," he said as he finally pulled away. "I can't help myself. Whenever I see you I have the urge to taste you, and Lucy's designs aren't helping." He kissed me again softly. "Have I completely ruined your lipstick?"

"Umm...not at all," as I licked my lips.

"Just when I think it isn't possible for you to be any more gorgeous, the light changes, or you smile at me differently or you wear something like this."

"I'm glad you like it. Now, as I was saying, at this rate we're going to be late. We should go."

"You're right. Let me grab the gift and we'll hit the road."

"How far do your parents live from here?"

"Only about half hour or so."

"That's not too bad. What did you get them for their anniversary present?"

"I put together a monogrammed album and DVD of pictures of them over the past forty years. I'll probably show the DVD tonight. It's already wrapped. You ready?"

"Yes. Should I bring my things now or will we come back here tonight?"

He gave me a wicked smile. "I don't think I'm the best person to answer that question. I would be inclined to say that you should come back here tonight. The guest room is still available."

"Let's plan on me coming back here to pick up my things, but I probably can't spend the night, there are few things I need to deal with before meeting my grandparents tomorrow."

"That's fine," he said as he took my hand. He picked up the gift, locked the door and helped me into the car.

On the way to his parents he gave me a brief rundown on his family. The party would be surprisingly small since only the immediate family was invited. Jonathan turned into the driveway about twenty minutes after six. A man walked up and opened my door and I had the quick feeling of déjà vu.

"Good Evening, Señorita," the gentleman said as he held the door and helped me out of the car.

"Good Evening," I responded.

"How's it going Mr. Hamilton."

"Not bad, Ramon. How about you, how's your family?"

"They are good. My youngest one started the first grade this month," he said with a proud smile.

Jonathan squeezed his shoulder and said, "That's great news. Ramon, this is Diamond Chantiel. Dye, this is my father's trusted chauffeur, Ramon Herrera."

"It's very nice to meet you, Ramon," I said with a smile.

"The pleasure is mine," he said as he took my hand and kissed the back of it.

"Woah, partner," Jonathan said with a laugh, taking my hand away from Ramon's lips, "She's taken." Turning to me, he said with a wink, "We've got to keep our eyes on him." We all laughed then.

"Have a good evening Mr. H."

"You too, Ramon."

As we walked up the steps, there were butterflies in my stomach. I was nervous. For the first time in my life, I *wanted* these people to like me.

Jonathan stopped at the door. "Dye, are you okay?"

I cleared my throat, "Um, yes, why do you ask?"

"Because, you're shaking."

I gave him a nervous smile, "I'll be fine. This is just a first for me."

"You'll be more than fine. I know they're going to love you."

"We'll see," I responded as he opened the door.

I could hear talking and laughter coming from the room and my heart was pounding in my ears. For Christ's sake Diamond, pull yourself together. It's just dinner. If Michelle were here she would whip you into shape. Jonathan gave my hand a gentle squeeze and we walked in. Within seconds the room was completely silent as everyone's attention was focus on us standing in the doorway.

"Well, don't stop talking on my account," Jonathan announced with a smile. There was an outburst of "Hi's'" and "what took you so long?" I had no intention of letting anyone see how nervous I was. Jonathan led me over to a very attractive older couple, who I assumed were his parents. They were standing in a small group as we walked up. A man had left the group just as we arrived.

"Happy anniversary, Mom and Dad," Jonathan said as he gave his mom a huge hug and kiss and shook his father's hand. "Umm, this is Diamond Chantiel. Dye this is my mom Elizabeth, my father Liam, my Aunt Susan, the man that just walked away was my Uncle Leland, and this is my great Aunt Rosa." He greeted everyone as he introduced them.

"It's a pleasure meeting all of you. Happy anniversary, Mr. and Mrs. Hamilton." It was a short while before they spoke. It was almost like they were in shock.

"Please call me Beth and my husband Liam," Jonathan's mother said with warm smile, giving me a hug. She held on longer than strangers meeting for the first time should. There was something strange about how they were looking as me, as if they hadn't seen me in a long time. They were trying to hide their shock, but I picked up on it.

"Dye, would you like some wine?" Jonathan asked, apparently oblivious to the reaction his parents were having to me.

"That would be nice," I replied.

"Red or white?"

"It doesn't matter. I'll have whatever you're having."

"I won't be long. Aunt Rosa, try not to tell her any embarrassing stories while I'm gone."

Aunt Rosa playfully pouted as Jonathan walked away. There was an uncomfortable silence that remained.

"So, Diamond, do you work with Jonathan?" his Aunt Susan asked.

"No, I don't, my best friend works at his firm."

"Oh, really?" asked his father, "What's her name?"

"Michelle Noir. She joined about six months ago."

"Noir? Michelle Noir. Yes, yes I know who she is. She's a very talented young woman. She just landed the DiAngelo case, didn't she?"

"Yes, she did."

"I must say," said Aunt Susan, cutting in, "that is an absolutely stunning dress? The colors and the way it fits you are perfect! "

"Umm, thank you," I said with a smile. "Yours is very beautiful as well. How did you leave the weather in California?"

"How did you know we live in California?"

"Jonathan had mentioned to me that's where you were from."

"Awww, that's so sweet of him. The weather never really changes where we are. When we left it was in the seventies," replied Susan.

"That's my type of weather, not too hot and not too cold," interjected Aunt Rosa. "Lord knows depending on the weather, places on my body either shrink, swell, become too moist or dry up like a soda cracker," she said as she made an obvious wink in my direction. I couldn't help but laugh.

Jonathan returned with our drinks, "I hope I wasn't gone too long."

"Not at all," I replied.

"So, Mom and Dad, other than tonight do you guys have any plans to celebrate?"

"No, we just want to relax this time around," replied his father, giving his mom's shoulders a squeeze. "It looks like your partner in crime is here," as he motioned with his head toward the door. We all turned to see Quinn at the door with none other than Michelle on his arm. I almost did a cartwheel. Michelle's eyes popped out of her head when she saw me standing there. She walked right over and gave me a hug, whispering in my ear that we would talk later.

Quinn walked up and greeted the group. "Hello, everyone. Happy anniversary Mr. and Mrs. H," he said as he gave Beth a hug and shook Liam's hand. "This is Michelle Noir."

"Wow, that's weird?" Liam exclaimed. "We were just talking about you."

"Really? Me?" Michelle asked, "I hope they were all good things."

"Yes, they were," he replied with a smile.

"Well, it's nice to meet you. Happy anniversary to both of you."

"Thank you," Beth and Liam said simultaneously. Turning her attention to her husband, she said, "Well, honey, I think we're going to have to start mingling. As much as I love my sister, we can't talk to them all night. We will see you all later." And with that our little group dispersed, leaving Jonathan, Quinn, Michelle and I.

Quinn turned to me and gave me a smile. "Diamond, I got your lovely gift this afternoon. That really wasn't necessary."

"Dye, he loved it. He talked about it the entire ride here."

"It was my pleasure."

"What gift?" Jonathan asked.

"An apology gift, I had delivered today, for the scene I caused last night."

"How did you know I collected lighters?" Quinn asked.

"I have my sources," I said with a smile.

The four of us sat and talked. We were joined by a few of Jonathan's cousins. Everyone was really nice, and if they'd seen the news, they were polite enough not to mention it. Michelle asked me to come to the bathroom with her, so we excused ourselves and went to the powder room. The door hadn't closed fully, before she was jumping up and down and covering her mouth. I swear no one would ever believe this woman was a lawyer, at times she came across as such a teenager, but in a fun and carefree way.

"This is too good to be true. Why didn't you tell me you were coming?"

"I don't know, I just didn't think of it when we were talking. Meesh, you and Quinn look great together!"

"Forget Quinn and I. I want to know about you and Jonathan."

"I really don't think this is the time to go into it. He's just...he's so...I can't begin to explain it to you. I just know he makes me feel things I've never felt. It's corny, but he brings out the woman in me."

"Did you sleep with him?"

"What? No! Of course not! I haven't lost my senses that much." I was appalled that she even asked. "Why, did you sleep with Quinn?"

"No, I didn't. You would've been proud of me. It was hard, but I held out. Now back to you. Did you kiss him?"

"Yes." I closed me eyes and bit my bottom lip as I recalled this morning, "Yes, I did, and for the record, I was the person who initiated everything. I asked him to be my boyfriend too. How corny is that?"

"You did? Good God, I've created a monster! Going home with strangers, kissing on a first date, actually not even a first date!"

"Do you think I made a mistake? That's the question I've been asking myself all day? If it's right that I should be having these feelings after meeting the guy less than twenty-four hours ago. I'm worried this is purely physical."

"Dye, I'm so happy for you. You deserve this. He's a great guy. Armand is right, if there is anyone that is a great judge of character, it's you. If it were anyone else, I was say to slow it down, but I know you would never do anything you didn't really want to do and to tell you the truth, this is long overdue."

"That's the problem. Meesh, he is the most beautiful man I've ever seen. I find myself staring at him constantly. It's pretty embarrassing how much I want him. I'm afraid this good judgment that you and Armand keep talking about has flown the coop with my common sense and I'm going to make a ghastly mistake!"

"I have to agree with you on his looks. Quinn is gorgeous and Jonathan still blows him out of the water. Now you know how I feel about Quinn. Don't worry, you're going to be fine, and if it does turn out to be a mistake you are well overdue. People usually make these mistakes in their late teens."

"Listen, do you have to go to the bathroom or not? We've been in here for a few minutes. I don't want to draw attention to us. We should head back out there. How do I look?"

"You can't look any better, you blow my mind away. Where did you get that dress? No one out there can keep their eyes off of you. Jonathan looks like he wants to be under your skin. You look great!"

"Thanks. Lucy brought it over this afternoon. We'll talk more tonight or tomorrow." Michelle turned to open the door and I stopped her. "Meesh?"

"Umm"

"I'm sorry I got mad at you last night. Forgive me," and with that I hugged her.

"I'm sorry too; things could've turned out much worse with your grandfather. Now stop, you're going to make me cry." She smiled at me and we stepped out of the bathroom.

Diamond hadn't left the room completely before I was surrounded by my parents asking what the deal was with us.

"Jonathan, what's going on?" my mother asked.

"What do you mean, what's going on? Diamond and I are seeing each other and I brought her to your anniversary dinner? Is something wrong with that?"

"She could be easily the most gorgeous woman I've ever seen," said my twenty-year-old cousin, Ralph. To which there was verbal affirmation from everyone.

"Enough!" my mother said in a low firm voice. My mother's face was stern as she shooed my cousins away so she could talk to me.

"She doesn't know who we are, does she?"

"What do you mean? She knows that Quinn and I know Nathan, but that's it. I don't think she recognized you and Dad. Why?" Everyone was quiet and a few people were looking around to see if she was coming back.

"I hope you know that it's pure coincidence that Nathan and Viktoria aren't here tonight. He called earlier this afternoon to cancel since Viktoria wasn't feeling well."

"Shit. I didn't even think about them coming."

"That's what I'm worried about. When a girl's involved, you don't focus on anything except what *you* want. Jonathan, you're my son, but I swear to God if you hurt her, I never forgive you."

"Hurt her? Why do you think I would hurt her?" I was getting visibly upset.

"Sweetie, you have a reputation."

"A not so good reputation," countered Aunt Rosa.

"As a womanizer," Aunt Susan added.

"I don't believe this! That was in college."

"And grad school, and the first year of starting the firm," Quinn said with a laugh.

"That's not funny, Quinn. I've changed! Shit, you of all people should know that. And I don't give a rat's ass what any of you think! I can't believe this!" I was raising my voice when my father stepped in.

"Jonathan, no one is saying…"

I didn't let him finish. "I know exactly what you're all saying and it's pretty much that I don't deserve her."

"No one is saying that you don't deserve her, but what your mom is trying to say is that if you're bored and only want to sleep with her for a notch in your belt, then you should stop right now. This woman is not that type of person, and if you dash her away as you have so many other women, there could be serious repercussions for our family."

"My God! Is that what you all think of me? I cheated on Lola once. Don't believe every fucking thing you hear on Entertainment Television. Lola and I were on and off again so often no one ever knew when we were or weren't together."

"Jonathan, that's enough," his father said sternly.

"No. You're right! This is enough. I have nothing more to say about this," and with that I stormed out onto the patio. I couldn't believe what I was just hearing. My family thought I was a womanizer. Quinn came and stood beside me.

"J, don't take this the wrong way"

"Quinn, I already said I have nothing more to say about this," as I turned to walk away.

Holding my arm he said, "Listen to me. I know you love her."

"What? I barely even know her." Damn was it that obvious?

"You can't fool me. I've been your best friend since birth and I've never seen you look at anyone the way you've been looking at her, but people are going to talk. You do have a reputation and you know how hard it can be to shake those things. We were both wild."

"How do you feel about it?"

"I think if she's the one, you should go for it, but if I'm wrong and she isn't, then you should back off. Your dad is right, from what I've been hearing, she isn't someone you want to cross."

Chapter 12

I don't know what happened, but the atmosphere had definitely changed since Meesh and I had gone to the bathroom. I returned to find Jonathan having a drink alone out on the patio and I could tell he was upset from how he was standing and rigidness of his back.

"Hey," I said as I walked up behind him and placed my hand on his shoulder. "You okay?" He tried to put on a cheerful face but failed miserably. "What's wrong?"

"Nothing. Would you like another drink?"

"No, I don't want another drink, I want you to tell me what's wrong."

He took my face between his hands and kissed my forehead. "Absolutely, nothing. Let's go back inside."

"Jonathan," I said, but he was already heading back inside. I wasn't sure what happened, but I knew that something did. Jonathan was pretty quiet the rest of the evening and even though no one was rude to me, there was tension there. When I asked if he was going to show his DVD, he said probably not. Knowing that something was bothering him and he wouldn't tell me was making me upset. Just before dinner I pulled Michelle aside.

"Is it me or does everyone seem different?"

"Different how?"

"Since we came back from the bathroom, Jonathan's been really quiet, and it's almost as though his parents are upset with him."

"He does seem a little quiet, but everyone else is fine. Relax, you're probably reading too much into things." We rejoined the group and shortly after Jonathan's cell phone went off. He excused himself and took the call. His frown deepened as he whispered into the phone and angrily pressed the off button. He walked over and said something to the maid standing at the door and she smiled at him and nodded in agreement, patting his cheek. He rejoined the group and said something to Quinn who responded by rolling his eyes and twirling his index finger at his temple, implying that someone was crazy.

We walked into the formal dinning room and were all seated at an enormous rectangular dinner table enjoying our first course. I noticed that Jonathan's uncle had disappeared; his was the only vacant seat at the table. A couple of people asked, but no one was really sure what had happened to him. I thought it was strange, but his departure was soon forgotten when Beth and Liam began talking about the funny experiences they had on their honeymoon. Our salad plates were being cleared away when we heard the commotion in the foyer and someone slam the front door. There were feet scurrying down the hallway and then Lola barreled into the room, wearing the same trench coat from this morning, but thankfully I could see the hem of a dress.

"I'm sorry I'm late!" she said practically out of breath and soon the maid stormed into the dining room behind her, fixing her twisted apron as it became apparent Lola had obviously used force to by pass the little woman.

"I'm sorry, Señor Hamilton," she said with a heavy Spanish accent looking at Jonathan. "When I told her she was no invited and dinner was already in progress she knocka me to zee floor and came in anyway!"

"Wasn't invited? She's obviously mistaken; I told her I was here with you, Jonathan!" she said, glaring at the woman. Everyone's attention was now on Jonathan since he was standing.

"Lola, what the hell are you doing? You need to leave! I told you on the phone we have nothing more to discuss."

"Why are you being like this? You use me when you wish and then treat me like shit." Turning her attention to his parents she said, "We spent the day together making love and he told me..."

"What? You liar! That's it. I'm tired of these fucking games. I was trying to be nice with this whole thing, but you obviously don't get it! I don't love you anymore. It's been over for a long time!"

"And he told me he loved me and wanted to marry me!" she yelled over him.

"Now I'm convinced you're absolutely crazy!"

"Jonathan, is this true?" his mother asked, her hands balled into fist at either side of her plate. She was furious. The family was appalled but no one said anything, because they wanted to know what was going on.

"Of course it isn't true!"

"Why are you telling these lies?" Lola pleaded, with fake tears rolling down her cheeks.

"Mrs. H, she's lying," countered Quinn.

"Shut up, Quinn, you're his best friend! You'll say anything to protect him!"

Jonathan stepped from in front of his chair and turned, heading around the table, but I caught his arm.

"Don't do anything you'll regret," I said in a low voice. That's when Lola noticed me sitting there. She put two and two together that Jonathan and I came together.

"He brought you! *You?*" She looked like she was about to explode from rage. "Your bed isn't even cold yet from our day together and you already have this filthy whore lined up for tonight?"

"Wait one minute!" Michelle jumped up. My trusted friend was quick to my defense.

"That's it!" Liam said, slamming his hands on the table, "Lola, I don't know what's going on between you and Jonathan, but you are going to have to leave. This conversation, if you can even call it that, isn't going anywhere, and quite frankly you're being rude and quite offensive. I expected more from you."

"Well, I expected more from your son."

"You need to leave," Beth repeated, standing beside her husband.

Lola completely ignored them and turned her attention back to me. She was screaming, "You conniving bitch! You didn't waste any time at all, pretending you didn't know each other last night at dinner. Who are you anyway? Diamond who? Do you know who I am? No one steals *my* man and gets away with it! Do you hear me? No one! Did he tell you he was with me today? Well, did he?"

"Lola, I..." Jonathan stopped talking when I stood up.

My back was rigid as I glared at her across the table. My voice was eerily calm as I said, "He didn't have to tell me, because I already know the answer. You see, Lola, *I* spent the night in Jonathan's guest room. *I* was at the house this afternoon when you showed up unexpectedly. He didn't know I was at the top of the stairs when *you* removed your trench coat, stood naked in front of him and begged him to make love to you," I looked at his mother, "and he refused your advances." Turning my attention back to Lola, I continued, my voice cold and deliberate, "*I* was also there when he admitted to cheating on you once and never doing it again after you were engaged. *I* was there when you admitted to having several affairs with his colleagues because he was never around and traveled too much. *I* was there when he admitted that he'd made a mistake giving you the engagement ring and should've ended the relationship long before. And finally, Lola, *I* was there when he told you if you ever pulled anything like this again he would throw you out on your ass and fire you! *You're* the liar." I leaned forward with my palms flat against the table. She was speechless and obviously mortified. "Now, Lola, *I* must ask. Do *you* know who *I* am? I don't think you do, or else you wouldn't have walked in here and announced to a room full of people that I was a filthy whore. You and Jonathan need to sort out your issues, although at this point they appear to be more your issues than anyone else's. My patience is wearing thin for people who slander my name. When I am finished with you, there isn't a law firm in the world that would hire you. Do you hear me? Not just in New York City, but the entire world. Do you really want to come up against me?" She just stared at me, "Answer me! I need to know that we understand each other and that's there's no miscommunication as to where I've drawn this line that you are never to cross. Let this be the first and last time that my name ever crosses your lips or that you lose your senses long enough to threaten me. Do we understand each other?" Still she gave no answer, so I raised my voice again. "Do we? It's either yes or no. How hard can it be?" I asked, using her insult from last night.

"We understand each other perfectly." She turned her attention to Jonathan who was also staring at me. "Good riddance! You were a lousy lover anyway!" and with that she stormed out of the house. The room was in silence as everyone stared at me. I immediately turned to Jonathan.

"I'm sorry. I shouldn't have eavesdropped on your conversation. That was wrong of me. And I shouldn't have gotten involved just now, but she was wrong. Forgive me?"

His gaze softened as he took me in his arms. "You never cease to amaze me," and kissed me tenderly. "I'm the one that should be apologizing about all of this."

"Don't. Now we're even when it comes to public confrontations," I said with a smile, returning his kiss. It was as if we were the only two people in the room.

"Now that we've gotten this all cleared up, can I finish eating?" Aunt Rosa announced. "This is the best anniversary dinner I've ever been to in my eighty-seven years!" and the room erupted with laughter as we all took our seats, except Aunt Rosa.

"Umm, Umm," she cleared her throat. "I would like to propose a toast," and with that she raised her glass and we followed. "To love, happiness, honesty and makeup sex." She winked at me. "The best sex in the world!"

"Gross, nana!" announced Ralph. There wasn't a dry eye in the room when the laughing was finished. I was blushing uncontrollably and hiding my face in my napkin. My ribs hurt from laughing so hard.

After that there was no tension. Jonathan's mother had come around the table and given him a long hug. We ate, drank, talked and laughed all night. Watching his family made me miss mine even more. Is this what we would've been like? Before we realized, it was after eleven and time for us to go. I kissed his family goodbye and hugged Meesh before she left with Quinn.

"Do you think I should stay over at his house again?" I whispered, "I don't think he wants me to go home."

"If you want to, I think you should stay."

"You know I want to."

"Then there you have it. Don't worry about Armand." She smiled at me.

"I'm not worried about Armand. Get out of here. The love of your life is waiting." Turning my attention to Quinn, I told him goodbye.

"Bye, Diamond. Enjoy the rest of your weekend."

"You too." He and Jonathan shook hands as I walked toward the car. His mom and dad were standing at the top of the stairs waving to Aunt Rosa as Ramon helped her into the car. There was something so familiar about them. Rarely did I ever forget a face, but I couldn't place where I knew them from. We got in the car and left.

"Did you have fun?"

"I had a great time. You have a wonderful family."

"Good, I'm glad. They loved you."

"I think your parents are still warming up to me, but I definitely won Aunt Rosa over," I said with a laugh. "So are you going to tell me what happened when I went to the bathroom?"

"Are you still thinking about that?"

"Yes."

"You're a persistent devil, aren't you?"

"Yes, I am."

"If you really must know, my mother jumped on my case about what my intentions were for you because I had a reputation for being a womanizer and they didn't think you were that sort of girl. She also said if I hurt you, she would never forgive me and I was mad she had such a low opinion of me."

"Umm. Well what are your intentions for me?"

Looking straight ahead he said, "I have known you for one full day

90

and there isn't a doubt in my mind that I don't want to spend another day without you. I want to learn everything I can about you. I want to teach you."

If I wasn't sure before, I was sure now, that I couldn't go home with him tonight. If I did, I would most surely sleep with him. I needed time. I felt like I was losing control. I was falling in love with him. "Jonathan."

"Yes."

"I need you to take me home."

He hesitated for a moment then said, "Sure, if that's what you want."

I know he wanted to ask me why, but he didn't. I needed to think and I couldn't do it while I was with him. I gave him my address and we were in front of my building soon after midnight.

"Would you like to come up?" I asked.

"Uh, no, I shouldn't. Listen, unless you really want me to, I think you should go to dinner by yourself tomorrow night. I'm leaving on a business trip to Rome on Monday morning, but I think I'm going to try and leave tomorrow evening instead. So I won't be back for a week."

"A week?" I tried not to sound too disappointed.

"Yes. Maybe that will give you enough time to think this all through. I don't want to rush you and I can tell all of this is moving too fast for you."

Is he reading my mind? Or did I say my thoughts out loud.

"You're right. I should go to dinner alone. I just…don't take…I still…shit, I can't even organize my thoughts well enough to speak!" He drove me insane.

"You don't have to say anything." He placed his fingers across my lips and before he knew what happened, I slipped my tongue down between the middle of his four fingers and had taken his middle and index fingers into my mouth, sucking on them gently.

"Dye…" he whispered, but I ignored him. He closed his eyes and I held his wrist, slowly moving my tongue around this two fingers. Knuckle to nail and back again, then around each of them individually, dragging my tongue down the length of his middle finger and flicking it over the web between his fingers. He shuddered. "Dye…"

I sucked them both one final time trying to get as much saliva off of them before I slipped them out of my mouth. I felt sorry for him. He had unleashed something within me and now it would be his responsibility to tame it.

"Goodnight, Jonathan." I opened the door, got out, and never looked back.

Chapter 13

The concierge said "goodnight" as Quinn and I walked in. We got upstairs, and he waited as I fumbled with my keys. I knew what I wanted to happen and it made me nervous as hell.

"Michelle, let me help you," Quinn said as he took the keys, unlocked the door and held it open for me. I stepped inside and caught a whiff of lavender. Thank God Gertrude had been there today, which meant my house was spotless.

"Come on in. Have a seat and make yourself comfortable," I said as I took his coat.

"This is a beautiful apartment."

"Thanks. Did I ever thank you for another wonderful evening. You can't keep spoiling me like this because I'll expect something similar next weekend."

"Really, next weekend you say? I think I could swing that."

"Do you want a drink? Nightcap maybe?"

"I don't think I can hold another drop. Actually, I think I need to borrow your little girl's room."

"Sure. It's down the hall there. The second door on your left."

As I watched him walk away, I knew I was fighting a losing battle thinking I wouldn't sleep with him tonight. Sooner or later he would meet the real me. The fly by the seat of her pants kind of girl that I am, couldn't hide for long. I took the pins out of my hair and let it fall down around my shoulders, hung our coats up in the closet, and went into the kitchen to pour myself a glass of wine. I stepped out of my shoes, leaned against the island and took a sip of wine. I heard the bathroom door open.

"Michelle?"

"I'm in the kitchen." I was putting the bottle of wine back on the rack when Quinn came up behind and snaked his arms around my waist and began to nibble on my neck. I couldn't help the low moan that escaped my lips.

"You…looked…beautiful tonight."

"Thanks, I try," I said with a smile as I turned to face him, wrapping my arms around his neck.

"I want you right now," he breathed.

"That's good to know, because I want you too, so let's cut this talking short."

"Where's the bedroom?"

"At the end of the hall past the bathroom."

"Finish your wine."

"What?"

"Finish your wine now, because you won't have any time later," he said with a laugh. "Here, I'll help you," and with one gulp he drank half my glass.

"Bottom's up," and I finished the rest.

"Now where were we?"

"Somewhere around here," I said as I took his mouth in mine. There was a sense of urgency to our kissing, our lips were twisting and turning around each others. My lips and tongue were sweet from the wine. He picked me up and I swung my legs around his hips as he palmed my cheeks and pressed me into his groin. I continued to kiss him as I slipped his dinner jacket off his shoulders and he walked toward my room. He held one hand over my left butt cheek as he used the other to unzip my skirt.

"Hurry," I said. I couldn't wait a moment longer to feel him inside me, filling the painfully empty walls of my womb.

"I'm sorry, but I have plans for you, so if you were expecting a quickie you're in for a rude awakening."

"Oh really?"

He threw me onto my bed and I let out a playful scream. As he kicked off his shoes and started to unbutton his shirt, I unbuckled his pants and pulled the zipper down, tugging his pants off his hips. I could see his erection straining against his tight jockey shorts and, my oh my, what an erection it was. Now I knew for sure he was perfect. He kicked his trousers from around his feet and I bent my head and took the tip of him into my mouth through his underwear and gently sucked. He moaned and stepped back.

"Oh no, me first!" he said. I must be dreaming as he pushed me onto my back and slipped my skirt off. I untied the neck of my shirt and pulled it over my head, then bent my arm behind my back to unclasp my bra, but he stopped me.

"I don't think so, Ms. Noir. I told you I'm running this show." He was firm and tender all at the same time. I moved up toward the head of the bed and we kissed, less urgent this time as he ran his hands over my breasts. My nipples were already standing at attention and awaiting their marching orders. I was rubbing his back as he bent his head and started to lick my neck, slowly moving down to my shoulder, planting a mixture of bites and kisses across my clavicle. I was in Heaven. Then he slipped his hand behind me and unclasped my bra, throwing it across the room. Straddling me, he brought my hands above my head as he sucked and bit my nipples, giving each one equal attention. I was going crazy. He brought his face back to my lips as one of his hands made their way down my body and rested on my hips. He slid off me without our lips parting and placed most of his weight on my right side, using his free hand he spread my legs, bringing my left leg up. Oh, he was moving painfully slow. It was almost as though he was doing it on purpose. He made a trail of kisses down my neck and between my breasts. Releasing my arms above my head, he slowly made his way over my navel, then to my hips and inner thighs. He kissed and licked every spot except the one that was yearning for his attention. He was torturing me. I ran my hands through his hair as he raised my legs up and pulled my panties off. He moaned as he hovered over my bare mound. He seemed to be taking in the scent of me and obviously loving it.

"You're a peach. Just the way I like it," he whispered, lowering my right leg onto his shoulder.

"Quinn...please."

"Don't worry, Michelle, I intend to."

And with that he ran his tongue from the base of my opening up to my clit, parting my moist lips with his tongue. He made tiny circles around her little head, applying just the right amount of pressure.

"Ah...Ah...Ah," I squealed in a breathless voice with each delicious circle. "Ooohhh, Quinn, just like that." He steadily made those circles. At first they were small, using just the tip of his tongue, and then he made larger ones, relaxing his tongue so that it was flat and wide.

"Ummmm," I moaned.

Small circle, large circle, small circle, small circle. I started to rotate my hips, but he stopped me, placing his forearm, of the shoulder supporting my right leg, just below my navel and across my abdomen to hold me steady. That was worse, I couldn't move as he licked and lapped at me from bow to sternum, pushing his tongue as deep into me as it could go. He curled and twirled his tongue like a true linguist speaking the language of cunnilingus. I could feel my sea pulling away from the shore as the trough of the tidal wave of my orgasm deepened. Just when I thought I could take no more, he slid his finger into my ocean. One, then two, in, then out, up, then down. Two, then three, slow, then with increasing speed. This man had skills because he hadn't missed a beat giving my little friend all the attention she needed. Uh oh...the trough was too deep and the crest of my wave was reaching new heights. I was holding my breath, my stomach muscles were tightening, and as I held a handful of his curly hair in both hands the inevitable happened. He continued to pump his digits into me, the crest broke, and the massive wave rushed toward my beach.

"Qu…Qu…Quinnnnnn!" I screamed as my body shook and convulsed against the waves that ravished my womb. I pressed my hand against his forehead to push him away because his tongue was still causing small but violent shock waves to ripple across my body, but he wouldn't move. He held his mouth in place until the last orgasmic wave broke onto my shore.

"Umm," he moaned as he drank, "I love how you taste."

"I'm glad," I whispered in a barely audible voice. "Normally this is where I say your turn, but I am literally drained. You've exhausted me and I didn't even do anything." He wiped his mouth on my leg, bit me and laughed.

"You can make it up to me in the morning when we wake up, because I'm exhausted as well."

"Are you sure you don't mind?"

"Mind? Of course not! I'm a lawyer, I make mental notes of everything, believe me when I say you'll both make it up to me," as he planted a kiss on my slightly swollen lips and scooted up in the bed to lie beside me. I kissed him deeply, tasting myself, and thought of Diamond. She didn't know what she was missing out on, but I was confident Jonathan would enlighten her. We slipped under my covers, and holding me close, I fell asleep in Quinn's arms.

I had found my Poseidon.

The light in Armand's room was on, which meant he was still up. I took a deep breath, went in and told him everything. Every detail from the party last night, to what happened at Jonathan's house and his parents' dinner, to just now in the car.

"What do you think?"

"What do you mean, what do I think?" He was staring out the window with a smile on his face.

"Armand, I need you to tell me what to do."

"Dye, I can't. You've never needed me to tell you what to do."

"Well, now I do! Am I behaving irrationally? Is the lack of sex catching up to me? Is that all this is about? You have tons of experience with women and men. I just want you to analyze this for me."

"That's the thing, Dye, when you're dealing with love it can't be analyzed and I think that's going to be the hardest part for you."

"Love? So you do think I'm in love with him? But I can't be…I've only known him a day." I sounded desperate, which is how I felt.

"Yes, I do. You can't put a time on something like this."

"That's what he said."

"So is he in love with you?"

"I don't know. We didn't talk about love—just the fact that we'd both never felt this way. He can't be in love with me…"

"I think the only reason you aren't lying in his arms right now is because you're afraid of what people would think, seeing that you just met him a day ago."

"That's true."

"For the record, I've had a woman with her legs up in the fitting room at Barney's after knowing her for ten minutes. I don't think this is just sex. You've been around numerous sexy, charming and charismatic men before and they've never had this kind of effect on you. So no, I don't think this has anything to do with your lack of sex catching up to you." He walked over placed his hand under my chin, tilting my head upward. "Any man that can make you not even mention a television station that ripped your family apart today is just the type of man you need in your life. I couldn't believe you didn't call me once."

"I know. When I'm with him things don't seem to matter as much. I swear to you on any other day I would've had them all fired and cut Lola's heart out with a spoon."

"Well, that bitch would've deserved it. What do you really want to do?"

"Really, really?"

"Yes."

"I want to be lying in Jonathan's arms right now. I want to go to Rome with him. I want to have dinner with my grandparents and put this tragedy behind me for good. *Quite honestly, I want to live.*"

"Good. Rome sounds like an excellent vacation for us."

"Us?"

"Don't worry I have no intention of being anywhere close to you two lovebirds. I haven't seen my lover Minerva in a very long time. Go to bed and get some sleep. I'll make all the arrangements."

"Thanks, Armand."

"It's my pleasure, sweetie. I've been waiting a long time to give you some love advice."

Chapter 14

The clock on the end table said 7:18; I don't think I'd slept a wink, just stared at the ceiling. My thoughts were in shambles, from Jonathan, to yesterday, to my grandparents, and then to Liam and Elizabeth Hamilton. It was bothering me that I couldn't remember where I knew them from. The phone rang and brought me back to reality. I scooted across the bed and answered before it could ring again. I had heard Armand go to his room only a few hours before.

"Hello?"

"Dye?"

"Hey, Meesh, what's going on? Are you all right?"

"I'm grrrreeat," she said with a chuckle.

"I can tell. What's up?"

"First things first, why are you home? Didn't you spend the night at Jonathan's?"

"Umm, no. I thought against it."

"That's your problem, you think too bloody much."

"How about you? You're home."

"Yeah I'm home, but I'm not alone. The man of my dreams is lying in my bed."

"What?" I dropped my voice as though I thought Quinn could hear me. "Quinn's there? You slept with him?"

"Yes, he's here and I kind of sorta slept with him."

"And you called me a tart! How was it? What does sort of mean? I want details. You know I live vicariously through you."

"I should make you pay me for what I'm about to tell you," she laughed, and over the next ten minutes gave me a blow by blow, or should I say a lick by lick, account of her rendezvous with Quinn. I think I was actually sweating on my upper lip.

"Good God, woman, talents like that should be illegal."

"I know. I thought I would get up early, have a bath and prepare for breakfast."

"Breakfast, breakfast," I asked in a high pitched squeaky voice, "or breakfast, breakfast," I asked in my deep sexy voice. We both burst out laughing.

"I was hoping for the later type of breakfast, plus, you know I don't cook."

"That's great. I'm happy for you."

"What about you?"

"What about me?"

"Diamond, I hope you aren't holding out on me."

"Why would I hold out on you? Nothing happened. I think we're both trying to slow things down because they're just moving too fast."

"Bullshit! You mean *you* are trying to slow things down and *you* think things are moving too fast. I saw how you two were looking at each other last night and you aren't fooling anyone. I just hope you don't over think this and lose a great thing. You know smart people can sometimes be really stupid. You've found a really good thing in him, Dye. Just trust your heart."

"Michelle, I'm not going to lose him. I am trying—in fact, I invited myself along on his business trip next week to Rome. I just haven't told him yet."

"You did what? That's what I'm talking about. You've got to take charge."

"Sure, Ms. 'Please can you come with me, I can't do this on my own.' You're really full of shit you know that?"

"I am not. Anyway, I didn't get to tell you how fantastic you were last night with that whole Lola situation. She had it coming. She's actually lucky it was you on a good day and not someone's wife that got to her first." I spent the next half hour hearing all the dirt on Lola and filling Meesh in on what happened at Jonathan's house.

"Dye, I've got to go. I just thought of a nice way to wake up Quinn."

"Oh, you naughty, naughty girl! Have fun and I'll talk to you later today after dinner with my grandparents."

"Okay. Good luck with that by the way. I think you're doing the right thing."

"I knew you would. Love ya."

"Love you too."

I hung up and for the first time in my life, I was jealous of Michelle.

I had to force myself not to call Jonathan all day. I spent most of the morning locked up in my office talking to Dr. Kimora and reading through the files Armand had put together. I still hadn't gotten out of my pajamas and didn't care. It was a little after three when Armand knocked on the door.

"Come on in." Armand opened the door and stepped in. "What's up?"

"You've got a visitor."

"What kind of visitor? Who? I'm really not in the mood to..." Armand stepped aside and Jonathan walked in carrying a bouquet of roses.

"I could always come back later," he said with a smile.

"No. I didn't know it was you," as I stuck my tongue out at Armand. "Armand, this is Jonathan Hamilton. Jonathan, this is one of my dearest friends, Armand."

"Diamond, we've met. Jonathan got here about forty-five minutes ago, so I took the liberty of talking to him and showing him some baby pictures before bringing him up," he said with a smile.

"Tell me you aren't serious. Jonathan?"

"Well, we did have a nice chat, but I didn't get a chance to see all the pictures."

"Armand, you little…"

I didn't finish before he said, "Just kidding. We talked, but I held back on the pictures. I'll leave you two alone."

"It was a pleasure meeting you," Jonathan said with a smile.

"Same here." They shook hands.

"Armand, would you mind putting these in some water for me?"

"Not at all." He took the bouquet and went back downstairs.

"The flowers are beautiful, thank you. What are you doing here?"

"I brought your things over, but it was just an excuse to see you before I left this evening and to wish you good luck tonight."

"Oh, thank you. Do you know where you're staying in Rome?"

"Umm…at the Hassler Villa Medici in Spagna."

"That's funny."

"What?"

"I think the Hassler could quite easily be Armand's favorite hotel in Rome."

"Umm… he seems like a really great guy."

"He is when he has to be." I turned and walked over to the window. We were silent for a little while. "Jonathan, just so you know, I didn't want to leave you last night."

"Then why did you?"

"I was afraid of what might happen."

"I wouldn't have let anything happen that you didn't want to. Don't you trust me? "

"No…yes…I mean I do trust you, I just don't trust myself around you."

"Umm…I understand. Well, listen I won't keep you. I really just wanted to see you before I left and drop your things off." He took his keys out of his pocket.

"Wait, please don't go. Stay a little while longer." I didn't care if I was begging, but I'd been thinking about him all day and now that he was here I didn't want him to leave.

"Come here," his voice was deep and coarse as he held his hand out for me and I took it. "Why? Why do you want me to stay?"

He was holding me in his arms and I couldn't think, I couldn't breathe, I closed my eyes and tried to turn away, but he didn't let me.

"Don't turn away. Say it…tell me what you want." He smelt so good and his body was so hard against mine. I couldn't concentrate, the words wouldn't form on my tongue, and the tightening in my lower abdomen was becoming more intense. "Why do you want me to stay, Diamond?"

"I…" *Open your mouth damn it! Say something!* Michelle was right; I was going to ruin this! I pushed out of his arms and walked over to the window. I was gasping for air as though I was holding my breath. Maybe I should let him leave, I obviously can't handle this and my inexperience was honestly pissing me off. I'm accustomed to being the expert. I am one of the most powerful women in the world, but when he touches me I turn into bumbling idiot. I hope he gives up and leaves. Who the hell wants to put up with this. Stay, no go, no stay, please go!

He walked up behind me. He didn't touch me, but I could feel him there. Damn he was persistent.

"I, what?" he asked. I still didn't answer. "Where is she? Where is that bold woman that sat in my car two nights ago and invited herself over to my house? She knew exactly what she wanted." He didn't seem angry, just frustrated.

I closed my eyes and leaned back into him. "I honestly don't know who she is. That was the first time I'd met her. Jonathan, I don't want you to go, but in the same breath, I can't handle it if you stay. I've been thinking about you all day and the minute I see you or get close to you this is what you do me." I took his hand and brought it up to my chest placing it over my heart as it pounded against my rib cage, like it was trying to escape the confines of my body. "I try to talk and act rational, but," moving his hand up to my forehead as the beads of sweat continued to form I dragged his hand across it, "this is what you do me." I brought his hand down and slipped it into the waistband of my silk pajama pants, opening my legs slightly so that we could cup my womanhood and he could feel the dampness against my thighs and moisture that had now soaked my panties. I heard him gasp. "I try to think and articulate and this is what happens. I try to ignore how my body reacts to you and I fail miserably. This is what you do to me. With each smile or touch you give me, *this* gets worse," I said pressing his hand into me and moving it back and forth. "What should I do? I can't handle it."

"Dye...I...we...let's." He was breathing quickly as though he couldn't get enough air and was struggling to form his words.

"Lost for words or does my cat have your tongue? Now you know how I feel," I responded, pulling my hand out of my pants and leaving his there.

"Yes. Now I do indeed." His voice was deep and coated with the sweetness of his arousal. "Do you know what you're doing to me right now? What you did to me last night before you got out of the car?" he said as he turned me around to face him.

"I can only imagine."

"Imagine, no more," and with that he pulled me into him, kissing me deeply, I gladly returned it. He pushed me against the window and brought my leg up so that his hand rested under my bottom and I was at the perfect height to feel his arousal. God, he felt good. His other hand was flat against the window as he pressed into me. I now had both hands on his butt cheeks, pulling him to me. We were feverish and frantic. Without stopping he picked me up and moved me over to the leather sofa, lying down so that I was on top of him. I could feel his member swelling as it lay across his thigh just below his belt. Holy mackerel! I was a lucky woman. He had raised my shirt and had taken one of my breasts into his mouth. His mouth was hot against my flesh and the sensations were incredible. I was holding my breath as he squeezed and rubbed my nipples. I had to stop, I was losing control. We couldn't do this here, could we?

"Jon...athan."

He moaned in response as he continued to set my senses ablaze with his tongue on my flesh.

"Jonathan," I breathed again as I pulled back away from him so I could look at his face. "We can't do this here. Not now. I'm not ready."

"For the record, your body is ready, but your mind isn't," he said, his voice soft and caring.

"I'm sorry."

"Don't be, it's okay," he said, trying to sit up. I thought I detected some disappointment, but it was slight as he kissed my neck and my face. "When you're completely ready, you tell me. All right?"

"Thank you for being so understanding."

"It's really okay, take as long as you need. When it happens I don't want you to have any regrets. You're worth the wait."

"How do you know?"

He sat up so that my legs were around his waist. "I've been with enough women to know how incredibly special you are. Right now I feel like the luckiest man in the world and I don't want to do anything that could ruin this. I know it's hard."

"It is *hard*, pardon the pun." We looked at each other and started laughing.

"Are you teasing me, Ms. Chantiel?"

"I wouldn't dream of it, Mr. Hamilton," I said with a smile. We hugged and stood up.

"I don't know if I can go a full week without seeing you. Shit, I couldn't go twenty-four hours," he said with a chuckle.

"You can call me anytime, day or night. Is your week filled with business?"

"Actually, no. My assistant had set up meetings for the first two days there, and even then they are only in the morning so I have all these tourists activities planned for the afternoon and the rest of the week. She thought I needed a vacation. I'll have her fax over my itinerary for the week, that way you will know where to reach me."

"That would be perfect."

"All right, I'm going to go. We'll talk later," he said, kissing me tenderly.

"Mmmm, have a safe trip and call me as soon as you get in."

"I will." He stopped to adjust his pants before opening the door and we both smiled.

I walked him to the front door and kissed him goodbye. I waited until the elevator door closed and then I ran to Armand's office, but he wasn't there.

"Armand?"

"I'm in my room." I opened the door and saw him taking shirts out of the closet and throwing them onto his bed.

"Have you already made the flight arrangements?"

"Yes. We leave tomorrow at four."

"Nothing sooner?"

"The only time earlier would be a 6:00 a.m. flight tomorrow morning and I didn't think so."

"All right then. Where are we staying?"

"You know I only stay one place when I visit Rome, but this time around I'll be staying with a friend so you'll be on your own at the Hassler."

"Excellent, I was hoping you would say that. Jonathan is staying at the same hotel."

"Did you tell him you were coming?"

"No. I want to surprise him."

"I guess it's a good thing I didn't open my big mouth."

"So what did you think?"

"He's even sexier in person. I think you've both got it bad. Hook, line and sinker. You've just given every woman on earth another reason to hate you."

"I don't care."

"I know you don't. Are you ready for tonight?"

"Yes. I spent most of the morning going over some things with Dr. Kimora." Armand and I spent the next hour talking about my grandparents and how I would handle tonight.

Chapter 15

I walked into the Peabody at 6:45 and was shown to our table. The stares were obvious and the whispering had begun. I ordered a Bailey's and began to organize my thoughts. My grandparents arrived on time and were directed to our table. My grandmother was in a wheelchair, and even though you could see how the cancer had caused her to wither, her beauty shown through. She was still beautiful, with her head wrapped in a colorful scarf. My grandfather was pushing the wheelchair, and for the first time I realized how old they were. I stood up and held my hand out for my grandmother, but she didn't take it.

"May I have a hug, instead?" Her voice barely audible as she choked back on her tears. Without saying a word I walked around the table, knelt in front of her and she hugged me. She was sobbing and I hugged her back. As she continued to sob, I held her tighter. After a couple minutes she released me. "Do you know how long I've been dreaming of this day? I thought it would never come. I thought I would die…"

"I am sorry," I said. My voice had little emotion, but it wasn't on purpose. I just didn't know how to feel. I had questions that needed to be answered. For the first time I acknowledged my grandfather. I looked up at him, "Would you like one as well?"

"More than anything," he replied. I stood up and gave him a hug and the restaurant broke out in thunderous applause. I didn't really notice it. I was in my own world. We released each other and I walked back around the table to my seat.

"I have heard rumors of your beauty, but now that I've seen you, I know they are true. You *are* the most beautiful woman I have ever laid my eyes on," said my grandmother.

"No. That's not true. Beauty is in the eye of the beholder. I had beautiful parents. I am a reflection of them." There I'd said it. I had brought up my parents. The reason we were here. They spent the next hour asking about my life, career, husband, and children; obviously I gave them the edited version, politely answering their questions. I didn't tell them about Jonathan. I wanted to hold some information back. Our main course had just arrived and we started our meal.

"It's now my turn to ask the questions. Is that all right?" I asked between bites.

They hesitated, but then my grandmother took my grandfather's hand and responded, "You can ask us anything. I'll be damned if I'll lose you again. Right, Nathan?"

"Right." He didn't sound as convincing, but the point is he answered.

"Where do I start?"

"At the beginning is as good a place as any," replied my grandfather.

"Okay. I'll start at the beginning. Why didn't you just give them the oil field?"

"Wow! You just jumped right into it didn't you?" I ignored his shock.

"That's all they wanted. You had a hundred other fields."

"I honestly didn't think they would hurt you. Various people had tried on several attempts to extract money out of me over the years by blackmail and it always worked out in my favor and to their detriment."

"Had your family ever been involved in any of these attempts?"

"No," he said as he solemnly lowered his head.

"So what made you think you could take that type of gamble with our lives?"

"Diamond, we got bad information," interjected my grandmother.

"Viktoria." My grandfather stopped her. He was obviously trying not to get her to say too much.

"What information?" I pressed.

"Do you know what's funny?" my grandmother asked. "Nathan was getting requests to buy that oilfield for months, but refused. We should've sold it when we had the chance."

"Why didn't you?"

"I wanted to keep it. It was good for Ramantu, his tribe and Africa as a whole. We were going to be constantly in Africa anyway to visit our extended family, so I didn't see any reason to get rid of it."

"Not to mention it was the most lucrative of your fields," I interjected.

"Yes. Not to mention it was the most lucrative of my fields."

"Who wanted to buy it?"

"The usual people, other oil companies, except," he paused and something flickered in his eyes.

"Except what?"

"It's strange now that you mentioned it, a month or two before you were kidnapped I got a call from someone who wanted to buy it. He wasn't from any company, but had become belligerent when I refused, saying that I would be sorry, but I didn't pay him any attention. It was your typical call."

"But it wasn't a typical call, because he wasn't calling from one of the usual oil companies and had actually gone as far as to threaten you. Correct?"

"Well, yes, when you put it like that I guess you're right."

"Do you remember his name?"

"No, no it was too long ago."

"You never answered me. What was the bad information that you got," I asked, turning to my grandmother.

She sighed, "It wasn't bad information as much as it was different. For years when anyone tried to extort money from us, our advisor

110

would tell us to refuse. We would find them and make them pay, but this time he didn't even get a complete rundown of what had happened to you before he wanted Nathan to give up the oil field. This was a man that wouldn't have given his mother a penny if he didn't think she deserved it and out of the blue he wanted us to pay," said my grandmother. "Now, in retrospect, I wonder if he was that way because our family was involved, but at the time it didn't sit well with me."

"I didn't take his advice, and I've regretted it ever since," added my grandfather.

"Who is this advisor?"

"No one you know. No more questions. Anyway we really want to try and put this all behind us. You need to let it go," said my grandmother. "Life is too short. Look at me."

"Don't worry. I will let it go when all my questions have been answered."

"You are stubborn just like your father."

"So I've been told. This isn't easy for me." Turning to Nathan, I said, "What you did scarred me deeply. I can't forget about it overnight. Do you understand that? I know you made a mistake and you've been hurting like I have, but I lost more than an oil field."

"So did I, Diamond," he replied.

The remainder of dinner went well, except for all the questions now floating in my head. They asked about Armand and I told my grandmother about the clinical trial I'd signed her up for. They were amazed at how much I knew about everything.

"Diamond, thank you for your suggestions, but I'm tired. I can't do this anymore. No more chemo and no more treatments."

"But, sweetie, she thinks she can help you. Why won't you give this a shot?"

"Because I'm tired, Nathan, these therapies drain the life out of me."

"Nana," I think I shocked myself more than I did them, hearing myself call her the way I used to when I was younger, "try this for me. I know it will work. I've been researching this for years. Let me help you." She exhaled a long deep breath and closed her eyes.

"All right. It's the least I can do after all we've put you through." I reached under the table and took out a leather bound folder and slid it across the table.

"Good. All the arrangements have been made and they are expecting you in Dallas on Tuesday morning."

"This Tuesday? I can't. I have to talk to Dr. Fre…"

"Dr. Fredrick? I've already spoken to him and he's in complete agreement. Your chart has already been sent over to Genesis."

"How did…when did you?"

"I am very persuasive as well," I said with a smile. "That I think I got from my grandfathers." Nathan made a small laugh.

"We are so very proud of you," he said. "It brings my heart great joy to be here with you. Just so you know, my lawyer has been in touch with the news stations that aired that erroneous story yesterday." I smiled inwardly.

"Thank you." Our waiter who had been successful at being invisible most of the night showed up to ask us if we would like dessert. We made our selections and he left.

"Diamond, can you join us at the cancer center?"

"I'm sorry, but I'm actually leaving tomorrow to go to Rome for a week, but I will come straight there upon my return. If that's all right with you? I need to organize my thoughts. I need more time. Eighteen years is a long time to hold on to something."

She didn't try to hide her disappointment. "We understand. Are you sure you'll come?"

"I promise. I'm done running."

She reached across the table and squeezed my hand. "Good now we can all heal from this. We love you so very much."

"I know you do, but keep in mind even after you heal from something, a painful scar can still remain." They both nodded, accepting the fact that I wasn't going to make this so easy for them.

We talked some more, finished up dessert, and I requested the check. Both my grandfather and I reached for it at the same time.

"No, Diamond, this is on me."

"No. I was the one that invited you both. Let me." Neither of us would let go and playfully went back and forth until my grandfather gave in. I took out my card to give it to the waiter, but he was nowhere to be found. "Where did he go?" I asked looking at my grandmother.

"Do you really think I had all night to sit here while you two stubborn people fought over the bill? I gave him *my* card," she said with a smile. My grandfather and I started laughing. "What? You didn't think I walked with my own money? I may be sick, but I know better. Now dinner is on me," she said with a broad smile. She was still a beautiful woman.

We exchanged numbers and I instructed them that they could call me anytime and they did the same. They hugged and kissed me as I tried not to seem so cold. I waited with them while their car was brought around.

Before my grandfather got in the car, he turned to me and asked, "Is the Genesis Cancer Research Institute associated with the Genesis Company?"

I hesitated for a second, "Yes, it is."

"Are you…my God…are you the…"

"Yes. I am the founder and CEO of the Genesis Company," I said with pride.

"Somehow I knew. I just knew it had to be linked to you. Your father would have been proud of all you've accomplished. Do you know how many deals you've beat me out of?"

"Thirty-seven," I said without hesitation. He laughed.

"Those television stations couldn't have been more wrong about you."

"Thank you."

"You're welcome," and with that he kissed me on my forehead, got in the car and drove away. I closed my eyes and turned my head up to the sky and asked in a soft voice, "Would you be proud of me?" I wrapped my arms around my body and squeezed, there was a chill in the air. *Diamond, you did it. You took the first step tonight towards burying your past for good. It may not be easy, but you did it.* I got in my car and headed home.

Chapter 16

I had my seat on the plane fully reclined looking out the window. Armand was so good. He had requested a complete wardrobe from Lucy and when I woke up this morning he had already packed my things. Jonathan's itinerary was sitting on the fax bright and early and Armand had gone ahead and made the reservations for me so I could join him on his excursions. I couldn't wait to see him. I wanted to be in his arms. I wanted to taste his lips.

"Ms. Chantiel?"

"Umm, yes?" I didn't mean to jump, but I did. I thought maybe I was talking out loud.

"You have a call coming through," said the flight attendant.

"Oh. Okay, thank you." I picked up the receiver next to my chair.

"This is Diamond."

"Diamond, it's your grandmother."

I sat up immediately.

"Hello. What's wrong?"

"Nothing, nothing at all. I just wanted to call and thank you for last night."

I breathed a tiny sigh of relief.

"I should be thanking you."

"No. I know how hard it was for you and I wanted you to know that you made me a very happy old woman, plus, I wanted to check that you hadn't given us wrong numbers."

We both started to laugh, because we knew she was serious.

"Now that you know I haven't, are you all set for tomorrow?"

"Yes, we've just landed in Texas."

"You're in excellent hands. Dr. Kimora is a wonderful doctor. Trust me."

"I do. Well, I'll let you go. We'll talk again soon. Promise?"

"Promise. Viktoria, I mean, Nana?"

"Yes, Diamond."

"You can call me anytime."

"I know, thank you."

"Bye."

"Bye."

I hung up and relaxed back in my chair.

"Is everything all right?" asked Armand.

"Everything is fine, that was Viktoria calling."

"Are you all right? You told me things went well last night, but since we left you seemed deep in thought. Is something bothering you?"

"I'm fine. Thinking about Jonathan mostly, but there are a couple things from last night that I want you to look into. They can wait until we get back they aren't pressing."

"Okay. What's up?"

"It maybe hard to get some of this information since it was so long ago, but I want to find out the companies that offered to buy the oil field prior to our kidnapping. More specifically there was apparently a man that called trying to get Nathan to sell it and actually became belligerent when Nathan turned him down. I want you to try and find out who it was. Who *did* he sell it to after the funeral? And last, but not least, who was Nathan's advisor?"

"Well, I can give a possible three out of four, but I will verify it all. I remember your father mentioning AOX, Vitax, Petrum, and Energim as the oil companies that had offered to buy the field. I had never heard of AOX or Petrum, but the other two are fairly large companies, but not as big as Nathan's or yours."

"Okay, I need details on all four for that year."

"Believe it or not, he sold the field to a friend of the family. It wasn't an oil company, but I'm not sure of the name. That I can find out, and his advisor was Laird Hamilton. Wait a minute, I think that's Jonathan grandfather. That's where I knew him from. Damn it I'm getting old. Don't you remember spending the summer at his family's house? Jonathan wasn't there at the time, but his parents were. You, Nyrobi, Zachary, and I had visited for a month when you were six or seven. His Uncle Leland and his wife Susie or Sue Ellen was there as well."

"Susan."

"That's it."

"Armand, they were all there at the party on Saturday. I recognized them but didn't know from where. That means they all knew me. Why didn't they say anything?"

"Dye, relax. It was just all over the news that you had a huge blowout with your grandfather over your parents' death and you expected them to bring it up? They probably didn't say anything because they didn't know how you would react. Not to mention being taken off guard that Jonathan even showed up with you."

"There is more to this than meets the eye. I don't think that's all there is to it, but as I said, it's not pressing and we can find out when we get back." I needed to end this conversation so I could think. Beth and Liam knew me. They all knew me. Why did his uncle leave and never come back?

It was a little before eight in the morning on Tuesday when we landed in Rome. I checked Jonathan's itinerary and saw that he had an investor meeting from nine to twelve followed by a quiet lunch at the Agata e Romeo. I decided I would join him there, hopefully he won't mind.

"Diamond, I've imported the numbers at Minerva's house into your phone. Call me anytime, although I would really prefer you call only if there's an emergency. For Christ's sake please try to have some fun!"

I laughed. "Something tells me you plan on having enough fun for the both of us."

"Something tells me you're right. Maybe we could meet for dinner on Friday or Saturday."

"That sounds nice, I will call you. Where are you going? Aren't you riding with me in the car?"

"No. I have my own ride," he said, motioning with head to an attractive big-boned woman sitting on the roof of her red convertible smoking a cigarette. She could've easily been a size fourteen; and I could swear the pants suit she was wearing was see-through. Her red hair was blowing carefree in the wind.

"Don't have too much fun."

"There's no such thing," he said over his shoulder and waved goodbye.

"Bye," I yelled, waving past him to Minerva who couldn't hide her excitement and was running to meet him. I got in the car and drove to the Hassler.

I watched as Diamond drove away and turned my attention to Minerva. She had put on a little weight since I last saw her, but there was a firm thickness to it that I loved. To me she looked even better. She swung her arms around my neck and kissed me deeply. No hello, no nothing, she found little need for words, she took pleasure in *expressing* how she felt.

"I'm happy to see you too." I said when she pulled away.

"It's been too long," she breathed. "I love the salt and pepper look," she said, touching the hair at my temples. "You are aging well."

"That's a matter of opinion," I said with a smile. "I love your new look as well," I responded as I squeezed her thigh. "You look great."

"That too is also a matter of opinion, but I'm glad you like. Do you think you can drive?"

"When, now?"

"Yes. I wanted to show you how much I missed you and I can't do that while I'm driving."

She was a girl after my own heart. "Do you live the same place?"

"No. I'm even closer. I just bought an apartment. It's located in Fiume Square, Piazza Fiume, between Nizza street and Bergamo street. Do you know where that is?"

"By the bakery?"

"Yes, exactly," she said, throwing me the keys. I told the attendant where the luggage should be brought and we were off. As soon as we pulled off, she pressed the button bringing the top up on the convertible and turned in the passenger seat so that she was facing me.

"Have you missed me, Armand?"

"Yes, I have." It was the truth. Minerva was one of my favorite lovers.

"Buono, good." She kicked her shoes off and knelt in her seat, kissing me softly on my neck. "Why do you persist in wearing these things," she whispered, trying to unbuckle my seatbelt.

"Because it's the law where I come from."

"Such nonsense," she scoffed, rubbing my crotch with her hand as she trailed the outline of my ear with her tongue, nibbling on the lobe. That drove me over the moon and she knew it. She continued to work my ear while skillfully with her free hand she unbuckled and unzipped my pants, slipping my now swollen member out of the confines of my slacks. "I've missed you," she whispered again, not talking to me, but to her long lost friend. She was stroking him gently, looking at me she asked, "You won't kill us will you?"

"No. Not intentionally," I replied with a smile.

"Buono." She bent her head and in one fell swoop took me in her mouth. The sensation seemed to travel immediately down my inner thighs to my big toes and then up toward my back. My entire body tingled from the warmth of her mouth as she moved her tongue and teeth over the sensitive tip of my meaty head and shaft. Up and down. Minerva was expertly using a small amount of pressure with her lips as she dragged them upward to my engorged head, and her hands were working my base. Twisting and pulling, she pumped me up and I instinctively pinched my butt cheeks together.

"Oh my…when did… you pierce your tongue?" I asked, but she didn't answer me. She never talked during sex, she was too focused.

The cool tip of her tongue ring against my warm penis was tantalizing. I had forgotten how much of an expert she was in the art of fellaito. I had to concentrate on keeping my eyes on the road as I fought the urge to lean back and close my eyes. Did I just run that red light? Bloody hell! My toes were bent in my loafers as she sucked and licked at my member. I was now fully engorged as she ran the stainless steel ball on her tongue ring just under the rim of my German helmet. She was using her hands and tongue to massage me.

"Arrhh, Minerva!" I took one hand off the wheel and grabbed as much of her hair as I could, resting my hand on the top of her mane as she sucked my head, licking and twirling her tongue around, up and down my veiny erection. I gently pushed on her head and she knew that it meant I wanted her to take as much of my erection as she could into her mouth and she obediently did it, opening her mouth wider as I hit the back of her throat with each thrust upward. On my fourth thrust she gagged and I eased back, letting her catch her breath. There was nothing I found more arousing than the sound of a woman gagging on me. It did a tremendous amount for the male ego, for my ego especially. I could feel her saliva trickling down underneath my sacks, they were slightly jealous. Almost as though she read my thoughts, she pulled me out of her mouth and took up a new profession as a juggler simultaneously stroking my member as she lavished Mutt and Jeff with all the attention they needed, using her teeth to gingerly pull at the sensitive flesh.

"Min! darling…I don't…know how much…more I can take." An annoyed driver blew his horn at me. Where the hell am I? I was trying to get my bearings and she was making it close to impossible. She took my bulbous head into her mouth again and while she stroked the base of my shaft, she diligently polished my knob, urging me to a climax. I could feel my lower abdomen and testicles tighten. I couldn't risk it! I pressed on the hazards and pulled off to the side of the road, switching the car into park. Taking her head in both my hands, I anchored my heels into the floor of the car, pushed back into the car seat, closed my eyes and pumped as hard and fast into her mouth as I could. She was a true expert. She didn't pull away once and it almost seemed like she was pressing into it encouraging me deeper and deeper down her throat. I saw tiny fireworks behind my eyelids as I exploded in her mouth. I felt lightheaded as the blood rushed from all over my body and my scrotum shuddered against her chin. She didn't waste a drop, reaping the creamy liquid reward for all her hard work. She moaned and licked her lips.

"You still put my skills to the test, Armand," she sighed once I'd relaxed enough to release the grip I had on her hair. "Any other man would've had an orgasm ages ago, but I enjoyed every minute of it."

"I know you did, that's why I tried to hold out as long as I could," I replied, taking her bottom lip in my mouth. "I love your piercing."

"I knew you would. Where are we?" she asked, looking around. "Christ, Armand, you went in the opposite direction," she said with a laugh.

"Listen, after what I just went through, you're lucky we're alive," I said, playfully rubbing her inner thigh.

"True. Take me home. I don't like to wait too long after my appetizer for the main course," she said with a wicked smile, tucking my now flaccid appendage, back into my slacks. I closed my eyes briefly and thought how much I was going to enjoy the next week.

The Presidential Suite Armand had arranged at the Hassler was a bit much, but had a spectacular view. I tipped the attendant and ran myself a bath. I felt good. I wasn't here for work or research. I was just there to have fun, which was a first for me so I was looking forward to it. I heard a knock on the door and slid farther down into the tub so that the bubbles were up to my chin. Who the hell is that?

"Yes?"

"Dye? It's Esdras."

"Oh my God! Come in!" Esdras had been our maid whenever we visited Rome for as far back as I could remember, and had worked her way up to management at the Hassler. We would spend weeks at a time here and she loved Armand. She walked in and screamed when she saw me, flailing her arms.

"Ciao Bella!" she said, reaching over and planting a kiss on my cheek.

"I can't believe you're still here! How long as it been?"

"Four years since we last saw each other and thirty years total at the Hassler. I started here when I was sixteen, working after school."

"That's amazing to me. You haven't changed a bit."

"Me? You are still magnificent. I talked to Armand and he told me to take good care of you. You're here for a man, no?"

"Jesus, is that how he put it?" We both laughed, "Yes. In all honesty I'm here for a man."

"Well, it's about time. No?"

"Umm, I guess."

"You finish up in here and I'll put your things together for your lunch."

"Thank you."

"No need to thank me. You know I would do anything for you and my Armand." She gave me a loving smile and closed the door. I leaned back into the gigantic tub and closed my eyes, thinking about Jonathan. I couldn't wait to see him.

Chapter 17

The driver pulled up in front of the restaurant and already I was having second thoughts.

"Signora, we are here. Should I wait?" asked the driver.

"No, that's not necessary. Thank you." I passed him a generous tip and got out of the car. The Maître d's eyes lit up when I walked through the doors.

"La signora di pomeriggio buona. La tavola per un?"

"Good afternoon to you too," I replied. "No table for me, thank you I'm looking for someone."

"Americano? I'm sorry. Who are you looking for, maybe I can help you."

"Ah, no. I see him right now." I had just spotted Jonathan seated at a large table in the corner with several people. Maybe this was a bad idea.

"Would you like me to let someone know you're here?"

"No. If it's okay with you I would just like to join them."

"Absolutely. Which group is it? I'll have the waiter bring over a chair."

"Thank you. The large one in the corner," I replied, walking into the main dining room and because the maître d' was standing in front of a wall I hadn't noticed how packed the restaurant was. Everyone's eyes were following me. Men were visibly turning their heads as I walked by and women were trying to appear like they didn't notice me by glancing at me through slanted eyes. As I approached the table eyes started to open in obvious amazement.

"Va va voom," a man on the far side of the table exclaimed.

"Jonathan, you have got to see the beautiful specimen standing behind you!" added another man.

"Uh no, Fabian, I'll let you do enough staring for the both of us. Plus, I told you I'm not shopping anymore," Jonathan said, dipping the end of his bread into the olive oil and garlic plate in front of him.

"Well, that's too bad," I said, standing with one hand akimbo, "because I came with the intention of selling my wares."

"Diamond?" he asked without turning around.

"Yes. I hope you weren't expecting someone else." He jumped up and turned around, dragging me into his arms. "I take it this is a good surprise?"

"Good? This is fantastic!" kissing me at the corner of my mouth.

"Don't tell me this is your new girlfriend!" shouted the first man. "Jesus, Mary mother of Joseph! How the hell do you do it?"

"You are the luckiest man alive," countered the first man.

"I am, aren't I?" asked Jonathan, kissing me again. "When did you get in?"

"This morning," I replied.

"Well, don't be rude, introduce us to the lovely lady before the boys have a heart attack!" said one of the women sitting in the corner, with a playful smile on her face.

"I'm sorry. Dye, this is Lollia, Fabian, Claudius, Damian, Justin, and Candace. These lovely people happen to be my dear friends who run my firms in Europe. Everyone, this is my girlfriend Diamond Chantiel," Jonathan said with a proud smile. *Girlfriend*. That sounded lovely to my ears.

"It's wonderful to meet all of you. I'm sorry. Had I known you were having lunch with friends I wouldn't have interrupted. Your itinerary said a quiet lunch."

"A quiet lunch?" Claudius yelled, "Is that assistant playing tricks on you again?"

"I think she was being sarcastic! Nothing involving this group could ever by quiet," Jonathan said, making everyone laugh. The waiter showed up with an extra chair and they shifted down so I could sit.

Turning to me, Jonathan asked, "Where are you staying?"

"I'm at the Hassler as well," I replied, giving him a smile.

"Great! I can't believe you're actually here." He couldn't hide his excitement.

I squeezed his hand, "Well, I am."

His friends were so down-to-earth and very boisterous. Definitely a different crowd from what I was accustomed to, but I was enjoying their company and watching Jonathan interact with them. We talked and drank the afternoon away. We had just finished dessert and the coffee the others had ordered was brought over to the table when a second waiter showed up, looking extremely uncomfortable.

"Signora?" He was looking at me and holding a tray with a Bailey's on the rock.

"Per me? I'm sorry, I didn't order anything," I said with a smile, shaking my head.

"I know. This is compliments the gentiluomo over there," he said motioning over to a man sitting in the center of the restaurant. I could tell the man was not a local. He reminded me of the arrogant prince from the Shrek movie. He had sandy blonde hair and tanned skin, with 'tooth-achingly' sweet features, and lips that were far too glossy for a man's.

"I'm sorry, but can you let the gentleman know that I can't accept the drink. Thank you." I nodded in his direction and turned back to the table. The waiter left to deliver the message and Claudius was making it very obvious that he was interested in the man's reaction.

"He's coming over!" Fabian announced.

"What?" Jonathan said under his breath.

The man was now standing directly beside me and in a heavy

Australian or South African accent said, "Your majesty. I apologize; I should've brought this over myself. I..."

I didn't want him to finish. "Don't call me that! I'm sorry but I don't think you bringing it over here in person is going to help much," I said, glaring at him. Jonathan was getting up, but I stopped him.

"Are you not the daughter of Princess Nyrobi Chantiel?" he pressed.

I was taken aback. I hesitated before answering, "Yes, I am, but what does this have to do with you? Who are you?"

"My name is Chad. Chad Smith. My father was one of your tutors when you were growing up. You probably don't remember me since I was away at boarding school most of the time."

"I do remember Mr. Smith. He taught me calculus and trigonometry. It's nice to see you. I apologize for being rude, but maybe next time you should just come over and say hi. Don't attempt to buy me a drink."

"You probably get that a lot. I just can't believe how gorgeous you are. I mean, you were a pretty kid, but I never imaged, you would..." he stopped and looked around like he was seeing the people seated at the table for the first time. "Listen, I can see you're in the middle of lunch with friends. Why don't you give me your number and we can catch up sometime." Claudius and Fabian were trying their best to hold in their laughs. Cameron scoffed at this point when he asked for my number.

I was still pretty serious. "Catch up on what exactly? I don't really know you."

"I don't know. I just thought..."

"You thought wrong. I don't think that's a good idea. It was really nice seeing you, though. Please remember to Professor Smith for me." I turned and sat back down.

"Maybe I could give you my..."

Jonathan finally stood up. "Chad is it? The lady is with me and I would definitely agree that exchanging numbers is not a good idea. Good bye." Jonathan was not trying to hide how aggravated he was by the entire exchange. I smiled inwardly, my protector. With his tail tucked between his legs Chad retreated.

"My oh my, Diamond, do you always demand so much attention?" Candace asked with a laugh.

"I try not to demand it, but sometimes I fail miserably," I responded with sarcasm, giving her a wink. I couldn't believe I was actually joking about getting too much attention. It was almost as though I was a different person. I liked her…who ever she was.

Our lunch was finally over and it was a little after four when we walked out of the restaurant.

"We'll talk soon," Jonathan announced to his friends as they all piled into the limo waiting for them.

"It was a pleasure meeting all you," I added. "Hopefully I will see you again, sooner rather than later."

"Definitely," said Damian and Justin simultaneously, the others all nodded and smiled.

"Give my love to Quinn. Okay?" said Lollia, winking at Jonathan.

"I will." He closed the door and they drove off. He turned to me and took me into his arms. "Thank you," he whispered before giving me a warm sweet kiss. I could taste a hint of brandy on his tongue and I loved it. I couldn't get enough of him.

"Thank you, for what?" I breathed as he let me go.

"For this, coming here, my surprise. I can't tell you how much it means to me."

"If you can't tell me, then you will have to show me," I responded, giving him a sweet smile. And show me he did. Slipping his arms tightly around my waist he pulled me into his body, kissing me passionately. I willingly opened my mouth and received his warm delicious tongue. I didn't care that I was kissing in the middle of the street in broad daylight. I was in love. We were interrupted by the low buzz of my mobile. I gently pulled away.

"I'm sorry, only a few people have this number. I have to take it."

"Go ahead, that's fine." I turned so that my back was resting against his chest. His arms were laced around my waist as he kissed my free ear. Gently taking the lobe, diamond stud and all, and slipped it into his mouth.

"Di…Diamond Chantiel."

"Diamond? It's Dr. Kimora."

"Hi there, is everything okay?"

"Yes, yes. Everything is fine. We began the infusion at 9:00 a.m. and she had a mild infusion reaction, some nausea, hives and dull headache."

"Did you decrease the infusion rate and medicate?"

"Yes. I decreased the rate to one milligram per minute and gave her 650 mg. of acetaminophen by mouth and she did fine, no further problems. I will go ahead and pre-medicate her one hour before tomorrow's infusion, but I don't think we will have any problems. I just wanted to give you an update."

"How do you think she'll do?"

"I really think she's going to get a great response. She has the perfect disease characteristics. Don't worry, she's in good hands."

"Well, thank you. Please don't hesitate to call me if anything else comes up."

"Don't worry I won't. Enjoy your holiday."

"Thank you."

I pressed off the phone and dropped it into my tote. "Mr. Hamilton, how do you expect me to concentrate when you're kissing me like that?"

"That's the thing, Ms. Chantiel, the last thing I want is for you to concentrate," he said with smile. "Is everything oayk?"

"Umm, yes. That was a doctor that I referred my grandmother to for treatment."

"I didn't even ask you how the dinner went."

"That's okay, it's not like we had the time to discuss it sitting at a table with six other people. The evening went well."

"Were all your questions answered?"

"Actually I think I ended up with *more* questions, but it's fine. Let's talk about something else." I honestly didn't want to start thinking about the past right now, because it would likely inundate my thoughts and at this point I was content to think about just him; Jonathan and Jonathan Hamilton alone.

"Okay, what's next on the agenda?" he asked.

"You're asking me? Your assistant is the one that planned the itinerary," I replied, playfully nudging him.

He quickly looked at his Blackberry and checked his schedule.

"Next is the five o'clock Tiber River sightseeing cruise!" he said with a broad smile. "Do you want to do go?"

"I would love too, but we're going to have to hurry, that's about twenty minutes away and it's already four-thirty."

Jonathan hailed a cab. Forty-five minutes later we were sailing down the Tiber River towards Tiber Island. We were sharing a seating area with a family on holiday from England. The father was trying his best to control the two boys while the mom tried to soothe the crying infant. They were making it a little difficult to hear the captain, but I didn't mind. I was content just resting my head on Jonathan's shoulder and looking out the window. The kids were getting fidgety and it wasn't long before the eldest boy took off after a bird that he saw land on the railing and with the father in hot pursuit and the mother still trying to calm the baby down, the younger boy took the opportunity to strip all his clothes off. Jonathan and I were smiling at each other, while the little flasher started to get obvious stares from other passengers.

"Ummm, excuse me," I said, "but I think you've got an entertainer on your hands."

The mother turned to find her little boy bent over trying to kiss his own ass.

"Gawh Blimey! Have you gone bloody mad, Charles? Where are yah clothes 'eh?" She was frantically looking around for her husband, but from the sound of it, he was now on the second floor still trying to catch boy number one. She looked at me with desperation in her eyes.

"Would you mind terribly?" she asked, holding the wailing baby with outstretched arms. "I'm so sorry. I know you're trying to have a romantic ride with your husband."

"Oh, he's not...I don't mind at all," I replied taking the baby from her. She spread the burp cloth over my shoulder and before little Charles knew what happened he was up in arms with his naked backside being carried away to the nearest bathroom. The baby looked up at my face and almost immediately became quiet.

"Well, hello there," I whispered, standing up and walking to the nearby window. I instinctively started to sway from side to side, all the while cooing and cawing at the tiny person in my arms. I kept talking. Telling him a little about the sights we were passing. His eyes were starting to close. I looked a back at Jonathan, to find him just staring at me. '*I think he's falling to sleep*' I mouthed not even trying to hide the pride I had in my little accomplishment. His little hand had come to rest under his chubby chin. He was beautiful. I rocked him a little longer, then placed him over my shoulder. I turned to find his mom and dad staring at me in amazement.

"I'm sorry, I didn't know you were back," I said in a low voice, slipping him off my shoulder.

"No, please. We've been trying to get him to fall asleep like that for the past hour. If you don't mind holding him a little longer we can get these two settled," the mother replied.

"Sure. I don't mind at all," I said, snuggly fitting him back into the crook of my neck. Soon Charles was back in full attire and Marty was enjoying gold fish by the handfuls. Jonathan hadn't said a word and was still watching me. He didn't look upset, but then again I couldn't really tell. Once they were all seated the mother reached for him.

"Alrighty, I'm all set now," she said.

"Here you go," I said handing the little bundle back over to her.

"Thank you so much."

"Yes. Thank you," said the husband dramatically, wiping the back of his hand across his forehead with a smile. Turning to Jonathan, he said, "She's ready! I know that look; my wife gave it to me as well when she was ready for a baby. All I can say is, enjoy your vacation because this will likely be the last one you ever have alone if you have kids soon."

"Simon!" his wife gasped, playfully slapping his arm.

"Umm, we aren't married." I decided to speak up since Jonathan for the moment seemed speechless.

"Oh my! I apologize. I could've sworn you two were…" He looked completely embarrassed and his wife was glaring at him. "I've put me foot in me mouth, 'eh?"

"Forgive my husband."

"It's okay," I reassured them, but their embarrassment was obvious. Just in time the captain came on to announce we'd reached the island and everyone could get a better view on the top level. The family was up and heading upstairs before the announcement was finished.

I turned to Jonathan and he was still staring at me. "What's wrong? Why are you looking at me like that?" He took my hands in his, but still didn't say anything. "Jonathan, say something, plea…"

"I love you." He was staring at me intently trying to read something in my eyes. *"Did you hear me, Diamond? I said I love you. I don't care if it* scares you away, or if I've only known you five days. I can't hide it anymore. I don't want to go another day without you in my life."

He loved me! He must be mistaken. I wanted to respond but I couldn't. I wanted to tell him I loved him too, but I couldn't. *I* must be mistaken. "Now will you say something, anything?" His voice was coarse with emotion.

"I can't. I need you to give me more time. That's all I think I need, this week with you, here, alone. No distractions, just us here together, to learn about each other. Can you give me that?"

"I can give you that and so much more," he whispered, pulling my face into his. "That and so much more," he whispered again before tenderly taking my mouth in his. I closed my eyes. He loved me.

Chapter 18

After my big announcement Diamond had become obviously quiet. What the hell was I thinking? One minute I don't want to scare her away and the next I'm telling her I love her. Well, it's the truth and sooner or later she would have to know. I had called my driver to have him meet us back at the pier, so when we docked, he was waiting. I helped Diamond into the car and then got in. I wish she would just tell me what she was thinking. I wanted to know what was going on behind those eyes.

"Are you hungry," I asked, looking for any excuse to get her to talk to me.

"Actually, I'm still a little full from lunch. What time is it?" she asked, looking down at her watch.

"Six forty-five," we said simultaneously. We smiled at each other. "How about we go back to the hotel, freshen up and meet downstairs in the restaurant around eight for a light dinner?"

"That sounds nice. I'm sure I'll be hungry by then," she replied slipping her hand into mine and resting her head back on the seat.

"You look tired. We don't have to go to dinner if you're not up to it,"

I didn't want to end the night, but she really did look exhausted. I'd forgotten that she'd just flown in this morning.

"I am a little tired, but I don't want tonight to end just yet. Maybe we can have dinner brought up and arranged on my balcony. You seem to have a thing for balconies," she said with a smile.

"Now that sounds perfect." I kissed her on the corner of her mouth and turned to look out the window. What a view. She had no idea how happy I was that she was there with me. I truly would've been miserable if I had to go the entire week without seeing her. The others really liked her today and it takes a lot for that group to like anyone. They hated Lola, which always made it difficult to visit them in Europe. My friends liked her, my Aunt Rosa liked her, my parents seemed to like her, and I loved her, so there was no reason why this couldn't work.

"Jonathan?"

"Yes, baby," I said turning my attention to her.

"Earlier when you told me…when you said what you said…" She was starting to fidget the way she got when we were alone in her office.

"When I said I loved you," I wanted her to hear me say it again. I wasn't afraid to say it.

"Yes. When you said you loved me and I didn't…well, I wasn't able to respond. It wasn't because I don't have feelings for you as well. I hope you know that."

"Don't worry. I know. When you're ready we'll travel that road. All right?"

"All right."

We arrived at the Hassler a little after seven. "Is eight a stretch? Do we need more time?" I asked as the chauffeur helped Diamond out of the car.

"I don't need more time. We're just having a casual dinner right? I don't need to dress up, do I?"

"No, you could come in your birthday suit if you wanted to," I said, giving her a wink as we walked up the stairs to the glamorous entrance of the Hassler. This place never ceased to amaze me. It was worth every penny.

"Very funny. I'll order dinner. I think my friend Francesca Lapreda is still the chef here," Diamond was saying as she looked back at me.

"That would be great," I responded. We hadn't made it half way through lobby yet and already Diamond was getting stares. Guests were stopping mid-conversation to watch her walk by. Watching the men look at her with such obvious want made me furious. I was trying to be polite today at the restaurant, but blondy was really asking for trouble. I had the urge to quicken my step so that I was closer to her, so that everyone would know we were together, that she was taken, but I stopped myself. I would not become the boyfriend that needed to always make his presence known. I trusted Diamond and I was confident enough to let her walk ahead. We picked up our messages from the front desk and walked to the elevator.

"What floor are you on?" she asked.

"The 6th floor. I usually stay in the Trinità dei Monti suite. You?"

"I'm on the 7th floor. Armand has this thing for the penthouse," she said with an uncomfortable smile.

"Well let's head up. I'll be there at eight in casual dress," I said with a smile, slipping my arm around her waist as the elevator door closed.

I watched Jonathan wave as he got off the elevator. I couldn't press the 7th floor button enough. I had to call Armand. My shoes came off as soon as got through the front door and I ran to the phone in the sitting room. It rang six times before Minerva picked up, sounding completely out of breath.

"Ciao," she said.

"Ciao Minerva, it's Diamond. Can I speak with Armand?"

"Oooh, Diamond, Armand is a little tied up at the moment," she replied with a little giggle.

"Minerva, I'm sorry, but I really need to speak to him." What the hell was he doing? I could hear them laughing in the background. He finally came to the phone.

"Hello, love."

"What the hell were you doing?"

"I don't think you want to know."

"I need your advice." I told Armand about our afternoon and what Jonathan said.

"And what did you say? Let me guess…nothing."

"Don't say it like that. I need more time, what did you expect me to say? Listen, that's actually not why I called, I want to know what you thought I should wear tonight."

"What do you think you should wear? I can't believe a woman of your intelligence is calling me with such stupid questions. Do you know what you're interrupting?"

I ignored him, "When he said I could wear my birthday suit I had the urge to do exactly that and I want you to talk me out of it! There I said it. Now tell me I'm crazy!"

"I think that could be the smartest thing you said all day. Just so you don't come across as being too brash, I would throw on the long ivory pajama shirt, the linen one. That should be translucent enough to drive him crazy. Do you know how inappropriate it is for your father figure to be giving you this type of advice?"

"Well, thank God I see you more as a friend and confidant than a father figure," I said with a laugh.

"Have fun love and use protection."

"I won't need protection. I don't plan on it going that far."

"Diamond, if you don't want it to go that far then put on some fucking clothes!" he said, abruptly hanging up.

I laughed to myself. I had managed to irritate Armand. I could tell he wanted me to admit I loved Jonathan and sleep with him already. Armand was not a man that liked games, at least not these types of games.

I quickly dialed down to Francesca, apologizing for the short notice, told her the occasion was a romantic dinner and requested that someone come up and set up the balcony for me. It seemed within a minute there was a team of people at my door, their hands filled with boxes, who quickly came in and started to rearrange the balcony. I left them to it and ran to the bathroom, giving myself a thorough shower. I had to be prepared for anything just incase things did go that far. I toweled dried my hair and stood naked in front of the huge Venetian mirror looking at myself for the first time as a woman. I had looked at myself before, but never with the intention of finding flaws. Right now I was looking for anything Jonathan could find remotely unappealing. Lola was so much thinner than I was. Maybe that's what he liked. She was the last person I wanted to think about right now, but I couldn't help it. I was never concerned about my weight and as I stood there turning from side to side, admiring my perfect hourglass shape, I trailed my finger tips up my thigh, over my hip and across my abdomen, I wondered if he would find me appealing. I looked at my light brown nipples pointing outward from my full 36D bosoms. My thighs were thick and toned from my running and weekly karate workouts. Then I looked *there*, so smooth and neatly shaven. Since Friday Jonathan had awakened something deep within me. I was eager to learn what treasures lay behind her thin curly veil. I pulled my wet hair up off my shoulders and turned so I could look at my back view. Enough! I needed to get dressed. I quickly brushed my teeth, moisturized with a honey butter Michelle wanted me to try, and slipped the soft nightshirt over my head. The material was almost like a cheese cloth and incredibly light. Armand was right, there was a simple elegance to it, but it would leave little to the imagination. I glanced at the grandfather clock in the hallway and noticed it was a couple minutes before eight. I took one last look at myself, tousled my hair one final time, put on a little MAC lip glass and went out to the balcony. They had transformed the already beautiful outdoor terrace into a soft romantic love nest, with candles, Toole, and beige linens. The linens on the outdoor bed were changed and now covered with a beige and gold cloud-like comforters and pillows. The dining table meant to seat six was collapsed and redecorated for an intimate dinner for two. A bottle of champagne was already being chilled with a sterling silver bowl filled with strawberries perched directly beside it. Everything looked perfect. There was a knock at the door and I jumped. Here we go…no turning back now.

"Come in," I yelled as I walked through the French doors and leaned against the grand Louis XV chair in the middle of the living room.

"I'd forgotten how beautiful this suite was," Jonathan announced as he came in and walked down the hall. "Dye?"

"I'm in here," I said in a sultry voice just as he entered the living room. He was a sight for sore eyes in khaki's and a thin cream sweater that fit his chest perfectly. He stopped in his tracks when he saw me. "Would you like some champagne?" I asked, but he didn't answer me, which meant he liked what he was seeing. "Jonathan?" I said as I walked towards him with an outstretched hand. His eyes followed the length of my body, top to bottom, pausing briefly at my breasts.

"What are you trying to do to me?" His voice barely audible.

"What am I trying to do to you like what? You're the one that suggested I wear my birthday suit," I said in a playful tone. "So I took you up on the offer. Should I get changed?" I asked, pretending to turn toward the bedroom. He grabbed my arm and dragged me into his arms.

"No, no, no. You don't change a thing. I'm going to issue this disclaimer early in the evening that I am not responsible for my actions after this minute." He had put on his courtroom voice and it was turning me on. "You look exquisite," he whispered, kissing me just below my earlobe.

"You look nice as well. Let me pour you a drink," I said, slipping out of his arms I walked out onto the terrace.

"D-A-M-N!" he exclaimed as I walked away, I turned to find him with his hand over his mouth, blatantly staring at my bottom.

"Stop it!" I said jokingly. "You're making me laugh."

"And you're making me swell." His tone was more serious. "I don't know if I can make it through dinner." There was another knock on the door and he abruptly turned around. "You pour the champagne, I'll get the door," he said over his shoulder. I was pleased with the effect I was having on him. It made me feel good knowing that he liked what he saw. A waiter walked in pushing a cart with dinner. It smelled wonderful.

"Thank you. You can leave it right here," I said, pointing next to the table, but the poor man didn't seem to be able to hear me or move for that matter. Jonathan quickly tapped on his shoulder, handed him some money and escorted him to the door.

"We will call down when we're ready for it to be picked up," Jonathan said as he closed the door.

"What was wrong with him?" I asked as Jonathan joined me on the balcony.

"In one word? You! You just don't realize the effect you have on people."

"Shit, I forgot what I was wearing, or should I say what I wasn't wearing." We both started to laugh. "Are you ready for dinner?"

"Yes, I'm starving. Did you do all of this?" he asked looking around the terrace.

"Uh no, I had someone come up while I took a shower."

"It's beautiful. The view alone is amazing," he said as he walked over to the railing. I could tell he was making a conscious effort not to be too close to me. I found it all rather amusing. I picked up the menu card to see what Francesca had sent up.

Steamed King Prawns served with Sicilian Couscous and garnished with Mozzarella and Basil

Buffalo Ricotta delight with White chocolate and Exotic Fruit

I uncovered the platters and beckoned Jonathan to come and sit tapping the back of the empty chair.

"That looks delicious," he remarked, sitting beside me.

"Well, let's eat before it gets cold," and with that we dug in.

There didn't seem to be anything we didn't talk about. We finished dessert and Jonathan called down to have the trays removed, while I went to the bathroom to wash my hands and freshen up. When I rejoined him on the balcony he was leaning back against the railing and drinking the cup of Irish coffee he had requested. I ambled over to the table, picked out the fattest strawberry remaining, leaned against the French doors and took a big bite, letting some of the juice trickled down my chin. I was stuffed, but purely using the strawberry for effect, knowing full well that Jonathan hadn't taken his eyes off me. He swallowed the coffee that was still in his mouth, walked over and put the cup on the table.

Looking down at me he said, "Thank you for a wonderful evening. I'm glad you're here. Maybe tomorrow we can do a little shopping?"

"Sure. That sounds like a plan," I responded, trying to figure out if that meant the evening was over and he was leaving.

"I'm going to head down and let you get some rest. You've had a long day," he said, kissing me on the top of my head. I guess it was over. Stop him, you know you don't want him to go. *For Christ's sake open your mouth and tell him how you feel.*

"All right then, I guess I'll see you tomorrow." Coward!

"Is ten okay?" he asked over his shoulder.

"Ten will be fine. Goodnight." *Super coward!*

"Goodnight." My eyes shut as I heard the door close. *What did I do wrong? Nothing,* I thought. *That's my problem. I did absolutely nothing. Jonathan wanted me to make the next move. He didn't want to be the one to give in to his urges again and I didn't want to be the one to make a mistake. Think, Diamond, think! He took his last chance today when he told you he loved you and you didn't respond. He is resenting himself for being so weak around you. What are you going to do? Damn it, I would be the one. I will be the one to take this leap. I will put my pride aside and tell this man how I feel.* I practically knocked the chairs over running to the door. I swung it open to find him standing there with his arms folded across his chest and a small smile played across his lips. He hadn't moved.

"Did you forget something?" he asked.

"No," I said with an embarrassed smile. "Actually, yes I did," jumping up into his arms and wrapping my legs around his waist. "I forgot this," kissing him deeply. "Come…back…inside." The Princess of Pride was no more.

He moaned, taking small steps back into the suite. I reached out and slammed the door once we were inside and he immediately backed me into the door, sliding his hands under the pajama shirt and cupping my naked cheeks. His hands were feverish against my skin and my tongue frantic in his mouth. I was savoring the taste of him running my hands through his thick dark hair as he slipped his hands up my back. I moaned as he brought his mouth down my neck and proceeded to suck and kiss the sensitive skin beneath my jaw line.

"Jonathan," I moaned, "I want you right now."

He pulled away looking at me intently, his eyes dark and glazed from his arousal. "Are you sure?"

"Why, aren't you?"

"Of course I am, but I've made it clear how I feel about you. I just want to make sure this isn't the bottle of champagne talking."

"No more talking. I want you to make love to me."

"No. We have to talk about this, because this is taking our relationship, if you can even call it that, to a new level. I don't want to make love to you if you don't feel remotely the same way about me, and I'm content to wait until you know how you feel."

"Why are you questioning me?" I was getting upset. "You're acting like you've never slept with someone you didn't care about. I just want you! Let's just do it!" Shit, that came out totally wrong. His face fell as he took my arms from around his neck and let my feet slip back down to the floor.

"Wow, if that's how you feel then you definitely don't want to lose your virginity to someone you don't even care about," he said, trying to step around me.

"Wait, God damnit!" I yelled, pushing his hand away from the door. "Let me organize my thoughts. That didn't come out right. It's not what I'm trying to say. What the hell is happening here?"

"I'll tell what's happening here from my perspective. You've finally met someone that you're attracted to and you're tired of not knowing what it feels like to *be* with someone. I just happen to be that someone. The only problem with that is if that's all you want then you've got the wrong guy. I want more, a lot more. I love you. I don't want just your body. I can have my physical needs met at any time with anyone. I want more than that. I want the whole thing. If you just want to have sex with me, I can't. I don't have time for these games."

"No. You've got it all wrong. I mean you're right about what you just said, but…"

"Am I wrong or right, Diamond? Do you just want to sleep with me? It's time to make a decision! One minute you're asking for more time and in the next you want to do something that would take our relationship to new heights. Am I wrong or right?"

"You're right." The tears began to fall as his shoulders dropped in disappointment and he walked into the hallway. "You're right about me being attracted to you and wanting to make love to you, but you're wrong if you don't think I want what you want out of this relationship." My back was still turned away from him. "I have Michelle and Armand telling me that I think too much and that if I keep thinking things through I'm going to lose you! So I take a chance tonight and I don't think things through and I tell you exactly what I'm feeling and what I want and now you're upset with me!" I walked out on the balcony and thankfully I heard the door close as Jonathan followed me inside. I spread my hands flat against the banister and lowered my head, the cool night air blowing through my slightly damp hair. "I want to tell you I love you and I want to tell you I want to marry you and spend the rest of my life with you and that after holding that baby today I know I want to have a whole brood of your children. And I want to tell you all this wealth, the companies, the clothes, the stupid penthouses I would give them all up in a heartbeat if it was a choice of me being with you or having them. But my brain won't let me say those things. My brain keeps saying, it's only been five days, what you're feeling isn't possible, you need to think this through." I turned to face him, the tears still falling as I was undoubtedly making some Godforsaken ugly face. "Tell me what you want me to do. Tell me what you want me to say. I'll do it. I'll say it. I suck at this! I've never been a relationship and at the rate I'm going, I'm going to lose you, and I can't bear that. I don't want to think, I just want to be with you. Can't you see that?"

He came toward me and took me into his arms. I cried into his sweater. I couldn't believe I just said all of those things to him.

"Baby, I'm sorry. Please don't cry. I just…I just want you to be sure. I didn't want you to have any regrets. I couldn't bear it if after everything happened you regretted being with me. I feel as though you're waiting for me to make all the moves. I don't want to pressure you."

I wiped my face and looked up at him. "I don't want to mess this up. You could very well be the best thing that ever happened to me." Touching his face, I added, "You make me so happy."

He picked me up and carried me over to the bed, lying down beside me; he wiped the tears off my cheeks.

"Do you really want to marry me?"

"Yes," I said without hesitation.

"Do you really want to have a brood of my children, even if they can turn out like little Charlie?" he asked with a smile.

"Yes."

"Do you still need more time?"

"No."

"What should we do now?"

"I think if there isn't a doubt in either of our minds as to whether we want to spend the rest of our lives together, then we should get married." I was touching his face and looking at him as intently as I could because I wanted him to see into the window of my heart. I didn't want to hide anything else from him ever again. He kissed me deeply, using his large hand to support my neck as he brought my face up to meet his.

"Did you just ask me to marry you?" he asked with a smile, lowering my head back to the pillow.

"I think I did," I replied.

"Are you serious, because…"

"As a heart attack."

"In that case, yes. I would love if you became Diamond Hamilton." Now it was my turn to kiss him.

"This may sound a little insensitive, even crude, but wouldn't you like to try my goods before signing your life over to me?"

"Don't *you* want to try *my* goods before you become my wife?"

"You have to understand; with me I have no starting reference, so you'll be it. You're my all. There is no way in Hell you could ever disappoint me. You, on the other hand, have a vast repertoire from which I could be catalogued, so again I ask; don't you want to try my goods before you commit to me?"

"No, you have to understand; with me it's much more than the physical. I will be content just having you. So again I ask, what do we do now?"

"Tomorrow we shop for a ring, on Friday we get married. When we return to New York, we plan the reception. How is that?"

"Are you going to tell anyone?"

"If you don't want me to, I won't, and we can wait to make the announcement together at home."

"Who would you tell?"

"I only have Armand, Michelle, my grandparents and Lucy." It felt nice to include my grandparents. I watched as Jonathan closed his eyes and ran his hands through his hair.

"Why Friday?" he asked.

"Well, today is Tuesday and if we got the ring tomorrow I figured we would have Wednesday and Thursday to learn as much about each other as possible, not to mention Friday would be a full week that we've known each other and it would sound nicer when we recap how we met to our children," I said with a laugh.

"Then in that case, Friday will be perfect. It would also give us a couple days to fly Michelle, Quinn, my parents and your grandparents in if you wanted"

"It maybe a stretch for my grandparents since my grandmother is having treatment through Thursday, but I can ask them. You really want everyone here, don't you?"

"I'm an only child. I don't think my mother will ever forgive me if I eloped."

"If that's how you feel, then they can come."

"You won't change your mind about marrying me, will you?"

"No, honey, I won't change my mind," I said with a smile.

Chapter 19

We lay in each others arms for awhile talking and looking up at the stars. I didn't know what time it was and I didn't care. He moved a tendril of hair away from my face.

"You're the most beautiful woman I've ever laid my eyes on. I'm going to make you so happy," he said, running his hand up my body and leaving it to rest over my breasts.

"I know you will," I responded, leaning forward trying to reach his bottom lip. He met me halfway and took my mouth in his, gently stroking my sensitive nipple with his thumb, as I sucked and nibbled on his bottom lip. A low moan escaped my lips, as he rose up on his elbow and swung his leg over to straddle me. He continued to kiss me and massage my breasts. I struggled to take his sweater off. Laughing he knelt over me and pulled it over his head, revealing the smooth olive skin of his wide chest and the dark hair that trailed from his navel to the growing member concealed in his trousers. I bit my lip as I could only imagine the treats he had in store for me. The moonlight had cast a warm glow on our bodies, making him appear even more Herculean.

"May I?" he asked gently pulling my night shirt from under his muscular thighs.

"Please do," I responded, making a small gasp as he pulled the shirt over my head and the cool night breeze blew across my warm flesh. With my arms still above my head, I rested my head on the pillows and gazed at him. He seemed to be just taking in the sight of me as well. Leaning forward, he placed his hand on my neck, using his trusty thumb to run back and forth along my jaw line. I closed my eyes as my stomach muscles were contracting and I could already feel the moisture between my legs.

"Open your eyes and look at me," Jonathan said in a soft firm voice. "I want you to look at me as I make love all over your body. I want you to see how much I love you," he said as he started to move down my body and I whispered his name.

"Jonathan…" but I could say no more as he had taken one nipple into his mouth and the other he was rubbing between his thumb and index finger. "Ooooohh," I breathed, arching my back as an electric shock walked up my spine. He was using his tongue to twirl and his teeth to graze and nibble. It felt so good. He moved back and forth between both my breasts for what seemed like an eternity. My stomach muscles were unbelievably tight and between my legs were drenched.

"Jonathan." He pulled my nipple out of his mouth and raised his head to look at me, still twirling and rubbing the other one between his fingers.

"How does this feel?" he asked.

"I can't describe it," I said without hesitation. He removed his hand from my breast and opened my thighs with his knee.

"And this?" he asked moving his hand to my mound and expertly slipping his long middle finger up between her drenched lips, making small deliberate circles as he opened my secretive folds, spreading the moisture over his finger. The sensation that came took me by complete surprise. I bit my lip and shot up further in the bed as the muscles in my lower abdomen contracted again. Immediately Jonathan pulled his hand away and looked as me with concern.

"Did I hurt you?"

"Uh, no…no. Not…at all. I just…you just surprised me and I jumped."

"Your lip is bleeding," he said as the frown in his brow deepened with concern.

"I know, I bit it," I replied in a small voice. I felt stupid.

"You've got to relax," he said lacing his fingers through mine.

"I know. I was…I am relaxed. It's just that you have all my nerves standing on edge and when you touch me they fire little shots of electricity up my spine. Please don't stop, I'll be fine."

"Don't worry, I have no intention to. Promise you'll let me know if I hurt you or you need me to stop."

"I promise." We kissed again, more tenderly this time and I tasted the hint of my blood on my lips. I turned on my side and looped my arms around his head, bringing my foot up to rest on the calf of my opposite leg. The cool breeze blew across my moist lips causing me to shiver. Jonathan drew me closer and almost as though he knew slipped his hand down over my vagina. Pressing his hand into me as he started to massage and knead my vagina with his palm, rubbing my clitoris and tapping my opening with his four fingers. That massage was unlike any other I had ever had. I still couldn't fathom how one small area could affect my entire body this way. We continued to kiss passionately, and then once, in his infinite wisdom, he felt I was ready, he slid his finger between my moist warm folds again. I moaned as he gently stroked me into oblivion. I could never have imagined how this would've felt. I was experiencing sensations that I didn't think were possible.

"You're…so…tight," he moaned kissing me a little harder. He slipped another finger inside me and I thought for sure I was going to fall over the edge of the cliff he had brought me to. Any discomfort disappeared before it was really noticed. As his fingers made a 'come here' motion inside of me, gently rubbing the roof of my womb, the friction his knuckles were having against the tight walls and soft lips of my vagina was pushing me closer and closer to insanity. He was moving at a steady pace, turning his wrist and bending his fingers.

"Oh God, Jonathan, that feels so bloody good," I moaned, as he was now sucking on my breasts again and now using his thumb to rub against the head of my rosebud. He was pressing down on it, while making quick deliberate circles. I started to rotate my hips as I could feel something strange start to happen, specifically low in my abdomen but generally all over my body. The sensation felt as though there was something building off in the distance, and with each circle Jonathan made or insertion of his fingers, it was coming closer and closer to the point of explosion. Then it happened, all those nerves I talked about had come to the surface of my skin and were now firing uncontrollably. My body wasn't my own. My toes pointed as I threw my head back and my stomach muscles drew together into one massive ball. I screamed and shook as my body convulsed between Jonathan and the bed. Beads of sweat had formed on my forehead and upper lip and *I* was trembling against his hand. Oh my God, what just happened? My eyes were closed and Jonathan was planting soft kisses all over my torso, as it took a few minutes for my convulsions to slow and finally go away. I opened my eyes to find the man of my dreams smiling down at me.

"Are you okay?" he asked in a soft voice.

"I'm better than okay. That was amazing." He lay back on the pillows and closed his eyes, making small circles around my navel. "Let me do something for you," I said in a sexy voice.

"You just did."

"No, I didn't. I didn't do a damn thing," I replied in a firm voice. I threw my leg over him, so that I was now straddling him, perfectly positioned over his enormous erection. "Please let me try. I've read books. Michelle has schooled me on technique. I can do this. I want to make you feel good." I began to unbuckle his belt and he held my hand.

"I have no doubt that you can *do* it, but you've gotten so far trying to save yourself, a few more days won't hurt."

"I wasn't saving myself for marriage, Jonathan, I was saving myself for the right man, and I've found him."

He was silent, lying there with his eyes closed and his hands behind his head.

"What's wrong?" He opened his eyes and looked at me.

"Lola."

I didn't try to hide the shock on my face. I knew he didn't still love her, but what was this about?

"What about Lola?" I asked as he sat up so that my legs were wrapped around his back.

"This isn't easy for me to say…"

"Say it for Christ's sake." I didn't mean to yell, but I did.

"She cheated on me numerous times."

"I know that…"

"Listen, people can rationalize it how they want, but to me that doesn't say something about Lola, as much as it says something about me. It says I couldn't satisfy her. I want to satisfy you." I closed my eyes in obvious relief.

I opened my eyes and pulled his face away from my chest. "Lola and I are two very different women." He opened his mouth to speak but I stopped him, placing my hand across his mouth. "Let me finish. Yes, she did cheat on you several times, but she was looking for something that you had stopped giving her long ago; your time and your affection. You didn't love her, but I know you love me. The woman I saw stand in front of you on Saturday afternoon was not an unsatisfied woman. The woman I saw yearning for you to make love to her like you had so long ago was not an unsatisfied woman. Lola didn't cheat on you because you couldn't satisfy her. She cheated on you because she couldn't satisfy you and she needed to be with men that she knew she satisfied and left begging for more." I took his hand and carefully started to suck on each finger, lingering on his middle and index fingers as I tasted myself for the first time. "You will satisfy me completely because I love you dearly and I know I will satisfy you, because on top of you loving me, I constantly strive for perfection and will try and try until I've given you perfect pleasure. Don't ever compare me to Lola. The funny thing is…tonight before you came up I stood naked in front of the bathroom mirror and compared myself to her, wondering and hoping that you would find me appealing."

"Dia…"

"No, listen, but after being with you tonight I wouldn't change a thing about myself, because the way you look at me is priceless and you never looked at her that way. You want me to trust that you will never intentionally hurt me and I want you to trust that I will always be honest with you. Now, if there's some other sentiment involved, like having your virgin wife on your wedding night for the first time, then let me know, because that I can definitely appreciate, from a man's point of view."

"I guess there is something special about waiting. Other than the fact that it's unheard of in this day and age, it would make our wedding night even more special. You would be giving me a part of yourself that no other man would ever have."

I was a little disappointed, but I understood where he was coming from.

"You're right, you're nothing compared to Lola and I'm sorry I even brought her up. I guess I don't want to disappoint you. If you don't want to wait, then we don't have to."

"No, I can tell you really want to. It will only be a few more days and I know you aren't going to disappoint me."

"Are you mad?"

"No, I'm not mad, a little disappointed maybe, but certainly not mad. I not accustomed to waiting for what I want, especially when I want something so badly."

He pulled me into his arms and kissed me tenderly. "Well, if it's any consolation, I plan on using the next couple days to do some prep work, so you can rest assured that the next few days won't be a complete waste," he said, gently massaging my breasts and sucking on my earlobe. "We can consider Friday night the finale to a week of simple pleasures."

"Ahh, Jonathan," I breathed, "when you put it like that, you actually have me looking forward to the next few days."

I slipped my nightshirt on against the cool night air and we lay in each others arms kissing, touching, and talking the night away.

Chapter 20

I awoke to the warmth of Jonathan against me and our bodies intertwined. I tried to slip out from under the comforter, but he pulled me closer.

"Where do you think you're going?" he asked in a low voice. I backed away, thinking neither of us wanted to smell each others breath at this time in the morning, but I didn't have time. I pulled the comforter up to my nose and turned to answer him.

"I was going to call my family and give them the good news and order us some breakfast." I replied, my voice muffled from under the comforter.

"Why do you have that thing over your face?"

"Ummm, morning breath."

"Do you realize you're going to spend the rest of your life with me?"

"Yes, I realize that, but…"

"And that you're going to be waking up beside me every morning?"

"Yes, but…"

"No buts," he said, dragging the comforter away and planting a wet kiss on my mouth. It wasn't as bad as I had imagined it could be, his breath was actually fresh. "How was that?"

"Not bad," I said, kissing him back. I got a waft of pancakes and bacon, "ummm what's that smell? Someone having breakfast, no doubt."

"Actually, I got up earlier, ran downstairs to freshen up and ordered us some breakfast. The breakfast just came and I sneaked back into bed, but I woke you."

"You already brushed your teeth?" I asked my eyes wide with amazement.

"Yep," he said with a wicked smile. "You don't think I wanted my first morning waking up next to you to be spoiled by bad breath, do you?"

"You little sneak!" I said through clenched teeth, playfully hitting him in the chest. "What about me?"

"What about you? I couldn't careless what your breath smells like," he said with a laugh, biting me on my shoulder. "Let's eat."

"What time is it?" I asked.

"Umm, a little after eight."

Jonathan fixed me a plate as I ran to the bathroom to brush my teeth and put my robe on. "Did you call your parents?" I yelled from the bedroom.

"Uh, no. I figured we could do it together, plus they're six hours behind. We can call this afternoon when we get back from shopping."

"I don't think I can wait that long to call Meesh," I said, sitting beside him. "I'll call her before we leave." We ate and while Jonathan ran downstairs to check his messages and get ready. I didn't waste anytime picking up the phone to dial Armand.

"Ciao," Minerva answered in a sleepy voice.

"Ciao, Minerva. I'm sorry for calling so early, but can I speak to Armand?"

"Certo." I could hear her telling him it was me.

"If you're calling me this early in the morning, then I know nothing happened, or Jonathan isn't as good as I had hoped, which I doubt. When are you going to relax and live life? You fly all the way to Rome and you probably aren't going to do half the things you intend on doing with that man. I don't know where I went wrong with you. You are fearless with everything else, but with him you turn to a bumbling piece of putty that needs me to tell her what to wear. Well, my trip won't be in vain. I am having a splendid time. Minerva is wearing me to the bone just the way I like it and she's even invited Esdras over this evening, so that will be double the trouble and twice the fun. Didn't I say this number was to be used for emergencies only?"

"Are you finished now?" I asked with a large smile spread across my face from listening to his spiel. "Armand, I'm getting married."

I could hear him sputtering on the other line. "I'm...I'm sorry, but I could swear you just told me you were getting married. Is that what I heard you say?"

"Yes."

"When?"

"Friday."

"Was it that good?"

"We didn't do anything."

"What?"

"Well, we did do some things, but not what you think."

"Who asked who?"

"I asked him."

"Jesus Christ! Now I know I went wrong with you! *You* asked *him*? You are smart enough to know that it's backwards. Good God! Are you certain?"

"As certain as I've ever been. I love him, Armand, and I don't want to go another day without being with him."

"But you haven't even tried the goods!"

"That's what I said, but he wants to wait," I replied with a chuckle. "And he saw me naked, so I'm not too sure what that says," I said, laughing even more.

"He saw you naked and he didn't want to sleep with you? What aren't you telling me?"

"We did other things, or should I say he did other things, but..."

"He really loves you if he can put his groin aside for three days so that he can have you completely on your wedding night."

"I know. The more I thought about it the more I appreciated his sentiment. I know you're having a wonderful vacation, but can you talk to Esdras and Francesca and have them pull something together for Friday night? I'll call Meesh and Lucy. Jonathan and I will tell his parents and my grandparents this afternoon and hopefully they can come. Once I get back to you on who's coming can you arrange my plane? I don't want them to have to make any arrangements since this is on extremely short notice. Okay?"

"Okay, love. I'm happy for you. I can't think of anyone who deserves this more."

"Thank you, Armand. Oh, I almost forgot, can you give me away?"

"I would be honored."

"Great. I'll be out most of the day shopping in town with Jonathan, so if you need me, try my mobile. I trust you completely, so please don't feel the need to check in with me on any of the frivolous deals, like flowers and colors."

"Me? Oh no…that will be in Lucy and Esdras' hands."

"Fine, whatever. I have to go. I want to call Michelle. I love you."

"I love you too, sweetie. We'll speak soon. And Diamond?"

"Yes?"

"Congratulations!"

"Thanks, Armand," and with that I hung up.

I immediately called Michelle and it took two tries before she picked up.

"This had better be good," she said in a groggy voice.

"Meesh, it's Dye."

"Hey, what's wrong?"

"Nothing's wrong."

"Then why the hell are you calling me at three in the morning?"

"Because I couldn't wait to tell you that Jonathan and I are getting married."

"What?" When the initial and follow up screaming was finished, I went into the details of the previous day, not leaving anything out. It's the least I could do after all, I had lived vicariously through Michelle's sexcapdes for so long it was only fair that I share my juicy details with her.

"Dye, I am so happy for you," she said in a choked up voice. "I wouldn't miss this for the world! Does Quinn know yet?"

"I'm not sure. Jonathan went downstairs to get changed so I don't know if he called him, but don't say anything. How are things going with you two anyway?"

"Great! Unlike you, we couldn't wait and have since had six delicious servings of breakfast since Sunday," she said with a giggle.

"Believe me, last night Jonathan was the only one with his head on his shoulders, or else I would've been having breakfast right along with you!" We both started to laugh.

"Are you nervous that you haven't known him long enough?"

"I was initially, but not anymore. I don't believe it is, but if it did turn out to be a mistake, I'm fine with that, because at this very moment it feels so right."

"Dye, does he make you happy?"

"Immensely."

"Then that's all that matters! I'll call Armand this afternoon to firm up the travel details. I love you, babe."

"I love you too."

"Ooohhh, no less than four carats!"

"Goodbye, Michelle!"

"Wait!" I had already hung up. I quickly stripped, shaved, and jumped into the shower. With my head down and my hands flat against the cool marble tile, I was enjoying the steaming water beating at the base of my neck and running down my back, washing away the thick lather of my soap.

"You're a sight for sore eyes," came a deep voice from behind me. I turned to find Jonathan gazing at me.

"You scared me. I didn't even hear you come in."

"I thought you would've been ready by now."

"I know, I'm sorry. I got caught up on the phone with Armand and Michelle. I won't be long."

"Did you tell them our good news?" he asked, while his eyes trailed my body.

"Of course, and they're thrilled. Close the door before you get soaked," I said as I started to rinse off.

"I already am. I'll wait for you outside before I jump in there with you."

"All right. I'll be out soon."

Jonathan and I had a lovely time shopping. When we went into the first jewelry store and began trying on rings, I was a little uncomfortable. I didn't want anything huge or flashy and that seemed to be all the attendants were bringing out for me to look at. I assumed we were going to pay for them together, but Jonathan had a different plan. I couldn't make up my mind. After visiting Harts, Cartier, and Christie's we ended up going back at Cartier and picking up diamond infinity bands we'd seen earlier. It was the only one I really liked. They were simply gorgeous. Mine was a platinum band made up of two rows of diamond clad infinity symbols. Jonathan's was a similar band with no diamonds and only one row of the infinity symbols etched into a platinum band. We loved them. Jonathan refused to let me pay for any, even his, so he paid and we left. We had a quick lunch and did a little more shopping and some sightseeing. It was after five when we returned to the hotel to find my room filled with white roses from Armand and Michelle. I was beginning to get excited. I was getting married. Jonathan had to return some calls for work and I still needed to call my grandparents, so we agreed to meet for dinner around seven-thirty.

I had close to a dozen messages between Lucy, Michelle and Esdras. I firmed up some details with Lucy on the dress and then gave Esdras a call. She was on her way over to Minerva's for their evening rendezvous, but had already finished up most of the arrangements this morning. I had forgotten how efficient she could be. I left a message for Michelle and then called my grandparents.

My grandfather picked up on the second ring.

"Hello?"

"Nathan? It's Diamond."

"Well, hello there. How's your trip going?"

"It's going really well. How about things with you and Nana at the hospital? Dr. Kimora told me after the mild infusion reaction yesterday, that she was doing fine."

"You are getting updates."

"Of course I am."

"She's resting now, but overall we've been very pleased. Dr. Kimora is right, except for the hiccup yesterday everything is going well. Viktoria seems more alive these past few days than over the past year, although I'm not sure if that has to do with you or the medicine. I'm hoping this works."

"It will. Listen, Nathan, the reason for my call is to…is well…I'm getting married." I announced in a low voice, not sure what I expected him to say.

"Married, to whom? When?"

"To Jonathan Hamilton on Friday."

"To Jonathan, this Friday? As in the day after tomorrow?"

"Yes. I know it's short notice, but I would really appreciate if you and Nana could come. I can have you flown out tomorrow night after her cycle with Dr. Kimora is completed. Please tell me you can come." He was silent for some time.

"I'm sorry I'm just a little taken aback. We didn't think you were seeing anyone at the moment after our dinner."

"I know. Honestly this all happened within the last couple days and we want to move ahead and do it quickly."

"Do you love him?"

"I do, and I believe he loves me as well."

"He's a good man. I lie, he's a great man. After his grandfather and I stopped speaking to each other, I didn't see him as much, but he was always one of my favorite people. You've chosen well."

"Thank you. So do you think you can make it? If not, we are planning on having a formal reception when we return to New York."

"No, I'll talk to Dr. Kimora, but if your grandmother continues to improve and feel the way she's been feeling I don't think it should be a problem. It isn't necessary for you to fly us out there; we can make our own arrangements."

"Please I insist! Don't argue with me on this."

"All right. Viktoria is going to be ecstatic when she hears the news and for it to be Jonathan, I know will make her heart soar."

"Do you really like him, Nathan?"

"Like him?" he was silent for a moment. "He reminds me so much of your father. That's why it hurt when our families were torn apart by Laird's and my conflict. Anyway, that's all in the past, God rest his soul. We will be there."

"I'll have Armand contact you with the details. Give Nana my love and I will see you both very soon."

"Okay. See you soon."

"Bye," and with that I hung up. There was a conflict between Jonathan's family and my grandfather? Once again I had more questions with no answers.

Chapter 21

I entered my suite after leaving Diamond upstairs and sat down intending to check my e-mail and call my parents. I couldn't believe all that had happened in the past five days. I was going to make her so happy. I would have to wait two more days before I could make love to her completely, but that was fine. Last night was one of the most beautiful experiences of my life, watching her respond to me and my touch was more satisfying than I could've ever imagined. She is going to be an excellent lover. Already her kisses left me on the edge, the way she flicked and twirled her tongue, the way she moaned when my fingers were inside her...ahhhhhh. It was the dial tone of the phone that brought me back to reality. I looked down between my legs as I had already started to swell as a result of my reminiscing. Yes, I had every intention of making her a very happy woman. Hanging up the phone I went to the bathroom to throw some cold water on my face. I needed to be in a different state of mind when I called my parents. I knew they would be happy for me, but there was something bothering me about the way my mother had reacted when she saw Diamond on Saturday. As quickly as I saw it flicker behind her eyes it disappeared. Maybe it was all in my mind, but she seemed afraid.

I responded to my e-mails and checked on things at the office before I dialed our home number and Rosa picked up and I asked for my father first.

"Son?"

"Hi, Dad."

"How's everything going?"

"Beautiful. I had lunch with the gang yesterday and they remembered to you and Mom. I sent you an e-mail this morning to go over a few things that came up from my meeting yesterday, but all in all things are going smoothly."

"That's great news."

"Dad?"

"Umm."

"Diamond is here with me. She came in yesterday morning to surprise me."

"Oh really? That must have been a nice surprise."

"It was. Listen…I have some news."

"What, are you okay?"

"I've never been better. Diamond and I are getting married on Friday and I want you and mom to fly down."

"What? Married? Isn't this a bit soon? Are you sure? This Friday? I didn't think things were this serious."

I went on to tell him how sure I was, and a little about the past five days and how I felt about her. He listened, only interrupting to ask a few questions.

"Dad, I'm so in love with her."

"She's an extremely beautiful woman."

"I know, but that's not it, her beauty is not what this is about. I'm no stranger to beautiful women, but I can tell you there's something special about her. She's beautiful on the outside, but even more so on the inside. She cares about people and her companies. I can't tell you how much she's done through her companies. She's just a good person."

"Jonathan, I'm happy for you. I really am. I don't think I've ever seen you act this way about a woman, and quite frankly that fact that you even want to marry her says something."

"Dad, I don't want to lose her."

"Son...there are a few things you should know..."

"The first being whether or not you and mom can leave tomorrow. Armand is making all the travel arrangements."

"Armand LaVoille?"

"Yes. He's been Diamond's caretaker since her parents died."

"I know exactly who he is. Listen..." I could hear my mother in the background asking if he was still talking to me that Rosa told her I just called. He must have mouthed to her that Diamond and I were getting married because the next thing I knew she was on the other line.

"Jonathan, is what your father saying true?"

"About Diamond and I getting married? Yes." There was silence. "This is where you tell me this is wonderful news and how happy you are for me, Mother." Nothing, just silence. "Well?"

"Jonathan, we're happy for you and we will be there for you," said my father.

"Dad, I know how *you* feel. I want to know how Mom feels. There's something neither of you are telling me."

"Sweetie, I am happy for you, but there *are* a few things you should know. We will leave tomorrow and be in Rome by Friday morning. We'll talk then," added my mother.

"No, I want to talk now!" I had raised my voice, but I didn't care. "What's this all about? Dad how do you know Armand?"

"Armand who? Armand LaVoille?" my mother interjected, her voice was almost incredulous.

"Yes," my father replied.

"The plot just thickens. Jonathan, I want you to stay away from him," said my mother.

"What plot? Why are you both so interested in Armand?"

"Jonathan..."my father began, but my mother cut him off.

"We shouldn't talk over the phone. Meet us at the airport, we'll go somewhere private and talk then."

"I'm telling you right now, I'm marrying her. Nothing you say is going to change my mind. Tell me what's going on!"

"You'll know soon enough," replied my mother. "Please don't take this the wrong way. We are happy for you."

"You could've fooled me! I guess we'll talk on Friday," I snapped, and with that I hung up. I could hear my mother and father both calling my name as I placed the phone on the receiver.

What the hell just happened? Why were my parents behaving like that? Why were they so interested in Armand? Why couldn't we talk on the phone? I wanted to get to the bottom of this. This must have something to do with Nathan, but I couldn't figure out what. I'll be damned if I'd let anything ruin this. My phone rang, but I didn't pick it up. Once it stopped, I called Quinn. His was the reaction I was waiting for. He was genuinely happy for me; I could hear it in his voice. I told him everything that happened from Sunday to yesterday to the conversation I just had with my parents.

When I was finished, I asked, "So what do you think?"

"What do I think? I think she's got it just as bad as you do."

"No, about my parents."

"Ah…I can't imagine what the big secret could be. I do agree with you that it likely has something to do with Nathan, but I still can't…"

"What?" Quinn has become quiet as though something had just crossed his mind. "Well, what is it?"

"Didn't Nathan have a falling out with your grandfather, where they didn't speak for years?"

"Yeah, they only reconciled a few months before my grandfather passed, but I don't see what that has to do with Diamond? I mean…"

"What?" Quinn asked.

"Do you remember when the problems began?"

"Yeah, only because it was our first year of college, so we really didn't know anything about it until we went home for the holidays."

"Exactly, our first year of college, was the same year Diamond was kidnapped." I couldn't process my thoughts fast enough.

"What are you saying? You think the kidnapping had something to do with why Laird and Nathan stopped speaking?"

"I mean, what else could it be? It happened around that time and those two had been lifelong friends. My grandfather was Nathan's advisor, for Christ's sake."

"What about your Uncle Leland? He was with your grandfather in London for some time. No one ever talks about that whole episode where he disappeared for six months. Just fell off the face of the earth." I was silent; my palms were starting to sweat.

"Quinn, what if Leland wasn't in London?" It was as though I had an epiphany.

"What do you mean?"

"That's where we all thought he was, but do you remember what Tanya Shore said that day we were in the library after we came back from spring break?"

"Who could forget? You almost punched her lights out for saying your family was scum and that you were exploiting the people in Africa. She said..." I finished his sentence.

"She said she'd spent her break in Africa volunteering for some United Nations group and while she was there she could've sworn she'd seen my uncle and he was consorting with rather seedy people. People, she thought, whose primary agenda was to take Africa for all it was worth and abused the natives. I told her my uncle was in London and she was mistaken, but she refused to accept it, saying she knew what she saw. All this time I thought she was a raving lunatic, what if he *was* in Africa?"

"If what she said was true, then that could mean he may know something about the kidnapping."

"Do you think my parents knew he was in Africa?" I had to sit down, what I was thinking couldn't be true.

"Jonathan, I can see where you're going with this. Let's just wait and see what your parents have to say on Friday and then we'll go from there. Okay?"

"You're right. These are all coincidences," I sounded as though I was trying to convince myself. "So listen, you'll be here on Friday, right?"

"Of course I'll be there."

"Armand will call you and give you the travel details."

"Great."

"All right, I'll see you soon."

"J?"

"Yeah?"

"Take it easy, I'm sure it's nothing."

"Yeah, I'm sure it's nothing too," I replied, but deep down I knew I was wrong.

My mind was so overwhelmed I was moving at a snail's pace. I finally got out of the shower and was brushing my teeth when there was a knock at the door.

"Who…is it?" I asked between rinsing my mouth.

"Jonathan, it's Dye."

I glanced at the clock and it was a little before eight. Shit! I'm late.

"Come on in," I yelled wiping my mouth. I walked out to find her leaning against door of the coat closet. Her hair was pulled into a pony tail and the strapless cocktail dress she was wearing hugged every beautiful curve. "I'm sorry, honey, I know I'm late, but I got caught up on the phone."

"That's fine, I made you wait this morning," she said with a smile. She hadn't taken her eyes off of me. Then it dawned on me that Dye had never seen me naked as I stood in front of her wearing nothing but the plush white hotel towel, I could see her eyes darken.

"Do you realize I've never seen you naked?" she asked as though she'd read my mind.

"I was just thinking that," I replied, the thought alone of her looking at me was making me erect.

"Would you mind if I watched you get dressed?" She was biting on her lower lip.

"No at all. I keep telling myself we only have two more days."

"We don't have to wait at all if you ask me."

"Patience is a virtue."

"Which I do not possess," she said with a smile. "You bring out that side of me. We could always do what we did last night and have dinner brought up that way we can just relax up here," she said with a wicked smile.

What would she do if my family had something to do with the kidnapping? I don't want to lose her. Why did my Uncle Leland up and disappear at my parents' anniversary dinner? Where was he for those six months? They must know something, and that's why they didn't want to talk on the phone. What was the big secret?

"Jonathan?" She was looking at me as though she realized I wasn't listening to what she was saying.

"I'm sorry, what..."

"What's wrong? You weren't listening to anything I just said." She was walking toward me and I tried to blink my thoughts away, running my hands through my hair. "Jonathan? Answer me, what's wrong? Are you okay?" She was standing in front of me and searching my eyes.

"Nothing, baby," I said reaching for her.

"Don't lie to me. We should be able to tell each other anything. I know you're lying to me and I don't like it. Talk to me." She was getting upset.

"Dye, I'm fine. I was just thinking about an e-mail I got, just work. I think I may have sent it to the wrong group of people. I'm sorry. Let's grab some dinner. I promise I'll stop thinking about work. No more checking e-mails." She wasn't buying it and I hated lying to her, but she didn't say anything. "I'll only be a couple minutes," as I ran into the bedroom to get dressed.

Chapter 22

The waitress was pouring our wine while Jonathan and I reviewed the menu.

"Did you speak to your parents?" I asked.

"Oh, yes, I forgot to mention it, they can come on Friday, so I guess we can forward their contact info to Armand for the flight."

"How did they take it?" I was looking for anything that would give me the slightest hint as to what was bothering him, since I wasn't buying the e-mail story.

"They thought it was soon, but were happy for me...for us. Quinn is beside himself. I think he could almost be as excited as I am. You already told Michelle, right?"

Did he just successfully change the subject? His parents had something to do with him being upset. "Yes, I told Meesh," I realized then as he was rubbing the back of my hand, that I didn't want to be in the restaurant, I wanted to be in the privacy of one of our rooms. I wanted to be alone with him. "Do you know what I was thinking about?"

"No, what?" he responded.

"Well, I was thinking about a couple things, actually. Are we going on a honeymoon?"

"You're right, I hadn't thought of that. We can, but I would be a week late, I have some meetings set up for next week that I really can't miss, unless you really wanted to leave then I would reschedule."

"Umm, no. I think we can put off the honeymoon for a week or two. That should give me enough time to plan the reception and then if anything we can leave right after that, like a real wedding," I said with a smile.

"That sounds like a great idea." Whatever was bothering him seemed to be slowly fading away.

"Question number two. Where are we going to live?" I didn't want to live in my apartment.

"You can move in with me, if you didn't mind of course. I could have the décor changed so that it was more feminine or neutral, but I really love that house and I can see us being happy in it." *I could see it too,* I thought with a smile.

"I was hoping you would say that. I don't care about the décor; I think you have a beautiful home."

"I'm glad," he said, reaching across the table and giving me a kiss. The waitress took our order and we continued making our plans. "Was that it?"

"Actually, I had one more, but it isn't related to the wedding."

"Well, hold that thought, I have a couple. Is the wedding going to be at the Hassler or were you looking at another location?"

"That was the plan, a simple garden wedding at the hotel. I thought their palatial grounds would be perfect. Is that okay with you?"

"Yes, that would be fine and how much will it cost? Have we gotten any estimates?"

"The cost is none of your concern; I'll be taking care of it?"

"Absolutely not! We can share!"

"Like how you shared the cost of the rings?" I said with a playful smile. "Anyway, that's how it's supposed to be done. The bride pays for the wedding and the groom handles the honeymoon."

"The honeymoon and reception."

"No, I will handle the wedding and the reception. That way we will both have two responsibilities."

"Yeah, except you have the two biggest responsibilities. I'm the man around here I should have the biggest responsibilities," he said, trying to hold a straight face.

"Honey, I'm not going to argue with you on this one. The bride takes care of the wedding and the reception. It's customary."

"Fine," he said with a laugh throwing his hands up in the air. "Is it also customary for the bride to ask the groom to marry her?"

"No," I said with a smile, "but that's different."

Our appetizers came shortly after and we were enjoying each others company. I was rubbing my feet around his ankle as he massaged my hand. I wanted to leave, and looking at him I could tell he wanted the same thing as well.

"Didn't you say you had one more question not related to the wedding?" Jonathan asked just as our dinner had arrived.

"Oh yes." I was a little hesitant, but I would have to ask at some time. "When I was at your parents' anniversary, it was subtle, but I got the impression they knew me from before. Did they?"

He immediately became uncomfortable. I could see in the way he began fidgeting.

"Well, like I told you before, Nathan has been a friend of my family for a long time. I think I mentioned him and my grandfather were friends. So they must have known you, especially with their frequent visits to Europe."

"That's what I thought, but I couldn't understand why they didn't mention it."

"I think they were just shocked to see us come in together. I mean I knew of you after everything happened with your parents, but I hadn't met you until Friday. And for me to just show up with you, they may just have been a little intimidated."

"A couple more questions and then I promise I'll stop. Do you know what caused the fall out between our grandfathers?" Jonathan almost choked on the wine in his mouth, resulting in him coughing and sputtering across table. "Are you okay?"

"Shit, I'm sorry. It went...down...the wrong tube," he said, wiping his eyes with his napkin once his coughing fit came under control.

"That's okay," I said rubbing the back of his hand. I knew then there was something he wasn't telling me.

"I honestly don't know what caused them to stop speaking. It all happened while I was away at college, and then once I came back there was an unspoken rule that it was not to be brought up. Why all the questions? What did Nathan say when you when you asked him at dinner?" he asked.

"That's the thing. I didn't realize how close our families were until yesterday when Armand told me that Laird was Nathan's advisor. I had no idea your family knew me until then. Your parents looked familiar to me, but I couldn't place where I knew them from. I assumed Nathan was at Quinn's dinner party because he's a relatively important guy, and not because he was a close friend of the family." I was looking off in the distance and trailing the rim of my wine glass with my middle finger. Jonathan squeezed my hand, bringing my mind back.

"This doesn't change anything between us does it?"

"No, of course not, I just want to tie up some of the loose ends in my head. I meant to ask you want happened to your Uncle Leland at the party on Saturday. He left as we walked up and then never came back."

"You know, I was thinking about that as well, I'm not sure what happened, maybe he got a call or something. He's a little weird like that."

"Oh, okay, for a moment I thought it was me."

"Why would you think that?"

"No reason. I guess it seemed as though he left as soon as we came. I don't know, I'm probably reading too much into things like Meesh and Armand told me. I'll get to the bottom of it soon enough."

Jonathan's face changed, "Get to the bottom of what exactly? My uncle?"

"No, no, no, all the questions I have, who was behind the murder of my family. I feel as though I let them down. All these years I didn't give it a single thought because I was consumed by hate for my grandparents and now that my issues with them have been resolved I feel as though

I owe it to my family to get to the bottom of this."

His voice was just above a whisper. "What will you do once you've found the person or persons responsible?"

"I'm not sure…Armand and I want different things. Let's not talk about it. I'm sorry for bringing up such a dreary subject," I said, kissing his knuckles.

"I want to know. What do you plan on doing?" He pulled his hand out of mine. Was he getting upset with me?

"If you really want to know, I personally want to destroy them. Crush them like the vermin they treated me and my family like, taking away every penny they own. Armand…well…his is another story, but it doesn't matter."

"Armand what?" He was upset I could see it in his eyes.

"It doesn't matter what Armand wants, let's eat."

"Diamond." His tone was firm and I knew he wouldn't drop it.

"Armand can be very vicious when he wants to be, when he needs to be. He will kill them, every last one of them. Torture them they way they tortured us."

"And that's fine with you?" he asked, his eyes wide with amazement.

"Of course it's fine with me, what do you want me to say? Forgive and forget? Let bygones be bygones? They murdered my family. They raped and tortured them! Cut my grandfather up like a slab of beef! My father blew his head off with a bullet! Because of them Armand lost his dearest friend and I lost a father. What the fuck do you want me to say? Of course it's fine with me if they all burn in Hell! I will personally destroy anyone who was involved or benefitted from my family's murder." I didn't notice how loud I was until I shut up and realized the restaurant had become quiet.

"Your father made the choice to kill himself; no one pulled the trigger for him. He did that on his own." The moment he said it I could tell he regretted it, but it was too late. The damage was done.

"Damn you!" I said through clenched teeth. I couldn't believe he said that, I immediately got up and ran out of the restaurant. Jonathan called for me to stop, but the waitress had stopped him for payment, which gave me enough time to jump in a taxi. How dare he? My eyes were cloudy from my tears, as I frantically wiped them away. The driver was asking where I would like to go so I called Minerva and got her address. My mobile wouldn't stop ringing, it was Jonathan. Without answering it, I turned it off. Twenty minutes later we were at Minerva's apartment. I tried to wipe my face before I entered the lobby. I couldn't remember the last time Armand had seen me cry, if ever. I took the elevator to the third floor where I found Armand standing in the doorway of the apartment. I ran into his arms and the tears came again.

"Did he hurt you?" he asked, his voice calm and deliberate as only Armand's could be.

"No…no he didn't hurt me," I replied between sniffles.

"Come in." Armand brought me in and closed the door. We went into a small sitting room and he left, coming back with a glass of water.

"Where are Minerva and Esdras?"

"I've sent them out." His voice was still calm.

"I'm sorry, you didn't have to do that."

"Its fine." His voice hadn't changed. "Now, tell me what happened." He sat down and I told him what happened at dinner. When I was finished he didn't say anything.

"Well, say something. Do you think I overreacted?"

"Yes."

"What?" I couldn't believe what I was hearing. I thought for sure he would've been on my side.

"Dye, you blatantly told the man we would kill and torture these people. That's not something normal people openly say. You probably shocked the shit out of him. How did you expect him to respond?"

"But it's the truth. Armand, they killed my family what does he expect me to say or do? I was just caught up in the moment."

"Yes, but we're from a different world. I'm from a different world. You can't forget yourself and what we're involved in."

"What about what he said about Daddy?"

Armand closed his eyes and let his head fall back. "Once again I could see why he would say something like that."

"Jesus Christ! What's the matter with you? Look at me and tell me you wouldn't have done the same thing my father did if it happened to you and your family!"

"I've asked myself that question a million times and I don't know what I would do. I've thought maybe I would've found and killed the bastards first, before taking my life, so that my family's death wouldn't be in vain. And then I've thought what's there to live for if all I hold dear is gone. You could look at it any way you like, but Jonathan's right, Zachary and Zachary alone made that choice. I wouldn't expect Jonathan to react any differently to what you said, but I'll tell you what is bothering me?"

"What?"

"This falling out between Laird and Nathan. I've been thinking more and more about it. Did your grandmother actually imply that Laird's advice was the reason why Nathan handled things the way he did?"

"Not really, she just said 'we got bad advice,' but wouldn't tell me who their advisor was."

"Dye, Nathan *gave* Laird the oil field after everyone was killed." Armand was now looking out the window and massaging his chin.

"What?" I was in disbelief.

"I made a few calls last night when I got home. Two months after everything happened, Nathan gave the field to Laird. Not sold, not loaned…gave. It was big news at the time because those companies I told you about yesterday were offering a pretty penny for that field. Rumor has it that Laird then took the field and three months later sold it for an incredible sum to a private party, without Nathan's knowledge."

"What? He turned around and sold it? To who?"

"A company called Nubian Oil."

"Well, what do the books say on this Nubian."

"I don't know. I requested all the info I could but it won't be here until late tomorrow."

"Why didn't you tell me all of this before?"

"I only found out about an hour ago. I made the calls last night and

I didn't get the followup calls until this evening."

"Do you think Jonathan's family knows all of this?"

"I don't know…I had to do *a lot* of searching to come up with any of this. You aren't going to let this affect you and Jonathan's relationship, are you? I can tell you right now he probably doesn't have anything to do with this. Don't look for a reason to back out of this Diamond."

"I am not looking for a reason to back out of this. For Christ's sake I asked the man to marry me. I love him, and that won't change. I just didn't appreciate what he said, but I have no plans on backing out of it. I came here because I needed to clear my head. I'm not running. My gut is telling me that there's something going on that he's not telling me about. My gut is telling me that his parents weren't as happy as he led me to believe. And my gut is telling me that his family knows something about what happened in Africa. And you know what Armand? In twenty-eight years my gut has never stirred me wrong."

"Okay. I'll try to get to the bottom of this by Friday when the others get here. I want you to go into this marriage worry free. He's a good man. I've looked into every facet of his life and found nothing."

"You checked him out?"

"Of course I did. What did you think that I was just going to take yours and Michelle's word for it that he was a fantastic human being? I don't think so," he said with a smile. Armand and I talked a little longer about everything. I was getting tired.

"All right, where's the guest room?" I asked.

"Why? I hope you don't think you're staying here tonight."

"I…uh…well…why not?"

"Why not? Because I've arranged for you to stay at the best hotel in Rome and your fiancé is probably worried sick. Go to him. This won't work if you two can't talk to each other. Plus, I didn't send Minerva and Esdras away all night. I have every intention of picking up where we left off."

"But…but…I was wrong. I overreacted. He probably thinks I'm crazy."

"So, this is the irrational side of the woman he loves and wants to marry, he'll have to see it sooner or later, now get out," his voice was serious again.

"I can't believe you're throwing me out," I said with a laugh.

"Believe it," he said with a smile, ushering me by the elbow to the door. "A driver is downstairs waiting to bring you back to the hotel."

I stopped when I got to the door and gave him hug. "Armand?"

"Yes, Dye."

"This morning when I said I considered you more a friend and confidant than my father figure, I lied. You've done so much for me, I…" He put his hand over my mouth planting a long kiss on my forehead.

"You don't have to say any more, I already know. I love you dearly. Everything will be fine," he said in a tender voice. "Bye."

"Goodnight, Armand."

"Goodnight, my love," and with that he closed the door.

Chapter 23

It was after midnight when I reached the Hassler and took the elevator up to my suite. I stepped into the private hallway to find Jonathan sitting on the floor in front of my door with his arms across his knees. He looked a mess, although I wasn't entirely sure that was possible. His dark hair was disheveled and he'd pulled his shirt out of his pants and had unbuttoned the first few buttons showing his white t-shirt. I could see the worry on his face as he got up on his feet, his eyes not leaving mine. I walked toward him fumbling with my room key.

"I'm sorry, I…" I began.

"Ssshhh," he said taking me into his arms. He was kissing my face and my neck frantically, finally taking my lips. I dropped the keys. There was an urgency to our kisses as our lips twisted around each other and our tongues delved deep into each other's mouths. He was rubbing my back and massaging my neck with his hands as I slipped my hand under the belt and waistband of his slacks trying to press him into me.

"Jona…"

"Ssshhh," he repeated.

He pulled down my zipper and tugged on the sides of my dress, letting it fall to the floor. He picked me up and I swung my legs around his waist. Walking over to the elegant lounge chair in front of the elevator he put me to sit down. I tried to unbutton the remaining buttons on his shirt but my fingers were clumsy and I was getting frustrated so I just ripped the shirt open, giving a little chuckle as the buttons danced around on the marble floor. Jonathan was kneeling in front of me and without breaking the momentum of our kisses slipped out of his shirt and as I unhooked my strapless bra, he took off his t-shirt.

I didn't care we were in the hallway, this was the only suite on this floor, so no one would be coming up, unless I called for them. Pulling me closer to him, the warmth of our flesh was making me more frantic. I wanted to feel him, touch and caress him, give him pleasure. He left a trail of wet kisses from my mouth down my neck and chest to my breasts, sucking on my nipples as though they were causing his saliva to turn into some delicious wine that he was addicted to. While he massaged one nipple, gently twisting it between his fingers, he had the other in his mouth, holding the nipple between his lips and front teeth as he flicked his tongue over it. He was bringing me to the edge and he hadn't even ventured to my valley yet. I took his head between my hands and brought his face up to mine, tasting his sweet lips. Reaching down, I unbuckled his belt and unfastened his pants, letting them fall around his knees. I slowly ran my hand over the length of his erection, smiling to myself when I felt the tiniest wet spot in his boxers. He began to moan as I continued rubbing him. I slipped off the chair so we were both kneeling on the floor.

"Sit down," I whispered breathlessly. He didn't move right away, but pulled away from me so he could look into my eyes. I turned my face to kiss the palm of his hand. "I said to sit down," I repeated in a soft firm voice. The second time was a charm, he quickly stood up and slipped his feet out of his trousers, sitting down. I lean forward and took his mouth again, this time sucking on his tongue as I pulled his boxers down. I could feel his large throbbing member hot against my abdomen, just below my breasts. I moved away from his mouth and did the same thing he had done to me. I left a trail of kisses down his neck, taking one of his nipples in my mouth and the other between my

174

fingers. His chest was so smooth. God, he was sexy. I could feel the muscles in his back as I held him and kissed his chest. I looked down at his luscious penis as it was now fully extended and lying up against Jonathan's stomach. It was beautiful. Big, but beautiful. I bent my head and kissed his navel, gently moving *him* out of the way, using my tongue to trail the rim of his belly button, while I slowly moved my hand up and down his thick shaft. I didn't have any idea what to do, so I was simply going to do what made sense. I was going to take my time and make love to him with my mouth. Everything I wanted to say to him right now or show him, I would do through my mouth, my lips and my tongue. I wanted to show him how sorry I was and how much I loved him. Michelle had always told me how important this skill is, so I had no intention of messing up, even if it was my first time. Slowly, but surely I would please him. Holding his shaft with both hands, I brought him to my mouth, opening wide so I could take his tantalizing head into my mouth. I could taste the hint of something salty, but it was quickly gone and replaced by the sweetness of my own saliva. I sucked and twirled my tongue all around it, up to the tip pressing my tongue against his tiny opening and down to the sensitive skin just under the head, being careful to watch the placement of my teeth.

"Dye…" he breathed.

Pulling him out of my mouth, I planted juicy wet kiss down his entire length, all the while, saying in my head with each kiss, *I love you, I love you, I love you.* With my mouth still open and my teeth slightly apart I ran my mouth from the base of his throbbing dick to the top and back again, grating my teeth gently against his flesh in the process. I was careful not to be too rough. Michelle had shared enough horror stories with me and I was determined not to make the same mistakes she had.

"Aaahh," he breathed between clenched teeth. On my third ascent I took him into my mouth again, this time taking as much into my mouth as I could, sucking and twirling my tongue around him. My hand was still around his base as his head pressed against the back of my soft palate, so I knew there was a good four inches left, I was determined to take all of him. I steadily continued to do that driving him to the brink of insanity and then bringing him back with a mixture of bites and kisses on his shaft. He was calling my name and letting out intermittent swears. He had released my ponytail and subsequently had handfuls of my thick hair. I was loving this, I didn't see any reason to get up, I could do this all night. After a few minutes practicing I perfected my breathing. As I came up his shaft, bringing his thick member from the back of my throat I took a deep breath, releasing it through my nose as I went back down. My hand was soaked from my saliva, but I didn't care.

Finally I rose up off my heels, and brought him forward a little more so that I was directly over his erection. Taking a deep breath, I opened my mouth even wider, if that was possible, and slowly lowered my mouth onto him. When his head hit the back of my throat I shifted, relaxed my jaw muscles, and flattened my tongue, drawing it down into my lower jaw. There was some resistance, but it wasn't painful so I pressed on feeling my muscles give way as inch by inch of his thick rod guided down my throat. He shuddered and movement caused him to jerk in my mouth, making me gag.

"I'm sorry," he whispered.

I pulled him out of my mouth and sucked around his shaft, trying to catch my breath.

"Don't be," I replied breathlessly. I was a little embarrassed, but he didn't seem to care, if anything he was becoming more enthralled. My eyes were watering and my nose was starting to run, must be the gravity. I ventured back, repeating each movement and concentrating on my breathing. I continued to do it until I could relax my throat long enough so he could bring my head up and down his shaft four to five times without me gagging. I didn't know how long I did that for, but Jonathan was becoming more excited, holding my head in place if he liked something I was doing. I loved that. I wanted to know what he liked. After a while I turned my attention to his sack, gently sucking away my warm saliva as I continued to move my hand up and down his length slowly at first, and then with increasing speed as I realized he was close to an orgasm. I was looking up at him as he stared at me, his eyes completely dark and glazed over from his arousal. He mouthed *I love you,* then biting on his lower lip he closed his eyes. He couldn't call my name enough, telling me how good it felt, only then did I realize how much between my legs ached for him.

I was pressing my tongue into the sensitive area just below the testicles that Michelle had told me about and Jonathan exclaimed, "Baby I can't take much more!" With that I took him in to my mouth again, making sloppy slurping noises as I moved quickly up and down his shaft urged him into an orgasm. When it happened he squeezed his thighs together under my arms, pinching his butt cheeks together as he pressed deeper into my mouth.

"Aaarrhhhh!" he exclaimed. The warm thick liquid shot into my mouth with repeated bursts, it was slightly acidic and creamy, reminding me of plain yogurt. Thank goodness, I *love* plain yogurt. I drank all he had to offer as he shuddered in my mouth. I had done it! I didn't stop until I was sure he was finished. His eyes were closed as his hands rested on my shoulders. I reached for his t-shirt, wiping my mouth and then the remaining saliva from him. He was looking at me with so much love in his eyes. As I stood up, my knees cracked.

"Oooohh," I moaned with a laugh, "my knees are killing me."

"I'm sorry," he said, leaning forward to rub them as he planted kisses across my abdomen.

"It's fine. They didn't bother me until I got up," I said, straddling him. He kissed me deeply, rubbing his palms over my lace panties. "I don't think I'll be able to look at a hotel chair the same ever again," I added with a smile.

He finally pulled his face away from mine. "Dye, I am so sorry about what I said earlier at the restaurant. I shouldn't have said that. I don't know what the hell I was thinking. All I could was sit here and think of what I would do if you didn't come back. I love you so much," he said, kissing me again, while massaging my back.

"I'm sorry if I made you worry. What you said hurt me, but I appreciate your honesty. Not once did I ever think my father could've handled that situation any differently. He had lost his family, and I thought for sure I would've done the same thing, but that's just me. I should apologize as well because I overreacted. I want you to feel as though you can tell me anything and I got off to a bad start tonight by exploding when you gave me your opinion. I would never leave you. I want to make you happy," I said, kissing his forehead and cheeks.

"Oh, believe me, you have made me a very, very happy man. I don't think I've ever been this happy."

"Really, was it good?"

"Good? I can't begin to describe to you what that was like. Where did you learn how to do that?"

"Some stuff I read, some Michelle told me, but the majority of it I really just did what I thought would make you feel good."

"Baby, you were wonderful. The best." I didn't hide the huge cheese-it smile on my face was inwardly giving myself high-fives. *I was the best!*

"I'm glad. Let's go inside," I said.

Picking up our things we went inside. We had a shower and were wrapped in each others arms, laying in the king sized bed soon after looking out onto the patio as the moonlight shone in.

"Jonathan,"

"Yes, love," he said, slipping his hand from under my head so he could look at me.

"We have to be honest with each other or else this isn't going to work. I can feel that you're hiding something from me and I don't like it. This isn't the way to start this marriage. We don't have to talk about it right now, but I expect it to be dealt with before we say '*I do*' on Friday, all right?"

He didn't say anything at first and then he answered, "Dye...I...all right." Pulling me into his arms and holding me close we fell asleep.

One more day and this man will be mine completely and I will be his.

Chapter 24

Thursday was a little hectic, but Jonathan and I still managed to get a lot of relaxing done. I went for a run and had a manicure and pedicure while he went to the gym and took care of some business in the morning. Then we went on a three hour walking tour of the Vatican City, which was pretty amazing. Both our phones kept ringing off the hook, but Jonathan refused to pick up any calls unless they were from Quinn or his other friends. I wasn't sure what that was about. Around four o'clock the calls stopped, since hopefully everyone was in the air. Lucy was flying in this evening so she would be at the hotel by the time we returned from our excursions. Armand hadn't called me all day and I hadn't heard from Esdras until midday. The poor thing sounded completely exhausted, but we managed to tie up what few loose ends there were for tomorrow. I arranged a family brunch around eleven in the morning and the wedding was scheduled for five in the garden. The entire area had been sealed off upon my announcement on Wednesday and plans were in full swing for whatever fairytale kingdom Esdras planned on bringing to life. Somehow the wedding had grown to include Jonathan's friends that we'd had lunch with on Tuesday. It was fine with me since they would not have been able to make the trip to New York in a week or two for the formal reception.

I was contemplating whether or not I should have my things packed up and brought over to Jonathan's house so that when we got home on Sunday there wouldn't be much for us to do. He thought it was a great idea, so I used a company that had done some work for me in the past and a friend of Armand and Lucy's was arranging everything on that end. Things were coming together perfectly. The wine and cheese had just been delivered to my room and Jonathan and I were laying on the lounge chairs out on the terrace watching the sunset.

"Dye?"

"Umm?"

"This maybe a little late, but we haven't talked about money."

"What about money?" I asked, sounding a little nervous.

"Didn't Armand suggest you have me sign a prenuptial agreement?"

"What? Of course not, why would he suggest something like that?"

"I guess I don't want people to think that I'm doing this for the money."

I put my wine glass down and reached for his hand, "Do you remember what I told you on Tuesday night when we were out here? I would give this all up for you. Everything. The money has never been important to me, and if you want it you won't have to fight very hard for it because you can have it all right now. I love you; I couldn't care less what people think. We know the truth," I said with a smile. "You're talking, but maybe I should be the one signing a prenup, you aren't so poor yourself!"

"Yeah, but I'm sure nothing in comparison to you."

"Can I tell you something?"

"Of course you can."

"I know it shouldn't, but talking about money or my wealth always makes me uncomfortable. It's almost a little embarrassing."

"I can see how that could happen. We don't have to talk about it."

"No. I guess if you're going to marry me we should get this all out in the open so there are not misunderstandings. Do you know how much the books say I'm worth?"

"Umm...no."

"Somewhere in the vicinity of eighty-seven-thousand dollars. There is only one account existing that actually has *my* name on it, and I've kept it for sentimental reasons since it was opened for me on the day I was born by my parents."

"And if someone were to disregard the books and ask?"

"Well, if someone asked, I probably would tell them to mind their own business, but if that someone was you, I would have to say that the last report I got sometime last week said I was worth a little over four -hundred and ninety-three-billion dollars, but who's counting?" I said with a small smile.

"Holy shit! I mean...I thought...I mean I knew you were wealthy, but I wasn't expecting you to be a multi-billionaire." He was not trying to hide his obvious shock.

"Well, if it's any consolation, you're a multi-billionaire too," I said with a laugh. Now he was the one that seemed uncomfortable.

"Would you do something for me?" he asked.

"Anything."

"Once we're married, we will open a new account and that will be *our* money. I don't want you to use your money for anything. Starting tomorrow it will come out of our account."

"Jonathan, there is no *your* money, it's ours."

"Dye, please. I want to provide all that you need."

"And I'm sure you will, but, Jonathan, are you saying that anything in your bank account before tomorrow is *your* money?"

"Of course not! What's mine is yours..."

"And what's yours is mine," I said, finishing his quote. "I feel no differently than you do. I may have more, but it means *nothing* if I don't have you in my life. I won't let you make this an issue, please. I am content to live off of you if you wish," I said, playfully kissing his hand.

"I guess all that matters to me is that you know I'm not interested in your money."

"I know, darling."

There was a knock on the door and I jumped up. It had to be Lucy, and sure enough it was. After the hugs and congratulations she got right to business telling Jonathan what he would be wearing tomorrow. The rest of the evening was spent with me in Lucy's suite fitting my dress and Jonathan having dinner with some friends.

It was well after midnight when I returned to my room and got ready for bed. I was slipping under the covers when the phone rang.

"Hello?"

"Hi, love." It was Jonathan.

"Hi, yourself," I said with a huge smile. Just hearing his voice made my heart soar.

"I've been calling, but I figured you were still downstairs with Lucy. Were you in bed?"

"Almost. I was just about the curl up under the covers when the phone rang. How was dinner?"

"It was fun. And how about you? Did Lucy have a lot to do?

"Actually, I was pretty surprised how much she's already completed. It was literally a fitting with her tweaking her design once she saw it on my body."

"Well, I'm sure you'll be exquisite," he said.

"I hope so." There was some silence as I could tell he was about to say something.

"Diamond?"

"Umm."

"We're getting married today," he said in a soft voice, and immediately my stomach started to flutter.

"Yes, we are," I replied, my voice becoming a little emotional.

"I'm going to make you so happy."

"I know you are and I'm hoping to do the same," I said, closing my eyes as I made the silent oath to myself. "Are you already in bed?"

"I've been in bed for the past hour, but couldn't fall asleep. I guess I just needed to hear your voice."

"Do you want me to come down?" I asked, feeling my skin tingle at the thought of being in his arms.

"Yes."

"**I'm on my way,**" **I said, hanging up without waiting for his** response.

I was knocking on his door a minute later.

"God, that was quick," he said, opening the door wearing just a pair of blue and gray flannel pajama pants.

"I took the stairs. I couldn't wait for the elevator," I said, stepping into his arms as he kissed me deeply. His tongue was so delicious as it trailed mine and we sucked on each others lips.

"I feel as though we've hardly seen each other today," he said.

"I know," I responded as I placed my hands along his jaw line, running my thumb across his lips. "I never thought it was possible to love someone as much I love you right at this moment," I said, my eyes becoming moist.

"I know exactly how you feel. Let's go to bed, Mrs. Hamilton," he said as he picked me up effortlessly and carried me to his bed. And for the third night in a row we slept in each others arms.

I could hear the low buzz of my blackberry vibrating on the antique end table. Slipping my arms from around Diamond, I skillfully got out of bed without waking her. I recognized the number, a local number. Walking into the living room, I took the call.

"Hello?"

"Jonathan?" came the deep voice on the other end of the phone.

"Yes. Who is this?"

"It's Armand. We ne…"

"Oh, hello, how's everything going?"

"They're going. We need to talk immediately."

"Immediately?"

"Yes, as in right now," he replied, his voice still not changing.

"What's wrong?"

"Is Diamond close by?"

"No, she's asleep in the bedroom and I'm in the living room."

"Good. Leave her a note that you've gone for a run and meet me at the east entrance of the hotel."

"Now? Why? What's going on Armand?"

"Jonathan, I'm here right now and I'm waiting. No more questions." He didn't raise his voice, but his tone had definitely changed.

"All right, I'm on my way." And without waiting for a response I hung up. Something was wrong, I could hear it in his voice, but I didn't waste any time pondering. I quickly wrote the note to Diamond, changed into my sweats and ran to the east entrance as Armand had instructed.

As I approached, I saw no one waiting, but there was a lone black Mercedes sedan with heavy tinted windows parked in front of the gate. I looked around more closely to make sure he wasn't waiting off in the distance and then walked towards the car. When I was within a few feet, the passenger door opened and I heard Armand's voice in the driver's seat.

"Get in," he said, still looking straight ahead.

I looked around one final time before I got in. He said nothing else at first once we drove off, which didn't help ease my discomfort. I was already thinking worse case scenario and my gut was telling me this meeting had something to do with my family.

"What's this about, Armand?" I asked. "Where are we going?" my voice sounding more nervous than I intended.

"Is there anything you want to tell me, Jonathan?" he asked in a calm voice.

"Anything like what? I don't know what this is all about."

"Okay, then I'll be more specific. Do you know anything about the connection between your family and the kidnapping of Diamond and her family?"

My worst fear had now been confirmed as I felt the blood draining from my face. Armand was watching my every reaction.

"You see, Jonathan, if you don't say another word, from the look on your face I can already see that you know something. So before you even think of lying to me I want to warn you against it. This is serious, in fact, it's a matter of life and death, and unless you want to lose the woman lying in your bed right this minute, I suggest you tell me everything you know." I couldn't talk, looking out the window as we pulled into a nearby park.

"I don't know anything," I began. Armand slammed his fists on the steering wheel and turned to face me, his eyes cold and deadly. Even though I was proud of myself for not flinching, for the first time I was afraid.

"Don't fucking lie to me! You know something and you're going to tell me! I don't have time for these games. You have three choices; you can tell me what you know, I can go to Diamond with what *I* know, or I can make you tell me." His face was menacing as I felt my heart skip a beat. "And as much as I like you, Jonathan, I *will* make you tell me."

"Go to Diamond with what exactly? There's nothing to tell!" I yelled. Armand closed his eyes and his features hardened as I saw his jaw begin to clench. Taking his hands from the wheel he began to slowly take off his black leather gloves. I was petrified. Who is this man?

His voice was dangerously low and his eyes cold and piercing as he began, "Don't let the clothes, the lifestyle, or my smiles fool you. I am the filthiest human being you will probably ever meet." He hadn't taken his eyes off of me. "I've spent my entire life protecting Diamond from people that would cause her harm. I would do *anything* for her, do you understand me? *Anything.* Don't make me do anything, Jonathan, because I won't hesitate to make this *all* go away." The lines on his forehead and around his mouth softened ever so slightly as the beads of sweat continued to form on my skin. "It may not seem that way, but I am trying to help you. I've never seen Diamond this happy. I know you love her and she loves you, but as much as it may hurt her, she will walk away from you and never look back. I've seen her do it to close friends, what little family she had in Africa, look at her grandparents for Heaven's sake! I know these past eighteen years have been torture for her, but did she show it? Not once. It tore her apart, but even as a child she had the ability to bury her thoughts and feelings into some deep and forbidden abyss that even myself and Michelle couldn't enter. Don't let her do the same thing to you, because as God as my witness she will. Tell me what you know, it's the only way I can help you." I could tell by the tone of his voice that he was serious. I massaged my temples as the pounding between my ears intensified.

"I will tell you what I've been speculating about these past few days, but I *know* nothing. Like Dye, since Saturday I've had more questions then answers." I started at the beginning, from my mother's reaction at the party, to what they'd said on the phone after I told them we were getting married, my Uncle Leland's untimely disappearance, and my conversation with Quinn. He just listened, not saying a word. "The plan was for me to get to the bottom of this when I met with my parents at the airport this morning."

"And that's it?" He didn't seem doubtful, but he was expecting more.

"Yes, that's it! I'm not stupid enough to lie to you," my eyes wide with frustration.

"I know you aren't."

"I love her. Tell me what you want me to do—at this point I'm lost. Some of the things I've been thinking are crazy!"

"What about Nubian Oil, you've said nothing about that."

"That's because I don't know anything about Nubian…" My mouth went dry and my palms started to sweat as once again I had yet another epiphany. "Is that a company in Texas?"

"Texas? No. It's the small company that now owns Nathan Skovachy's Prumol oil field in Africa," his tone was laced with frustration. "The same oil field that Dye and her family were kidnapped over. The same oil field you've owned for the past seventeen years." I almost choked on the small amount of saliva I was managing to produce to soothe my painfully dry throat.

"What? You're mistaken. I don't own any oil fields. I'm a lawyer, always have been. My uncle is the oiler, not me!" I could feel my pulse pounding in my temples.

"Then explain this," and with that he threw a leather bound folder onto my lap. I was hesitant as I opened it and looked at the papers within. What I was reading was impossible, bank statements, contracts, and money transfers all with my name and signatures, listed as the CEO and owner of Nubian Oil.

"I can't explain this."

"Try, God dammit, think! I can't begin to explain to you how this looks."

I couldn't think straight, my mind was going a million miles a minute as I tried to slow my thoughts and think logically. Who would have access to my signature? Leland. Who close to me has experience with the oil industry and has worked in Africa? Leland. When could he have done this? Seventeen years ago? Seventeen years ago I was a sophomore in college. That's it!

"One night during my sophomore year of college, shortly after my uncle had reappeared from where we thought was England and Europe, he called my apartment and asked me to meet him. He said he wasn't speaking to my father and was in the process of trying something new, buying a cosmetic company called Nubian out of Texas. He wanted me to sign on as his number two guy, more like a contact or backup in case he couldn't be reached. I thought nothing of it. I had seen my father sign as my uncle's backup on several occasions and vice versa. In some instances I had even signed for my father. I told him it wouldn't be a problem. He asked me not to tell my father because it was a new industry and he didn't want to hear him say how much of a bad idea he thought it was getting involved in the cosmetic industry. I told him it was fine. I never heard another thing about it. Not a piece of correspondence, bank statement, nothing. I signed the papers right there, went back to my room and that was the last I ever heard of Nubian."

"And you never asked about it?"

"No, there weren't any problems, and honestly I didn't give it a second thought. Between Laird, my father and Uncle Leland they were always trying their hands at something new." The pieces of the puzzle were falling into place. "Did my uncle have something to do with the kidnapping?"

Armand had now taken to rubbing his temples and looking out the window. His frown deepened and features again grew hard. His knuckles whitened as his grip on the staring wheel tightened.

"Son of a bitch! Your uncle has to be involved with the kidnapping. Not only did I find out that he was in Africa months before and after the kidnapping meeting frequently with Rono Montandu, the leader of the militia, but I also trailed large sums of money coming out of Africa to an account in your name…" I didn't wait for him to finish. I didn't care who he was, but I had no intention of letting him continue with his implications.

"I told you already I don't know anything about this. I've never taken money from my uncle."

He raised his voice over mine, "An account in your name, with your uncle listed as the custodian of that account. I know you aren't involved, Jonathan, but he has everything set up to lead away from him. What I don't understand is how Laird was involved. He tried to get Nathan to give up the oil field after the kidnapping. Something isn't right. The two of them were close enough that Nathan would've given him anything if he asked for it. Let's head to the airport, we can speculate as much as we want, but we won't get to the bottom of his until we speak with Nathan and your parents. I want to get to the bottom of this before the wedding."

I didn't say anything as he started the car and we went to airport. I was sick with fear, disappointment and worry. No wonder my parents reacted that way when I called his name, they must know what type of man Armand Lavoille is. What if Diamond found out all of this? How could my family do this to me? They must know something. I went through every possible scenario in my mind and came to the conclusion that everything I had with Diamond could be gone in the blink of an eye if she ever found out my family's involvement.

Chapter 25

The plane had just landed when we got to the airport. Armand made a call asking that everyone stay on board and for the flight staff to get off until we got there. Everyone was a little shocked when they saw us come through the door together. Before we'd even gotten on board, Armand had instructed me to let him do the talking. That was fine with me. I couldn't look at my parents or face Nathan.

Without any pleasantries, Armand began, "Michelle, Viktoria and Quinn, there is a sedan waiting outside to bring you to the hotel." His voice was firm and unflinching.

"What's going on?" asked Viktoria almost immediately.

"I need to talk to the others," Armand responded.

"Well, I'm not leaving my husband. Anything you have to say to him can be said in my presence." Her voice was stern. I hadn't seen Viktoria in a long time and as I looked at her cancer ravished body and her aging face I immediately became angry at how much my family had to do with their unhappiness.

"Does this have to do with Diamond?" asked Michelle, the next one to inquire.

"It's none of your concern, Meesh. Go to the hotel." Armand was not trying to hide the annoyance in his voice.

"If it *is* about Diamond, then it *is* my concern. I'm her best friend and I'm not going to leave you lot to make any decision about her."

"Armand, I actually want Quinn to stay," I added.

"God dammit! If you all want to stay, then fine. You had your opportunity to leave. But know this, if you stay, you are *all* involved. Any decisions we make here will be done on a collective basis. Am I understood?" There were affirmations all around. My parents looked extremely uncomfortable. Armand spent the next fifteen minutes going over everything we had just discussed. "Now that you all know where we stand I need some answers. First, I'll start with you, Nathan. Why did you stop speaking to Laird?"

Nathan took a deep breath and began, "Ultimately, it was because we didn't trust him anymore. My relationship with him was driving a wedge between Viktoria and I. She just couldn't get over his entire reaction to the kidnapping, and then when I gave him the oil field and he turned around and sold it…well, that was the straw that broke the camel's back. I wouldn't let myself believe that he had anything to do with it. Zachary was like a son to him. I was his best friend for over fifty years. But there were just too many questions left unanswered. Viktoria and I couldn't get over it." They both looked relieved to have gotten it off their chest. My father's eyes hadn't left Nathan's.

"All right, that puts that portion in perspective. Liam, Beth? Do you know anything about this?"

My father began almost immediately and described the few situations after the kidnapping that had sent up red flags in his mind. My uncle's initial disappearance, the visit they had shortly after the murders by a group of men with heavy South African accents looking or my uncle, his unexplained return, the questions he was told by Laird not to ask, and Leland's newfound wealth months later. My father suspected that my grandfather's businesses were all in trouble, between his gambling and one too many bad deals. He was broke, although no one would've been able to tell, how he was living. My father said all their problems seemed to go away within six months to a year of the incident.

"Deep down inside I knew something wasn't right, but I stayed out of it. Actually, my father kept me out of it. Never once did he ask for my opinion or for me to join him on one of his trips. Then everything changed, him and Nathan had a falling out. He refused to see my brother and then I became his all for the next fifteen years until he became ill. I never asked and he never volunteered any information. If I had known Leland was using your name, Jonathan, I would've put a stop to it. You have to believe me when we say we knew nothing about the kidnapping."

"I knew," my mother added in a barely audible voice, looking out the window as the tears rolled down her cheek.

"Knew what?" everyone said simultaneously.

"I knew Laird and Leland were involved."

"What?" growled my father.

"How long have you known?" I asked, my blood once again beginning to boil.

"Laird said things before he died."

Viktoria was now wailing uncontrollably as Michelle tried to comfort her. Armand's phone was ringing as both Nathan and my father tried to talk to my mother. I saw Armand glance at the phone and his eyes turned to slits. Then his voice thundered over everyone else's.

"BE QUIET! Diamond is calling." He hurried toward the cockpit as Viktoria physically covered her mouth. We could only hear his end of the conversation.

"Hi, honey."

"He's with me, I picked him up."

"Yes they're already here. We had a couple things that needed to be taken care of before we headed to the hotel."

"Everyone is fine. Listen, the reception is pretty bad over here. We should be back at the hotel within an hour."

"Well, you know traffic and so on, but we'll hurry. Promise. I love you too."

He was quiet for some time as he listened to what she was saying and his eyes closed.

"Of course I'll tell him."

Armand hung up and his shoulders fell. Turning his attention to me, he said, "Diamond said to tell you she loves you more today than she did yesterday and that she hopes you enjoyed your run."

My face was hard as I turned to my mother, "Spill it! You tell us everything you know right now, or I swear to God I'll never speak to you again." She broke down then, falling into my father's arms, but he wouldn't hold her. We all stood there as she cried. I refused to comfort her as did my father.

Armand was the one that talked to her. "Beth, this is hard on all of us, but we don't have any more time. You have to tell us what you know." My mother stopped crying long enough to begin.

"I didn't know that much until I listened to what you had to say just now and filled in the blanks. You have to understand," her eyes were pleading with us as she looked from me to my father and then to Nathan. "I didn't know for sure. In Laird's last days he rambled a lot and was incoherent, but I guess that was as lucid as he'd ever been when he told me what happened." Over the next half hour she told us what my grandfather had told her. In his last days he refused to stay at the hospital or in a hospice so we brought him to stay with us. She said my father was busy tying up loose ends of my grandfather's businesses, so she spent most of the days with him and when he wasn't sleeping they would talk about everything. Sometimes he would ramble, so she could never be sure what was fact from fiction. One day in particular he started talking about Nathan and their relationship. He said his companies were going under and he didn't want Nathan to know how badly he'd messed things up. He thought all he needed was a cash cow to get back on track and, that oil field alone would've taken care of all his financial needs. He said it was Leland who told him to ask for the field, but he refused. She swore she had no idea which field he was talking about until he started throwing in tit-bits about the kidnapping as well. He said it was only on the day of the kidnapping that he learned Leland was involved. Leland had convinced the militia that Nathan always listened to his father and he would give up the field in a heartbeat for his family if that's what Laird told him to do. It didn't work out that way. No one expected them to be killed and we all knew what happened next. My mother seemed to think that both Laird and Leland were being blackmailed, hence my uncle's disappearance. It all seemed so farfetched to her that she never said anything about it. She had more questions than answers. Nathan's fists were curled into tight balls at his side as the rage burned behind his eyes and he listened to my mother. Viktoria was now hysterical as Quinn and Michelle tried to calm her down.

"How could you keep this from me?" asked my father.

"I didn't know how to tell you." They started to yell back and forth then until Armand finally interrupted.

"Okay, what we need to decide right now is if we tell Diamond any of this," yelled Armand. I could tell he was trying to contain his anger and the veins in his neck and forehead bulged.

"No, you can't!" Michelle didn't hesitate to say, her eyes wet from her own tears. Nathan and Viktoria felt the same way, adding if Diamond knew they'd suspected Laird's involvement and did nothing about it; she would never forgive them and be lost to them forever. They couldn't bear that. Diamond had suffered enough. My parents felt that she shouldn't be told because even though I wasn't involved, I was still *involved* and it would cast a shadow on our marriage. Quinn agreed.

Armand turned to me. "What do you think? Yours is the opinion that ultimately counts."

I was so confused—I didn't know what to think. "Diamond told me two nights ago that she could feel I was hiding something from her and it was a bad way to start a marriage going into it with secrets." My voice was choked up. "I love her more than words can express and it's killing me that I may have to keep this from her, but in the same breath, I saw her pain and felt her rage when she told me she would destroy anyone who had benefitted or was involved in her family's murder. Right now that's me and my family. As unintentional as it is on my end, it's the truth. I don't want to lose her, but I want this to go away. In such a short space of time she's become my all. I don't know what to do."

"I can make anything go away," Armand responded, looking at me intently. "The question is, do we *want* this to go away? What about your uncle? That bastard is responsible for the torture and murder of people I loved. If we decide that nothing is to be done then, *nothing* can be done. None of you can bring this up to him. I cannot touch him. When we step off this plane, it should be like nothing has happened. I'll figure out what to tell Diamond. She can never know any of this, even more important, if she does find out she must not know that we knew all along of Laird and Leland's involvement. Is that clear?" Everyone agreed. We got off the plane and with a solemn cloud hanging over us, drove to the Hassler.

It's not supposed to be like this, I thought to myself. Was I making a mistake? Would we live to regret this decision?

Chapter 26

Everyone was so happy to see me, but there was something strange in how Michelle was acting. I could sense it. I quickly pulled her aside at the hotel, but she played it off, saying she had a little tiff with Quinn. I wasn't buying it even though I could tell she had been crying. Quinn had better not hurt her.

Jonathan's parents seemed like different people, hugging me and kissing me as though they were genuinely thrilled for me. Maybe their first reaction to me was all in my mind like Michelle had thought. I think Beth and Liam also had a tiff because he seemed upset with her. My grandparents were doing well, rather emotional. Viktoria couldn't seem to stop crying. After a while the atmosphere became charged with the excitement of the upcoming wedding. Michelle was ecstatic and poor Quinn couldn't keep his hands off her, which led me to believe she'd forgiven him for their tiff earlier. Jonathan was a little distracted, but wouldn't leave my side. And Armand…well, he had disappeared. Everyone arrived at the hotel and immediately went to their rooms to freshen up before the brunch, but he was nowhere to be found. I thought he'd gone back to Minerva's to change but it was now twelve and he still hadn't returned. I wanted to get things started so I asked everyone to take their seats, tapping on my glass. Just then I saw Armand sneaking in and he gave me a wink. I was glad he'd made it in time.

"Umm umm," I said with a smile as I cleared my throat. "Can I have your attention please? I guess the first thing I want to start by doing is thanking you all for being here on such short notice, to share in what will most likely be one of the happiest days of my life."

"Our lives," Jonathan added with a laugh, squeezing my hand. There were small laughs all around.

"Yes, our lives," I said with a smile. "This is a big thing for me…"

"Big?" inserted Michelle.

"All right, huge!" I replied with a laugh as the others joined in. "Enough with the commentary, you know what I'm trying to say. What am I trying to say?" I asked jokingly, rubbing my temple as I looked up at the ceiling and the others continued laughing. Turning to Jonathan, I said, "What I'm trying to say is that I've never loved anyone the way I love you right now. It's only been a week, but I feel as though I've known you an eternity. I look at you or you hold me and all my problems seem to float away. You make me forget." Turning to his parents, I added, "I also want to thank you for supporting our decision, I know Jonathan is your only son and it means a lot to him for you to be here. It means a lot to us. I promise I will love, cherish, and be forever faithful to him. I'm not sure if you've all heard the story, but when I proposed…"

"*You* proposed?" interrupted Liam with a smile.

"I thought I trained her well, but I guess I was wrong. I told her she had it all backwards," Armand added with a smile and again the room erupted.

"Yes, I proposed and I'm proud of it," I replied as the laughter died down.

"For the record, I would've proposed eventually…just not after five days. That was a gutsy move, because deep down you would have to believe that the person would say yes and I did."

"I'm glad you did," I said bending my head to kiss his forehead. "Now, as I was saying. When I proposed, my original plan was for us to just do it, nothing big, just the two of us, my Armand and a priest. We would announce it to everyone when we returned and have a reception in New York, but Jonathan said his mother would never forgive if he eloped, so we decided to do it this way. And I'm happy that we did."

"I am too," added both Michelle and Beth with a smile.

"I've said all of this to say welcome. It makes my heart soar to have you all here as my family." My eyes began to tear up as I felt my chest tighten. "As glorious as these past seven days have been, they have also been the most difficult," I was choking up. "I've fallen in love for the first and hopefully last time, I've never cried so much in my life, my grandparents are back and sharing in this day, and I've honestly never missed my parents more than I did this week." The tears were silently rolling down my cheeks as I tried not to focus on any faces and look up towards the ceiling. Jonathan was rubbing my hands. "Michelle has been my dearest friend for so long and Armand like a father to me. I wanted to thank you both from the bottom of my heart for your patience, unconditional love, and even more so, your honesty. Neither of you have ever steered me wrong or lied to me and for that I'm forever grateful." Michelle started to cry then, as did Beth and Viktoria. Reaching under my chair, I took out two black satin envelopes wrapped in a gold ribbon. "This represents the millions of times you both supported me, the millions of times you gave me advice, told me I was wrong, and made me forget my sorrows." I walked over and gave Michelle a kiss on the mouth and whispered, "Thank you," and then did the same to Armand. Wiping my tears away, I said, "Don't open that now, I'll be embarrassed. Now that the sappy part is finished, I propose a toast." As everyone reached for their Mimosas and raised their hands, I began, "To families, old and new or even better, as Aunt Rosa would say, to love, happiness, and makeup sex."

There were a few more emotional toasts throughout the afternoon, but overall everything was perfect. Francesca had certainly outdone herself and promised that our brunch was just the beginning to the splendid feast she had planned for us at the wedding this evening. We were all talking and laughing when the waiter approached with a phone, telling me I had an important call.

"For me?" I wondered who it could be, since anyone that I would've expected to interrupt me, was also sitting at the table. Armand was looking at me as I excused myself. I took the phone.

"This is Diamond."

"Don't say another word and don't look around, just listen."

My heart rate had increased, but I kept smiling as Armand and Jonathan were both looking at me.

"All right."

"If you want to know who killed your family come upstairs to your room, I'll be waiting for you. Come alone. Your friends and family aren't what they seem."

Then the line went dead. I continued to smile as I took the phone from my ear and went back to the table.

Armand was the first to ask, "Is everything all right?"

"Yes, but I have to run to my room. I'll be back shortly."

"Who was on the phone?" he pressed.

"Dr. Kimora."

"Oh."

"Don't be too long," Jonathan added as he kissed my hand.

"I won't," I replied as my mind sped to assess what just happened and who was waiting in my room. I detected a South African accent and felt adrenaline rushing as I exited our function room. As I passed the waiter packing up our lunch wares, I handed him the phone and asked that he return it to the front desk immediately. When he turned his back I slipped one of the dirty steak knives into a napkin and headed for the private elevator that would bring me to my floor. I had to be prepared, since I didn't know who the hell was waiting for me and my instincts were telling me to be careful. Clutching my purse a little tighter, I was prepared to jump on anyone as the door elevator door opened, but there was no one there, just the infamous lounge chair that brought back memories of my night with Jonathan and I quickly pushed those thoughts aside staying focused.

Walking up to my door I swiped my key and slowly let it open. I could see no one as I stepped inside and as the door closed the hairs on my neck stood up. There was someone behind me, but before I could turn his arms were already around me and his hand over my mouth.

"Don't even think about screaming. Do you hear me?" he asked, his voice firm and cold. I nodded as he slowly released my mouth. I was trying to catch my breath as he had still not removed his arms from around my chest.

"Take...your...hands...off me." His grip lessened slightly, but it was still intense. "Since...you...called me...with infor...mation that I'm interested in...I'm going to forget...what just happened. Take your hands...off me."

"They told me to be careful because you were dangerous. You're the farthest thing from dangerous," he said as he slowly began to grind against my back and I could feel his hardness pressing into my bottom. Now I was getting upset.

"Tell me what you came here to tell me or I'm going to kill you." My voice was steady.

"Kill me? I doubt it." He had now brought his arm up and had it across my breasts, squeezing and massaging them as you would if you were milking a cow. That's it. I raised my shoe and slammed my three inch heel into his foot, twisting it as he growled in pain.

"You stupid bitch," he yelled as he swung me around and drove his fist into my face. I heard the bones in my nose crack from the force and I fell to the floor. Not wasting any time he planted his boot squarely against my rib cage. I tried to scream in pain, but nothing came out, just the air he had knocked out of my lungs as I sputtered blood and saliva across the floor. Damn I was out of shape. Placing his knee in my back he put all his weight on me as he circled his meat hook of a left arm around my neck. I could feel the sharp edge of the knife in my purse pressing into my abdomen, where I'd landed on it.

"Now where were we? Aaaahhh, somewhere around here," he said as he reached back and slipped his hands under my dress, squeezing my thigh. My nose was still bleeding and I was having a hard time breathing as his two-hundred twenty-five pound frame crushed my diaphragm.

"Tell...me...why...you're here," I managed to force out.

"All business and no pleasure?" he growled against my ear as he continued to massage my inner thigh, flicking his tongue in my ear. "Your boy Armand has been snooping around so we had to wrap this up once and for all. Do you want to know who killed your family?"

"You know I do."

"Leland arranged the kidnapping, but his father didn't deliver, so we couldn't very well waste all that royal pussy and if we didn't think you were already dead we would've had yours as well." He laughed. "All the better though, I was an inexperienced buck back then, now I'm even more of a man. All I need is five minutes to make you wish you had died with your filthy family," he said, extending his large calloused fingers to rub them roughly against the thin covering of my silk panties. I flinched at his harsh touch, groaning in disgust. The pain between my ribs became obsolete as I turned my focus to how I was going to kill this motherfucker.

"What…does…this have…to do…with the Hamiltons?" I asked as I began to control my breathing.

"Everything. Everyone down there knows the Hamiltons were involved and they're swimming in your family's wealth, but they aren't going to say anything. Why? Because marrying the little princess will make it all go away." He had now removed his hand from under my dress as he straddled my bottom and leaned forward with is forearm against the back of my neck pushing me into the cold marble floor as he rubbed his growing manhood into my back.

"Is…Jonathan…involved?" My voice was barely audible as my throat pressed into the floor.

"They're all involved. The oil field is in Jonathan's name, with his uncle and my boss collecting the profits and splitting it down the middle."

"Who's your boss?"

"I probably shouldn't tell you, but there isn't much you will be able to do about it from a grave. He goes by Rono."

"Did you kill my parents?"

"Me personally? No. I had a piece of your mother's tight ass, but as I said, I was a rookie back then. I was the lucky one guarding the hut.

She was begging for more, like she wasn't used to a *real* man. She should've known some European billionaire couldn't satisfy her. Over the years I've moved up in the ranks. "

"Why did you come here? Why are you telling me this?"

"Don't you know? To tie up our loose ends. And you are definitely a loose end. I have to admit, you're being a very good girl. No yelling or screaming."

I began to cough and sputter as blood was now running down the back of my throat and I could feel the bits and pieces of bone and grizzle in my mouth. My intruder eased up ever so slightly and that was all I needed. Before he knew what had happened I had turned onto my back so that he was now sitting on my pelvis. He quickly put his hands around my throat, obviously upset that I was able to move at all.

"Woah, you're a fast one, huh?" he asked with a wicked smile, squeezing my neck. "But I like this position much better," he said as he started to tear my dress from my shoulders. "You're a beautiful woman; I'm going to enjoy every minute of this." I started to mouth words, but he couldn't hear me so keeping his hands around my neck, he leaned into me positioning his ear over my mouth. "What did you say?"

"I said so…am I!" and with that I took his ear in my mouth and with one bite and fierce pull I ripped the tiny appendage from the side of his head, while simultaneously driving the steak knife to the hilt into his side. He howled in pain as he fell off me, wildly grasping at the knife in his side and open wound at the side of his head. I was on my feet and over him immediately, spitting his ear out before I angrily began stomping on his head and chest with my heels, feeling his skin give way with each penetration of my heel. He swung at my feet, but I had already dropped to the floor so that his neck was clenched between my calves and with a quick twist of my hips, I snapped his neck. "So am I," I breathed, "so am I."

I sat there for a moment as my breathing returned to normal, blowing my nose into the hem of my dress. I picked up the phone and made two calls. I hung up and stood to my feet. Grabbing one foot I dragged the man out of my suite and into the elevator, pressing the down button. I exited into the hallway just outside the function room and thankfully none of the waiters were there, not that I gave a shit at this point. I opened the door and backed in, dragging my package with me.

"What the hell…" I heard Armand yell, followed by a few screams. I calmly stepped in and closed the door. Armand was over his table and standing in front of me before anyone could get to me.

"Oh, my God!" exclaimed Michelle as Jonathan rushed to me.

"Diamond, what happened to you? Are you all right? Who is this man?" asked Armand reaching to grab me.

"Don't any of you fucking touch me." My voice was low and lethal. "Sit down." No one moved. "I said to sit the fuck down, all of you!" Armand tried to wipe the blood from my face and I knocked his hand away. God, just a few days ago I was telling Jonathan to sit down before I took him in my mouth. I can't think straight, they had all deceived me. They betrayed me.

"Diamond, we have to get you to a hospital," said my grandfather.

"I don't need a doctor, I need the truth," I yelled. "This man was waiting in my room to rape and kill me, just like he did to my mother. Do you know what he told me? He told me that you all knew that Laird and Leland were responsible for my family's death. He told me that the Hamilton wealth is built on the blood of my family."

"Dye, I don't know what this man told you, but he's lying," Armand yelled, cursing under his breath. "Did he hurt you?"

"Hurt me? My physical pain does not compare to the pain of being betrayed by the men I loved. Jonathan, do you own my grandfather's oil field?" My tears were falling as his reaction gave me my answer before he'd even opened his mouth.

"Diamond, please, we can explain," Michelle interrupted.

"Meesh, stay out of his, you have nothing…" my eyes opened wider as the pain in my chest intensified. "Unless you knew as well. Did you? Did you know all along?"

"Diamond, please, we can explain," Jonathan said as he took my arm. I reacted and slapped him hard in the face, watching as he recovered from the shock, rubbing his cheek with his hand as the tiniest dribble of blood escaped the corner of his mouth. His mother was wailing like it was her son lying at my feet.

"If this man was lying and Jonathan does not own the oil field, and none of you knew of Laird and Leland's involvement, tell me now." No one moved, no one uttered a sound. The pain in my chest was now excruciating as I realized it was the truth. I turned to Armand, my tears pouring from the well of my eyes, "Him I've only known a week, and as much as this hurts and as much as I love him, I will get over his betrayal, like I've gotten over many things, but *you*?"

"Dye, please..." Jonathan began, but I raised my hand, silencing him.

"How could you keep this from me and let me fall in love with this man? Even encourage it."

My grandmother stepped forward, with outstretched hands, "Diamond, we made a mistake, but you're wrong."

"Please don't say another word. I can't trust anything you say. I need a minute to think and gather my thoughts. I'll be back."

"Darling, please let us explain. I love you so much. Don't leave me," Jonathan begged, sounding as though he was in genuine pain, but he was a good actor. With no pre-nup, his family would've had it made. I couldn't look at him. He had fooled me.

"I'll be back," I repeated, exiting the room, I stood there for a moment and then like I'd done almost twenty years ago, I walked away. Not looking back once, I left the Hassler and got in the car that was waiting for me.

"Did you do everything I requested?"

"Yes, Ms. Chantiel."

"Take me to the airport."

Chapter 27

She never came back. I waited in Rome for five days before it hit me she was gone. I guess I always knew she could walk away from me, but I never thought that she would. And as I sat in the leather seat opposite Armand on our way back to New York from Africa, after another lead turned up nothing. My thoughts as always, rested on her. Within in minutes of her walking out of the Hassler, the men from the government she had called showed up, closed off the function room and her suite and without a single question, cleaned up the mess that could've very easily ruined our families. Armand seemed to know the men and knew Diamond had called them, which meant that she walked into that room with her mind already made up that she was leaving. So no matter what we said the wheels were already in motion. Two weeks after Diamond so easily walked away from the Hassler and out of my life, Rono Montandu went missing. Armand was convinced Diamond was involved, but no one knew for sure. We had confronted Leland who was rightfully afraid for his life. My parents were a mess, especially my mother, who had taken everything to heart and seeing me sad and miserable didn't help. Michelle had attempted to quit her job to help us search, but I refused to let her do that. I hadn't physically been in my office in over three months, trusting Quinn and my father to handle everything for me. I followed Armand wherever he would let me. The Skovachys were heartbroken. Viktoria had stopped treatment and we were all now playing a waiting game with her health. With every day and week that went by that we didn't find Diamond, Armand became more withdrawn and bitter. He blamed himself for everything, and even though he could probably live, a miserable life, if Diamond never spoke to him again, he at least needed to know she was safe, and right now he didn't know that. We didn't know anything. On top of being worried, I think his pride was suffering. A man in his line of work should be able to find anyone, but he some how couldn't find her and it was tearing him apart inside.

How was *I* doing? Well, I knew I loved Diamond, I just didn't know how much until she walked out that door and never came back. I missed her terribly; I mean, my longing for her ached all the way to my bones. I was sick with worry as I fought to get out of bed in the mornings, smile when people asked how I was feeling and pretend like I didn't want to curl up and die. But the more I hurt, the angrier I became that it was so easy for her to just walk away from what we had and the promise of what was to come. The angrier I became at the thought that she really believed I was using her and only wanted her money. These past few months had been the worst of my life and I couldn't help but think that she didn't feel the same way about me as I had thought. Not a call or a note to let us know she was alive, nothing. But I would continue to search for her until I didn't have a single breath left in my body, why? Besides the fact that I loved her so much, I needed her to know that I hadn't betrayed her, even if she listened to what I had to say and then slammed the door in my face. It would hurt, but at least she would know I never meant to hurt her and that my family isn't what she thought. I needed her to hear my side of the story. We all did.

Chapter 28

I was looking out the window of a building, down at the street below. I could see for miles, but somehow I was at ground level as I saw Jonathan crossing the street. My heart still skips a beat and my stomach flutters when my eyes are on him. A bus had stopped to let him cross, but in the distance I could see a truck barreling towards the intersection. I began to bang on the window, screaming frantically as I realized he didn't hear me. My fists were stinging as I used every ounce of strength to try and break the glass. Jonathan couldn't see me; my eyes were wide with fear as the inevitable happened and the truck slammed into him, sending him flying several feet in the air. Time seemed to stand still as his body turned over and over in the air. My own screams were deafening to me. My heart stopped with the same thud Jonathan's body made as his body hit the pavement. At that moment I opened my eyes, sitting up in bed panting, beads of sweat running down my face and chest soaking my flannel nightshirt. The thunderous sound of my heartbeat pounding in my ears and slamming against the wall of my body enveloped me, as the realization came that I was dreaming again, or more accurately, having a nightmare. I couldn't catch my breath fast enough, my chest was heaving. Suddenly I was cold, trying to adjust my eyes to the early morning light. The snow was still falling outside from the storm that hit yesterday. The trees looked like beautiful chandeliers with ice crystals hanging from every branch. The glow of dawn cast little shimmers of light against the icicle pendulums illuminating my room. My blankets were strewn everywhere except over my body and the wood in the fireplace had burned out, leaving tiny orange ambers. Reaching for the closest blanket, I drew it around my shoulders. My tears came then, rocking back and forth I tried to calm down as my emotional pain wrought my body.

It had been a little over four months since I walked out of the Hassler and my family's lives and I hadn't been in contact with them since. And the one-hundred and twenty-forth day that Jonathan Hamilton had haunted my dreams, not counting the seconds of the day that his memory enveloped all my senses. I couldn't understand why he wouldn't just go away. I had only known him a week, seven days, I'd known my grandparents for ten years and it was easier to walk away from them after my parents' funeral. I was a stupid human being, that was clear to me now.

I had traveled to Africa immediately after I left Rome and it was shear determination that kept me from going to sleep and never waking up. I had never thought about killing myself so often in my life as I did during the past few months. But I was determined to find and kill Rono Montandu. Finding him took a lot longer than killing him. Once I got to him, the fact that the poor bastard had an affinity for prostitutes made it extremely easy for me to get him where I wanted him. With the help of a good friend, we offered our services and he willingly took the bait. I drugged and brought him to a secluded place in the jungle. He was fearless and brave, *at first*, calling me every name in the book and telling me all the different ways he would kill me once his men got there. I didn't eat, he didn't eat, when he did sleep, he would wake up to find me just staring at him. It went on like that for two days. Ah, tut-tut, on day two when the realization came that his men would not be coming and the woman that sat in front or him for two days straight without moving was a killer unlike any he had ever known, he became a different man, a coward even as he begged, promising me riches untold, the names of affluent people who knew of and were involved in his dirty deeds. He was afraid of me and rightfully so. I worked on him all day and all night.

One of the many pieces of information that Rono had given up in the futile effort to save his life, was that not only had he never met Jonathan, but it was *his* decision alone to kill my family. He was blackmailing Leland with an affair he had with a fourteen-year-old girl in Johannesburg who had become pregnant. That was how he'd enlisted his help. His number two guy that had met his untimely demise in my hotel room was mistaken and had a talent for embellishing; most of what he told me was wrong. Rono knew Leland was cooking the books, but he had no idea that all the trails lead to Jonathan as the CEO. All he knew was that his men had jobs and seventy percent of the money from the oil field came to him. I made sure he suffered, the same way my family had, and the same way I was suffering right now after walking out on the people I loved. I was afraid that killing Rono wouldn't satisfy me, nor make all the pain of the last eighteen years go away, and that I would still be unhappy. That was always a risk with killing someone, the fear that the scars they'd caused were too deep and nothing, not even their death could make the pain better. Thankfully, that wasn't the case, as with each pile of dirt I threw over his crushed and mutilated body I felt the weight of not having punished my family's killer lifted. It had now been three and a half months since I had buried Rono in the same soil he had drenched with my family's blood. In the end I felt better, but all that remained now was the excruciating pain in my heart. A pain that grew worse with each passing day.

The night I stood over Rono's defeated body I decided I would spare Leland's life, since in a small way, he was also a victim in this, although he would soon see all his money disappear. Once again I was wrong and had overreacted. The Hamilton's weren't involved to the extent that I implied that night in Rome, but the fact remained that they all knew and it was obvious that they planned on keeping it from me. But who could blame them? Look at what I did, how I reacted, I would've kept it from me as well. How could they ever forgive me? How could Jonathan forgive me for running off the way I did? I hadn't called or written. I knew Armand was at this wit's end. I hadn't touched any of my accounts or credit cards, emptying the safe at the hotel and the account my parents had opened for me.

I knew Armand and Jonathan were looking for me, but chances are they were looking in the wrong place. I had paid cash for a small cottage in Mont-Tremblant, Quebec, had a woman come and set it up for me with everything I would need, furniture, accessories, and the like. I kept to myself most of the time, venturing out only for groceries. I was miserable. I wanted to go home, but my pride wouldn't let me. I began my daily routine, crying until the sun had fully risen, replenished the stock of firewood, had a bath and returned to bed. Sometimes I ate, most of the time I didn't. I knew I'd lost several pounds, but since I rarely wore anything other than my pajamas I didn't notice as much. When the pain of not having Jonathan in my life became too intense to the point where it hurt to breathe, furthermore get out of bed, I would touch myself trying to recreate the sensations he so easily brought to life in me, crippling my body. In each instance I failed, snatching my hands away in embarrassment as my fingers began their unnatural probe. My hands weren't his. What I wouldn't give to have him hold me again. I was so close to having it all, love, happiness, and makeup sex, I thought with a smile, recalling Aunt Rosa's toast. A fresh wave of tears came upon me. I was driving myself crazy; I needed to get out of this house. It was still snowing outside, but I didn't care. It snowed here constantly; if I let that be a deterrent then I would probably be miserable for the rest of my life. I needed a hobby, a job or something to take my mind off of everything. Starting over wasn't as easy as I thought it would be. Or maybe that's because for the first time in my life I was truly alone. I had no one.

Finally I got up, dressed in umpteen layers, and went to shovel the walkway before the snow built up any more. My closest neighbors were almost two miles away and I actually preferred it that way. There was no chance of people popping up just to say hello.

It took me over an hour to do just the porch. I was halfway down steps when a truck pulled up and the driver yelled out in French, if I wanted him to plow my driveway. I had to think for a minute since French wasn't my strongest language and yelled that it wasn't necessary since I didn't have a car. Surprisingly he parked anyway and trudged through the snow up to porch.

"What the hell was he doing?" I muttered under my breath, pulling my scarf that was already wrapped around the lower part of my face, up to just below my eyes.

"You are new to the area?" he asked

"Yes."

"Are you from here?" God I wasn't in the mood for this.

"Here, meaning Canada? Umm, no. I've been living in America for almost a year. I'll apologize up front since my French isn't very good."

Switching to English, he responded, "It's not so bad, but I can speak in English if you prefer."

"That would help," I said.

"Let me help you. It doesn't look as though you've made much progress since I passed by the first time."

"No, no, that really isn't necessary. I probably would've been done by now if this bloody snow wasn't so heavy."

"That's why I offered my help. I know the damage this stuff can do to your back. My name is Crane Boudreux," he said with an outstretched hand. He was looking at me like he expected me to volunteer mine. This is exactly why I've stayed inside these past three months.

"Mr. Boudreux, I appreciate the offer, but I really have this under control," I responded, glancing away from his hand.

"Umm, all right," he said, lowering his hand in embarrassment. "Maybe I'll see you around," and with that he turned to leave. Why was I being such a bitch? I definitely wasn't worried about him hurting me; I just didn't want to answer any questions. I hadn't talked to someone in so long.

"Mr. Boudreux?"

"Yes," he replied turning to face me.

"I'm sorry. If there really wasn't anything more important that you could be doing right now, I wouldn't mind a little help. At this rate I'll be here all night."

"I don't mind at all. We'll be done in a jiffy. Let me grab my shovel and I'll work from the street in. And by the way, you can call me Crane." Before I could respond he was heading back to his truck.

He wasn't wrong we were finished in forty-five minutes, meeting in the middle of the walkway.

"Wow, thank you. You're a pro at this."

"It's no problem. I like this type of work."

"Well, if you hold on, I'll grab my purse."

"Purse? Oh, no, no, no. That's not how we do things around here. You don't need to pay me. It was my pleasure."

"Can I at least offer you a cup of coffee?" Did I just invite a stranger into my house? Do I even have coffee? "It's freezing out here. Please I insist."

"Sure," he replied, taking our shovels and leaning them alongside the wooden banister.

We slipped our boots off and then stepped inside.

"Make yourself comfortable. You can hang your coat on the rack beside you. Let me get things started in the kitchen and I'll be right out.

"Okay," he responded.

I put the coffee in the coffee maker and took my jacket off in the mud room. Up until that point I hadn't realized that my face was still wrapped with the scarf. Once the coffee was finished I set up the tray, dropped in a pinch of salt, and brought it out. Crane was kneeling down building a fire.

"That was fast," he said, looking at me over his shoulder. He was staring. After a few seconds he snatched his eyes away from mine.

"I have one of those super efficient coffee makers, which makes it easy," I replied. He finished building the fire as I put the tray down on the table. Once the fire was started, he sat next to me on the sofa as I poured him a large cup of coffee. I could still feel him staring at me.

"Thank you," he said taking the cup.

"Be careful it's very hot."

The fire finally kicked in as we enjoyed our coffee. Crane told me about his landscaping and towing business. Our conversation trailed to the news, but I volunteered that I didn't have a television or radio so I hadn't been keeping up to speed.

"If you don't have a television or radio, what do you do all day?"

"Sleep or read," I responded.

"That's not good. With this type of weather you should at least have a radio."

"I do have a little radio that the previous owners left, that I listen to at least a couple times a week for the weather, but that's it. It's a little archaic."

"You should get a television so you could at least watch the news." There was a hint of something hidden in his voice.

"Why, what's gong on in the world today?"

"I really should be going. Thanks for the coffee. I'll see you around." He was hurrying to the door.

"No, please wait. Am I missing something?"

"You aren't missing anything; I think I'm going crazy."

My voice became firm as the realization came that he recognized me. "You aren't going crazy. What's going on?"

"Are you who I think you are?" he asked, his eyes questioning mine.

"Who do you think I am?"

"Diamond Skovachy." My heart sank. I sat back down in the sofa and closed my eyes, dreading the thought of having to move again. Starting over this time was hard enough. "Don't worry, I'm not going to say anything," he added as though he read my mind. Turning to leave he said, "I'm sorry about what happened."

"Why? What happened?" I was prodding him since I wasn't sure what he was talking about. What happened at the Hassler was supposed to disappear. I'd made sure of that.

"It's been all over the news." My heart rate increased.

"I told you I don't watch the news," I yelled. "Tell me what happened."

"Your grandmother fell into a coma early this week. They don't expect her to live much longer. Your grandfather has been on all the major networks this week asking you to come home. The media has been camped outside the hospital waiting for news. As of this morning, nothing had changed." I was quiet for a long while. I had put them through so much and they still wanted me.

"Do you know where they are?" my vocal cords tight from the tears I was fighting to hold back.

"Umm, in New York I think, Memorial something Hospital."

I would not let my pride rule me any longer. I was going home.

"I'm sorry to ask, but do you think you could take me to the airport?"

"Sure. You can use my mobile if you need to check flights."

"Thank you. Give me one minute."

"Take your time."

I changed into some dry clothes and headed for the airport. As we pulled into the terminal I turned to Crane.

"Why did you help me?"

"I don't know. I was asking myself what the hell I was doing when you refused the snow plow and I pulled over anyway. Something was drawing me out of that car. Then once I saw your face I understood why. Your family really loves you. They need you. Go to them." I squeezed his hand.

"Thank you," I said and went to catch my flight.

I prayed all the way to Manhattan. I prayed she would hold on until I got there. Why would God listen to me after all I had done?

Chapter 29

When I arrived at Memorial Sloan-Kellering Cancer Center, the police had the entrance barricaded. The cabby told me that was as far as he was able to go, so I paid and walked up the entrance. A security officer at the door stopped me and asked where I was heading.

"I'm going to see my grandmother," I replied solemnly.

"Which floor?" he questioned, trying to see under my baseball hat.

"I don't know which floor. I have to find out from the front desk."

He was hesitant, "Umm, all right, go on in, but I'm watching you. No funny business."

There were two women at the front desk and I prayed they didn't give me a hard time.

"May I help you?" the one closest to me asked.

"Yes. Can you tell me which room Viktoria Skovachy is in?" Both women looked at each other and started to laugh.

"Let me guess," the other woman began, "you're her granddaughter and you're here to see her." Once again they burst out laughing. Was I missing something? "Do you really expect us to just give you the room number?"

Removing my baseball cap, I replied, "Yes. As a matter of fact I am her granddaughter and I would love to see her."

"Your name?" she asked, still laughing.

"Diamond Chantiel Skovachy."

"Do you have any I.D?" I took out my passport and handed it to her. They instantly stopped laughing, searching my face. She looked at it and immediately her demeanor changed. Handing it back to me she said, "I'm sorry Ms. Skovachy, your grandmother is on the 16th floor, room 1652. I will call up and let them know you're coming."

"Please don't. I want to…I don't want…let me surprise her." She placed the phone back on the receiver, looking at me with sad eyes.

"All right. The elevators are on your left."

The elevator was taking forever, as though it was urging me to turn back. When I exited onto the floor the staff at the nurse's station stopped talking. I was looking around for the room signs when an older nurse asked if she could help.

"Which way is room 1652?" I didn't think it was possible for a silent room to become even more silent, but it did.

"Are you a member of the family?" she asked, raising her eyebrows.

"Yes. Which way is the room?" Impatience was creeping into my voice.

"All the way down this hall. Ms. Skovachy is in the last suite on the right."

"Thank you."

As I reached her door it was closed and I could hear voices on the other side. I raised my hand to knock, and thought I couldn't do this. Drawing it back to my side, I turned to leave. Down the hall I could see all the nurses bent over the counters and standing in the hallway trying to get a better look at me, which stopped me in my tracks. They scurried when I saw them. Damn, nosey bitches! I sighed and walked back to the door, knocking before I could talk myself out of it again.

"Come in," said a deep male voice that I recognized as my grandfather's. Taking a deep breath I opened the door. The suite was huge, and at first glance didn't look like a hospital room. Once again the room went silent as I entered. There were several people standing and sitting, but I didn't focus on any of their faces, looking only at my grandmother's tiny frame in the bed and Nathan beside her.

My grandfather was the first to speak, "Diamond?"

"Yes, it's me." There were low gasps around the room, but again I only focused on my grandparents.

"You came," his voice cracked. "You finally came."

I wish I could cry, but the tears wouldn't fall. I know I came across as such a hard, evil person and for once I wanted to appear human, but as much as I willed it they wouldn't fall.

"I'm sorry it took me this long. Where I was staying there wasn't a television or radio. How is she?"

"Don't be sorry. She must've known you were coming because she came out of the coma this afternoon. She's been in and out of consciousness."

"Can I talk to her?"

"Of course you can. I don't know if she'll respond, but give it a try," he replied. I walked over to the sink to wash my hands and there was a man leaning against it.

"Excuse me," I said in a low voice, not looking up. He stepped aside and as I washed my hands I could feel his stare burning into my skin. I brought my shoulder up to my ear as though I thought that would help protect me, but I didn't. Reaching for a paper towel I quickly dried my hands and went over to the bed. Nathan got up so that I could sit down. I couldn't tell if she was awake or not, since her eyes appeared to be open, but all I could see were the whites of her eyes. I drew her frail hand to my lips.

"Nana…" Almost immediately her eyes started to flutter open. "Nana, it's me, Diamond." Her eyes were open now and I could tell she was trying to focus. Her hand was so cold.

"Dye…"she breathed.

"Yes," I said squeezing her hand a little tighter, happy that she recognized me so quickly.

"You're here?"

"I'm here. Nana…I know…that I don't have the right to ask anything of you, after all that I've put you through, but I'm going to ask anyway. Please don't leave me?"

"I knew...you...would come. We...were...so...worried."

"I know. I'm sorry. If I could take it all back, I would."

"I prayed that you would come back for his sake, if not for ours. You broke his heart terribly," she said, her voice barely audible as her breathing began to sound even more labored. I knew she was talking about Jonathan. "He loves...you so much. Don't...let us ruin it for you."

"Sssshh, don't talk any more. You should rest." My tears came then, at the thought that I'd hurt Jonathan so badly.

"I don't want to rest. I have an eternity of resting just around the corner." She closed her eyes and took a deep breath, "I've been waiting for you."

"I'm here now."

"He's a good man, Diamond. Do you love him?" I felt the urge to wail coming on as I cried into the back of her hand. "Diamond, it's a simple question, do you love him?"

"I don't want to! I don't want to love him. Loving him hurts too much," I said, pausing to catch my breath as I heard someone leave the room.

"Do you love him?"

"Yes, yes I love him, more than life itself," I sobbed. "I've been so miserable, Nana. Each day I thought it would get better, but it only became worse." I continued to cry into her hand as she smoothed my hair with her other hand.

"It hurts...when it's real," she began. "Promise me you'll try to be happy...and live life to the fullest. You've being through so much; it's time to turn a new leaf."

"I don't even know if he'll still have me. I've been so stupid, Nana. I walked out on him; I walked out on all of you. How can you ever forgive me?"

"Don't cry my love. There's nothing to forgive. We could never begin to understand all that you've been through. That night in Rome we were all angry with ourselves. Jonathan didn't know anything until that morning, he wanted to tell you, but like us, he was afraid, afraid of losing you. And then knowing that you could've been killed up in your room by that horrible man was a terrible pill for us to swallow. None of us are angry with you. We missed you. We wanted you to come home. It was more painful, not knowing if you were hurt or ill."

"I felt like I couldn't stay. I felt betrayed."

"And rightfully so, but you didn't give us a chance to explain. You automatically thought the worst of us all…including Jonathan, Michelle and Armand. While you were gone, did you bury all your demons?"

"Yes, one."

"Good. You know, he's been miserable without you."

"So have I. While I was gone, I came to the realization that I really don't deserve him."

"That's nonsense! I can't think of two people who deserve each other more than you two. Stop fighting this, looking for reasons to be alone, he is the only man for you."

"I would give up everything I own to have him love me, or even just forgive me."

"You will have to give up something…but not what you're expecting. You'll have to give up your heart…"

"I'm so afraid."

"Afraid of what, child?"

"Afraid of losing him, afraid of love, afraid of life. Life without hate. It's consumed me for so long, that now that it's gone, I'm not sure what to do," I was crying uncontrollably as I tried to form my words.

"Love him. That's all you need to do. Let the love for your family consume your heart now. We all love you so very much. My husband is a good man and he's made some terrible mistakes that he's paid for…but you must forgive him. I need you to take care of him."

"I will," I cried.

"It's natural to be afraid, but you can't let it consume you. You've done so much, for so many people. Let Jonathan love you." She took a deep breath and closed her eyes tightly with a grimace on her face. She was in pain.

"Nana, no more talking, I want you to rest," I said, patting her forehead.

"I don't have time to rest." Her breathing again sounded labored. "I know they already know, but when I see Zachary and Nyrobi, I will tell them all the great things you have done." She was smiling, then something behind me caught her eye, "Aaaahhh, I see them now," she whispered. "Zachary is that you, my love?" She was looking past me out the window.

"No, no," I wailed, "please don't go. Stay with me. I promise I'll never leave you again. I can't do this alone. Don't look at them. Look at me!" I cried as I tried to turn her face from the window to focus on me. I could hear people behind me crying and someone was comforting my grandfather.

"I've waited for this day all your life," she said with a weak smile. "And now it's finally here. Learn to love...keep me in your heart...and I will always be there with you," and with that she took a deep breath.

"No, wait!" I screamed. "It's not supposed to be like this. You were supposed to be at my wedding, hold my son in your arms. Please..." I begged, "don't leave me like this."

"You don't understand, do you? I've never left you," she whispered. My head was buried in the crook of her neck as I emptied my soul on shoulder. "Thank Crane for me," she said, placing her hand on my back, and then she was still.

It took a few moments for me to realize what she said but it was too late, she was gone. Crane? The doctor came to my side and checked her pulse, recording the time of death and then I heard him telling Nathan he would give us a few minutes. I wept until nothing was left in me. Finally I stood to my feet and turned to find Nathan in Armand's arms, Liam comforting Beth on the sofa, Quinn quietly consoling Michelle in the corner, and the man standing at the sink was gone. They were all there.

"You...you're all here?" I asked, my voice broken like it was the night at Jonathan's house. Both my grandfather and Armand looked at me. "Can you ever forgive me?" I asked as I ran into Armand's arms.

"The question is can you ever forgive me?" he cried then, like I'd never heard before. I just held him. My dear Armand.

Nathan walked over to my grandmother and took her hand, kissing

219

it tenderly. "Darling, you finally got your wish. I will miss you immensely," and leaning over, gave her a long deep kiss. "Let's go home," he said turning to face us. "Let's all go home."

Armand took my grandfather to meet the press while we all waited in lobby. Michelle and I had our tearful reunion in the hallway as she too let the tears wash away all the pain and worry of the past four months.

"Michelle Noir, will you still have me as your stupid best friend?" I asked, swinging both our hands between our bodies like we were little girls. To me she looked more beautiful than ever.

"Will I have *you*? Oh no, that question should be the other way around," she replied with a laugh and placing our hands over her lower abdomen, she tearfully whispered, "Will you have *us*?"

My eyes were wide, "Us? Are you…"

"Almost four months. Goddamn *breakfast*," she replied with a mixture of laughs and sobs.

"Oh my gosh! Does Quinn know?"

"Yes. He wants to get married."

"That's wonderful, but are you ready for that? A baby is no reason to rush into things."

"That's the same thing I would say, except he asked me before I found out I was pregnant. I'm so glad you're here Dye. I told Quinn I wouldn't marry him until you came back. Dye, we didn't want to lie to you and Jonathan just wanted…"

"Sssshh, don't say any more." Our tears fell anew as I silently buried the little piece of jealousy trying to creep into my heart. Could that have been me if I hadn't leave Rome and run away from everything I ever loved? Could I be carrying Jonathan's child?

"I am so happy for you," I said, hugging her tightly. I really was. Quinn came over and hugged me then as well, followed by Beth and Liam. Looking at all of them I said, "Thank you for making it so easy to come back."

Beth began, "Can you ever forgive me?" Her tears were streaming down her cheeks.

"There's nothing to forgive," I replied. I was looking around as I realized the man that was leaning against the sink never came back. "Umm…is…where is?"

"He left shortly after you came into the room," Quinn answered, his eyes were apologetic.

"Was he the man by the sink?"

"Yes," said Beth. "I'm not sure where he went. The last four months have been really tough on him. He closed himself off from us, shut up in that house, when he wasn't joining Armand on leads of your whereabouts."

Turning to Meesh, I asked, "How could I have been so stupid? You warned me. I…I just…"

"That's enough, Dye," Meesh said, holding my shoulders. "Viktoria was right. We could never imagine going through what you've been through. I'm not sure where Jonathan went, but I know he has a good reason and that he's still very much in love with you. We're just glad you're back here with us, safe and sound."

"She's right," added Quinn. "I can call him right now."

"No, don't do that. He obviously wants to be alone right now. Let's go home." Silently my heart and body ached for him. I just hope he forgave me as readily as the others did.

Chapter 30

Nathan was staying at our penthouse, so we all met there. Armand helped my grandfather to bed and then we all sat in the living room to go over the details for the funeral. Almost all the arrangements had already been made; her body would be flown back to London and buried in the lot both her and my grandfather had picked. Quinn and Michelle were busy notifying the people on the list Nathan had provided to us. The story had already hit the news and the Hamiltons were fielding those calls. Armand and I stole a moment to talk. I told him about the past four months and what happened with Rono. He wanted to know if Rono had hurt me and I told him he hadn't even gotten the opportunity to lay a finger on me. He was sorry that I had to do "that" alone. My businesses were doing better than ever, and other than the fact that everyone was miserable from my disappearance, things were going well. It was close to midnight and Jonathan still hadn't called or come by. Michelle was pretty tired so Quinn took her home and Beth and Liam left shortly after. I checked on Nathan and then joined Armand in the living room while he finished up some paperwork. As I looked out the window at the thriving city below, I thought about Jonathan and everything my grandmother told me.

"Are you all right?" asked Armand.

"As well as to be expected," I replied. "Where are all my things? I wanted to take a bath, but my drawers upstairs are empty."

"They're at your house."

"What do you mean?"

"When you were in Rome you had everything shipped to Jonathan's house, remember?"

"Oh yes."

"Well, they're still there. What are you waiting for?" he asked.

"What do you mean?"

"You sound like a broken record. You know what I mean. Go to him. Don't waste another second or another day." I closed my eyes, hating myself for being so transparent.

"Armand, I can't, not after what I did."

"Why not? That man loves you and I know you love him. In the end, that's all that matters. We've all made mistakes."

"You don't understand," I sobbed.

"I understand perfectly. You are too proud to admit to him that you were wrong. Too proud to be the one to go over there and beg for him to take you back after all that you've put him through. He has crawled continents upon continents, and country upon country looking for you. And you're going to sit there and wait for him to come to you?"

"That's not true. I would do anything to have him hold me again, or tell me that he loves me. Anything! How dare you presume that this has been easy for me? Not one second of any day as ever gone by without me thinking of him."

"And yet you still managed to go four months without a call or letter. Actions speak louder than words, Dye. Everyone in that hospital room knows you love him, but it's time to show it. Go to him." I was crying as I realized he was right. I was standing at that window hoping that Jonathan would call or come by, because I didn't want to be the one. "I know it's hard, but you have to swallow your pride and go to him."

"Will you be all right?" I asked, knowing full well what he was going to say.

"Of course, now go! I'll have Abram bring the car around."

"Thank you," I said, kissing his cheek.

"Diamond?"

"Yes."

"I love you so very much, but if you do anything like that again, I'll kill you myself."

"I love you too," I said with a warm smile. I blindly ran to the door, blowing him a kiss over my shoulder.

I don't know how fast I was driving, but it's a miracle I didn't get a ticket or crash. I drove up to the intercom at Jonathan's front gate and pressed the button twice. There was no answer, so I pressed it again.

"Hello?" came a groggy voice on the other end.

"Jonathan, it's Diamond. I know it's late…" I didn't finish as the gate opened and the intercom was cut off. I drove in and parked behind his car. The front door was unlocked, so I went in.

"Hello?" I called.

"I'm upstairs in the guest room," he yelled.

My heart was beating out of control. I had to hold on to the railing since I didn't trust my legs not to give way from underneath me. My palms were sweating as I knocked on the bedroom door.

"It's open." I took a deep breath and walked in. The bed was empty, but I could tell I must have woken him. There was a half empty bottle of whiskey and a glass on the end table and the bathroom light was on. "I'm out here, Diamond." Oh God, oh God, just breath, move your legs dammit! The door to the balcony was open and I could see Jonathan in his robe standing with his back to me. I stood in the entryway, waiting for him to turn around and say something, but he didn't.

"I'm sorry I woke you," I began.

"Its fine, I was barely sleeping anyway. I'm really sorry about Viktoria. I know it made her happy seeing you tonight." He still hadn't turned around.

"Jonathan…I," he cut me off.

"Diamond, this evening when I heard you tell Viktoria that it hurt too much to love me, I made a decision. I decided that I don't want to hurt you or cause you any more pain. I guess up to that point I'd only been concerned with what I wanted. In Rome I didn't want to tell you what I suspected, because *I* didn't want to lose you. I wasn't thinking of what you may have wanted. Sometimes being in a relationship isn't for every...one." His voice trailed off.

"Look at me. Please," I walked over and touched his shoulder and he jumped, "look at me." Still nothing, he just hung his head. He wouldn't look at me.

"You didn't even give me a chance to explain. You automatically assumed that I was out to hurt you, that our week together in Rome had been a lie, and all I wanted was your money. After all we had shared. Maybe it wasn't meant to be and my dreams weren't your dreams."

"Stop right there! Now look at me," I said, turning him around. My chest tightened when I saw the pain in his eyes. "I need you to listen to what I'm going to say. You left the room before you heard what else I said to my grandmother." I was rubbing the sides of his face with my thumbs. "Yes, I told her, it hurt to love you, because it's true. My feelings for you grip my heart like a vice and I can't escape it. I love you so very much, Jonathan, words can't begin to explain it. I am sorry I left Rome the way I did. At the time I felt as though I couldn't face any of you. I should've known that neither you nor Armand would hurt me, but I guess inside I was looking for anything that would give me reason to run away from you."

"But why, after all we had shared?"

"Because I was afraid. Afraid of losing myself to you. You have no idea what you do to me. When I'm with you nothing else matters. Each day for the past four months a piece of me has slowly died. I wanted to come back to you, but my pride wouldn't let me. I don't want to spend another second without you in my life. I've lost too many people I love and I refuse to lose you as well. Let me love you. I promise I'll never leave you again." Jonathan closed his eyes and turned his face into my palm, kissing me tenderly. "Give me another chance."

"I am the one that should be asking for another chance. I don't think I could've held out much longer if we didn't find you. When I saw you covered in blood and then you never came back, I didn't know what to think. The thought of that man with his hands on you was enough to drive me over the edge. Over the past four months I've known exactly how your father must have felt, far too many times."

"No, please don't say that. I couldn't bear to lose you like that. I am so very sorry. I need you to teach me, teach me how to love. If there is one thing I've learned over the past four months, it's that I can't live without you in my life," I cried. He took my hands from his face and wrapped them around his neck. And then we kissed, like we'd never kissed before. My mouth was the oasis that held the sweet liquid that could quench his thirst and give him life after the desert of the past few months. We drank, like we'd never drank before. And with each twirl of our tongues and nibble of each others lips the parts of us that had died since Rome, were slowly revived.

"Wait here," Jonathan said, finally pulling away. I was on fire. I didn't want him to leave my side. He ran to his bedroom and then came back on the balcony.

"Now, let's do this right," and getting down on one knee, he took my hand. "Diamond Chantiel Skovachy, will you marry me?" My heart was soaring as he took the band he'd bought in Rome out of the case and placed it on my finger. I had goose bumps as the chills walked up my spine. I dropped to my knees as we hugged in the spot where it had all began. The spot where I'd poured my soul out for the very first time in his arms.

"Yes, I will be your wife, today, tomorrow, and forever. You've made me so happy." He picked me up then and carried me down the hall to his bedroom, and as we walked in I realized it had been completely redecorated. Some of my art and furniture had been incorporated and the same lush neutral colors that were used on the terrace at the Hassler were now spread around the room. "Jonathan, this is beautiful! Did you do this?"

"Yes and no. I had Lucy arrange it before she flew to Rome for the wedding, and when I saw it I couldn't bring myself to sleep in here, so I've been sleeping in the guest room ever since. This was supposed to be *our* room, plus I felt like I was closer to you sleeping in the same bed you'd slept in when you were here. Either way, you're here now and we can enjoy it together."

"It's beautiful." I smiled, kissing him tenderly. "Let me have a bath and I'll join you, all right?"

"Sure. Everything is pretty easy to find in there, but if you need anything just yell."

"I will." I closed the door and stripped, quickly jumping out of my jeans and sweater. I lathered thoroughly, even my shower gels and hair products were in the bathroom. I heard the door open.

"Jonathan?"

"You're taking too long," he said with a smile, opening the shower door. He was already naked and obviously ready for me. I had to giggle as he stepped into the shower with me. I scurried over to the other side of the shower so he couldn't grab me.

"I have to rinse off and wash out my hair," I said with a laugh.

"Come here. I'll help you," he said, and stepped under the shower dragging me into him. "Turn around." His voice was firm. I did as I was told. Placing his hand on my lower back, he pushed me forward until the shower was barely hitting the back on my head and I was almost against the glass wall. "Hold your head back." Again I did as I was told and with slow deliberate fingers Jonathan rinsed the shampoo out of my hair. I don't know how he did it, but it was very arousing. When he was finished he turned me around and pulled me back towards him, taking his hand and wiping it across my face to get the excess water from my eyes. He took my wash rag off the shelf and rung it out, not taking his eyes off mine and washed all the remaining soap from my body. There wasn't a part of me that he didn't give the utmost attention. All I could do was close my eyes as he gently parted my lips and cleaned me. Jonathan continued to stroke me as I leaned back against the wall, standing on the tip of my toes, every nerve on edge. Not stopping his strokes, he covered his middle finger with the wash cloth and cleaned inside me. I couldn't breathe as he rotated his finger in and out. Rinsing the rag again he knelt down in front of me, opening my thighs enough to fit his hand and using the soaked cloth wiped away the suds that were left. When he was finished he brought me forward ever so slightly and covered my throbbing bud with his warm mouth, caressing it with his tongue. I couldn't help the sharp intake of breath that escaped my lips.

He lingered for a while and then stood up, taking my bottom lip in his mouth, nibbling on it as he slipped a long slender finger between my aching folds. It didn't hurt, but instead heightened every nerve or primitive sensation running through my body.

"Jona…than," I panted, but he didn't stop, instead pinning me against the shower with his hard body as he sucked on my ear and my neck. I was trying the hold back the urge I had to growl and scratch his back and he knew it.

"Diamond, you aren't breathing. You're holding back. I need you to relax," he said, pushing his finger deeper in me while staring at me. I was writhing against his hand as he coaxed me to an orgasm, grabbing his shoulders I pulled him to me trying to kiss him, but he moved his head. "No. No kissing, I want you to look at me, talk to me, and let me know what feels good." I closed my eyes relishing in the pleasure and bit my lip out of frustration. "Open your eyes, Diamond, look at me." His voice was firm, he was serious. You heard the man, Diamond, relax. I opened my eyes and continued to look at him as intently as he was looking at me. He'd seen me naked before, but tonight there was something different about him, something aggressive that I loved. Soon whatever was holding me back was replaced by intense passion.

"Right there," I said, holding his wrist as I kept his hand in the spot I knew would surely carry me over the edge. "Jona…than," I breathed, "Aah, ah," I was moaning and groaning loudly and I didn't care. And as I bucked like a wild animal between his body and the shower wall he began kissing me, but I couldn't close my mouth, feeling slightly stupid at the face I was making. I came then, the internal fireworks he'd launched ravished my womb over and over again, trembling against his hand. "Oh…baby," I whispered when he finally took his hand away. He pulled me under the steaming water and again washed away the new moisture between my legs, taking his time around my sensitive bud. He still didn't say anything as he turned the water off and wrapped me in the plush terry cloth robe folded neatly on the counter. I was thankful he picked me up since I didn't know if I could walk. He put me to stand on the bathroom mat and as tenderly as he bathed me, he dried every drop of water on my body. When he was finished, he left me standing there as he got back in the shower and bathed himself. Watching him bathe was unbelievably erotic. The dryness between my legs didn't last long as again the warm ambers of my desire, were fanned into raging flames.

"Jonathan," I whispered as I leaned back against the marble countertop, but again he didn't answer. He turned the water off, got out, and dripping wet, walked toward me and picked me up, carrying me into the bedroom. Even his silence was sensual as he opened my robe and let it fall to the floor. The bed had already been turned down and the sheets were cool against my warm flesh. Over the next hour Jonathan used his mouth to make love all over my body. There wasn't a toe or finger that he hadn't lovingly suckled, or joints and crevices that he didn't kiss and caress. He turned me on my back, then stomach, and then onto my back again as my body quivered against his muscular frame from its third climax. He took my mouth now, kissing me passionately.

"Are you ready?" he whispered, speaking for the first time since the shower.

"As ready as I'll ever be," I said with a smile. "No wait. Where is your ring?"

"In that drawer," he replied.

"Give it to me." Supporting his weight on his elbow he leaned over and took the velvet box out of the drawer and handed it to me. I took it and sat up in the bed facing him. "Give me your hand." Putting the ring on his finger I said with some degree of finality, "Now I'm ready. I don't care what the law says, as of this moment we are one. Man and wife. I am yours and you are mine. I will love no other."

"I am yours and you are mine. I will love no other," he repeated, and lacing our fingers together, we kissed again, lying down with him on top of me. "Tell me if you want me to stop."

"I'll be fine. Please…I can't wait any longer," I begged, and with that he came onto his knees and brought my legs up to rest on his thighs. Holding my waist he effortlessly lifted me up and forward so that I was perfectly inline with his throbbing manhood. He doubled the pillows behind my head and again asked if I was comfortable, I just smiled and kissed him, running my hands through his thick hair. I could feel him rubbing his large head against my opening, spreading some of the moisture onto himself, then pressing ever so gently until my lips gave way and he was in me. It hurt a tiny bit, but nothing like I was expecting. I smiled to myself as I immediately felt full and then empty as he pulled himself in and out. I thought I'd experienced it all with his hands and his mouth, but I knew now that was nothing in comparison to sensations gripping my body at this moment. I was moaning and groaning as he leaned back on his heels, squeezing his cheeks together as he penetrated me. It felt glorious.

"Are you okay?" he asked softly, not stopping.

"I'm great. This is so much better than I ever imagined and it didn't hurt as much as I thought it would," I said with a smile, bringing his hand to my lips.

"Well, that's good to know," he said with a little laugh, "but we haven't really started yet." I looked at him with questioning eyes.

"What do you mean?" He pressed into me a little farther and the tip of his penis hit something that made me flinch. "Ooohh, what was that?" Scooping his arms around my back he came forward, moving my hand from resting on his thigh he brought it up to his back.

"Hold on to me," he whispered into my ear. "The pain won't last long."

"Woah, wait a minute," I yelled, trying to scoot further up in the bed away from him. "What pain? Aren't we done? You're in there. I can feel *you*. What pain?" His strong arm held me in place.

"You can feel *me*, but that's not *all* of me," he said, bringing my hand to him. And as my hand explored him like a blind woman, it hit me that there was still a great deal of *him* left to go in, all this time it was just his head I was feeling. My eyes were wide with panic. I had *that* in my mouth, how could I have forgotten. I don't think I can do this. I started to squirm, but he continued to hold me in place on him. "Stop," he said lacing his fingers between mine above our heads. "Trust me."

"Jonathan, I can't."

"Yes, you can. Trust me. I promise I'll go slowly if you want me to."

"What do you mean if I want you to? Of course I want you to!"

"It's just that it tends to hurt more when you go slowly, kind of like taking off a band-aid or having your eyebrows waxed. It's better if you do it quickly; it hurts only for that instant and then gets better. Don't you trust me?"

"Yes, I trust you. I just…umm…I trust you. I'm sorry, you just tell me what to do and I'll do it. Millions of people do this every day, I can do this."

"Wrap your arms around my neck. Now kiss me and let me love you."

I closed my eyes and did just that, as he started to move in me again and the sensations immediately overtook my body. He pressed a little deeper and I tensed up. He groaned, telling me not to do that and then he eased back, moving in and out of me slowly.

"Look at me." I opened my eyes. "Do you love me?" he asked as he continued his steady movement.

"Ye…" before I could answer he'd made a sudden thrust covering my mouth with his, and a hot searing pain shot up my lower back. I screamed into his mouth, but he didn't stop kissing me, holding my hips in place as he drove into me. Inch by slowly inserted inch, he buried his thick shaft in me to the hilt, filling me to the brim. I could feel my eyes wet with tears as the pain slowly faded.

"Breathe, baby," he whispered against my ear. I hadn't even realized I'd been holding my breath all that time. He was kissing my face and neck as the initial shock of his penetration wore off. If anything it was now a dull sensation that was quickly being replaced by the indescribable pleasure and warmth between my legs. He continued to massage my cheeks and thighs, pressing deeper and deeper into me. He was right, the pain didn't last that long. "Are you all right?" he asked in a low voice, gently suckling on my earlobe. I was moaning as I started to rotate my hips, matching his rhythm. I was making love. His strokes where long and deliberate and he continued to rotate his hips upon withdrawal. "Dye…you're…so…tight." I dug my nails into his back as he touched somewhere deep inside me that I never knew existed.

"Aaahh, this feels sooo good. *You* feel so good," I moaned, finally opening my eyes so that I could see his handsome face. He was looking at me, his eyes dark with his arousal. Moving his hips, he thrust his hips towards the side of my womb.

"Here?" he asked with curious eyes. I didn't know that he was asking so I just moaned. Moving his hips to the opposite side he thrust into me again, hitting a spot that caused my body to shudder. The sensation was a thin line between pain and immense pleasure, although I was leaning more towards immense pleasure.

"How about there?" he asked, purposely aiming for it.

"Yes, that's it! There!" I squealed as his rhythm increased and I could feel him pounding my abdomen, hitting that spot with commendable precision each time. I buried my face into his muscular bicep, digging my teeth into his flesh, he growled, but seemed to enjoy it. I had taken all of him and it felt damn good. He was perfect, filling even. I fit him like a glove and as he drove into me, his brow furrowed in concentration and his testicles heavy with my reward, slapping against my bottom, we were engulfed with the sounds and smells of our lovemaking. Just when I thought I couldn't take it anymore, he would slow down to long deep strokes, reading my every move or groan, and then he would start again, pummeling the core of my being. This man was brilliant. How could I have ever thought I would survive without him? He was close to his climax and I admired his restraint. Wrapping my legs around his waist I pulled him into me, taking every inch of his luscious penis into me. I began to pump then, moving my hips and thighs against him, slamming our pelvises together, grinding and swirling my hips like I had been making love my entire life.

"Arrhh," he growled. Leaning back away from me onto his heels, he placed his large hand against my lower abdomen with firm pressure and with his thumb over my rosebud, he pressed down. I could feel him moving deep within me against his palm on the outside of my tummy, as he made tiny circles with his thumb. I could tell he liked being able to feel himself against the wall of my stomach and as I massaged and rubbed his nipples I could feel my climax building. I moved faster, urging him to cross the finish line with me.

"Dye...slow...down...I don't...want this...to end," he said, his voice barely audible. Slow down, I did, rotating my hips, moving them back and forth in a painfully slow and deliberate fashion. "Oh, oh, baby," he groaned. I was deep in concentration as I recalled the days when I was learning how to hula hoop with the girls in my grandparents' village. There was only one hula hoop to go around and it was pretty battered, but it did the trick. I moved my waist and hips in deep circles, simultaneously squeezing the muscles of my vagina around his pulsing rod. I could see the beads of sweat running down between my breasts. I didn't know how much longer I could hold on. We rode each other until I could bear no more. His coarse pubic hair rubbed against my clit, producing in itself another amazing sensation. I was on the verge of a cataclysmic eruption.

"Jonathan...I'm...ready," I moaned.

"So am I," he groaned. And with that he held me close as he pumped vigorously into me like a jack hammer operator on a New York street. It was coming, as if the spot he was hitting was sending out some type of pulse that would ultimately result in this explosion. I could feel it off in the distance, getting bigger than I ever imagined, nothing compared to three splendid orgasms I'd experienced only an hour or so before. Every nerve in my body was tingling, my toes, head, arms, breasts, abdomen, back, were all alive, firing premature blasts all over my body. We were making primitive sounds as our legs and arms intertwined. It was as though we were attempting to become even closer than physically possible. We wanted to be under each others skin. We were one, moving, groaning, and writhing together. I didn't think it was possible to love him any more than I did an hour ago, or a minute, or a second ago, but I did. "Dye...I'm...coming..." Jonathan exclaimed at the same moment the tightening in my lower abdomen became unbearable. Squeezing me tight, I closed my eyes as we exploded in each others arms, bucking and arching our backs like wild animals. I think I was screaming as he let out a guttural growl, his entire body stiffened as he pressed into me. I could feel the heat of his love juice explode in my womb, followed by the smaller bursts as I recalled how he came in my mouth. The fireworks blasted in waves and then slowly stopped. We were both soaking wet from our sweat, trying to catch our breath.

"I love you, I love you," I whispered, kissing any part of him I could reach.

"I…love…you too. You're going to have to forgive me, but I can't move just yet," he said with a little laugh. Easing onto his elbows he looked at me, wiping the wet tendrils of hair from my face. "Are you all right?"

"Umm, umm," I said, turning my face away, but it was too late, he'd seen my tears. My emotional orgasm came then.

"Baby?" He turned my face to his.

"It's nothing," I said.

"It's not nothing. Did I hurt you?"

"No, no. You didn't hurt me. You were wonderful. I can't describe what just happened and how you felt," I said breathlessly. "I just don't know how I can be so happy and still so sad all in the same breath." He wiped away my tears and brought my leg up to rest on his bottom.

"Please don't cry. I'm going to make you so happy. Let me make all your pain go away," and as he kissed me I could feel him inside me growing hard and thick. We made love again, this time more tenderly as my tears of joy and sorrow continued to fall and he continued to kiss them away. The walls of my womanhood were tight around him, stretched to accommodate his girth as he spread my cheeks. This time he only nudged that spot knowing exactly where it was, he merely massaged it. The immediate sensation of him rubbing against it wasn't as shocking, but still fantastic. His strokes were slow and deep as he sucked my breasts and I raised my hips to meet him. His breath became hot against my ear as we got nearer and nearer to the pinnacle of our love. We came together again, like a beautifully choreographed ballet. We held onto each other as the breaking waves of our less violent orgasm rolled over our bodies. I was shuddering against Jonathan and him against me. Our bodies exhausted from our lovemaking. After some time he withdrew his flaccid appendage from the silky grip of my vagina, but I held onto his arms, not wanting him to leave my side.

"Where are you going?" I asked.

"To run us a bath," he said with a smile.

"Umm, all right," I responded, and rubbing my thighs together felt the stickiness of our union. We bathed each other, washing away my blood and his semen, and there in his porcelain tub we made love for the third time. He couldn't stop kissing me. When we did manage to tear ourselves apart, we changed the linens on the bed and climbed under the sheets. The sky was ablaze with the colors of dawn. Naked and basking in the warmth of our bodies we wrapped ourselves in each others arms and fell asleep. The princess of pride was no more.

Printed in the United States
61698LVS00004B/28